# Splinter

## SEBASTIAN
## FITZEK

**Sebastian Fitzek** has worked as a journalist and author for radio and TV stations all around Europe, and is now head of programming at RTL, Berlin's leading radio station. His first and subsequent novels have become huge bestsellers in Germany, and he is currently working on his fifth.

# Splinter

## SEBASTIAN FITZEK

Translated by
John Brownjohn

CORVUS

First published in the English language in Great Britain in 2011
by Corvus, an imprint of Atlantic Books Ltd.

Originally published in German as *Splitter* in 2009
by Droemer Knaur.

1 3 5 7 9 10 8 6 4 2

A CIP catalogue record for this book is available from
the British Library.

ISBN: 978-1-84887-695-8

Printed in Great Britain by the MPG Books Group

Corvus
An imprint of Atlantic Books Ltd
Ormond House
26-27 Boswell Street
London WC1N 3JZ

www.corvus-books.co.uk

For Clemens

'What do you think?'

'Hm. . . I'd call it, well. . . an acquired taste?'

'Utterly hideous, more like.'

'Was it a present?'

'No, I bought it.'

'Just a minute. You paid good money for that thing?'

'Yes.'

'For a baby-blue, battery-operated dolphin bedside light which you yourself think is ugly?'

'Hideous.'

'Okay, so enlighten me. If that's feminine logic, I don't get it.'

'Come here.'

'I'm almost on top of you as it is.'

'Come closer all the same.'

'Don't tell me you bought it as a sex aid?'

'Dickhead.'

'Hey, what's the matter? Why are you looking at me like that?'

'Promise me. . .'

'What?'

'Promise you'll always turn the light on?'

'I. . . I don't get it. Scared of the dark suddenly?'

'No, but. . .'

'But what?'

'Well, I've been thinking how unbearable it would be if something happened to you. No, wait, don't pull away, I want to hold you tight.'

'What is it? Are you crying?'

'Look, I know it sounds a bit weird, but I'd like us to make a deal.'

'Okay.'

'If one of us dies – no, please hear me out – the first of us to go must give the other one a sign.'

'By turning the light on?'

'So we know we aren't alone. So we know we're thinking of each other even if we can't see each other.'

'Baby, I don't know if—'

'Ssh. Promise?'

'Okay.'

'Thank you.'

'Is that why it's so ugly?'

'Hideous.'

'Right. Good choice from that angle. We'd never turn on that monstrosity by mistake.'

'So you promise?'

'Of course, babe.'

'Thank you.'

'Still, what's likely to happen to us?'

# Splinter

It's either real or it's a dream,
there's nothing that is in between.

'Twilight', Electric Light Orchestra

The end justifies the means.

Proverb

# 1

## TODAY

Marc Lucas hesitated. The one uninjured finger of his broken hand hovered over the brass button of the antiquated doorbell for a long time before he pulled himself together and pressed it.

He didn't know what time it was. The horrors of the last few hours had robbed him of his sense of time as well. Out here in the middle of the forest, though, time seemed unimportant anyway.

The chill November wind and the sleet showers of the last few hours had subsided a little, and even the moon was only intermittently visible through rents in the clouds. It was the sole light source on a night that seemed as cold as it was dark. There was no indication that the ivy-covered, two-storeyed, timber-built house was occupied. Neither did the disproportionately large chimney jutting from the gabled roof appear to be in use, nor could Marc smell the characteristic scent of burning logs that had woken him in the house that morning – shortly after eleven, when they had brought him to the professor for the first time. He'd been feeling ill even at that stage, dangerously ill, but his condition had dramatically worsened since then.

A few hours ago his outward symptoms had been scarcely detectable. Now, blood was dripping on to his dirty trainers from his mouth and nose, his fractured ribs grated together at every breath, and his right arm hung limp at his side like an ill-fitting appendage.

Marc pressed the brass button once more, again without hearing a bell, buzzer or chime. He stepped back and looked up at the balcony. Beyond it lay the bedroom, which by day afforded a breathtaking view of the little forest lake whose surface at windless moments resembled a sheet of window glass – a smooth, dark pane that would shatter into a thousand fragments as soon someone tossed a stone into it.

The bedroom remained in darkness. Even the dog, whose name he had forgotten, failed to bark, and there were none of the other sounds that usually emanate from a house whose occupants have been roused from sleep in the middle of the night. No bare feet padding down the stairs, no slippers shuffling across the floorboards while their owner nervously clears his throat and tries to smooth his tousled hair with both hands and a modicum of spit.

Yet Marc was unsurprised, even for an instant, when the door suddenly opened as if by magic. Far too many inexplicable things had happened to him in the last few days for him to waste even a moment's thought on why the psychiatrist should be confronting him fully dressed in a suit and neatly knotted tie, as if he made a point of holding his consultations in the middle of the night. Perhaps he really had been working in the recesses of his little house – perusing old case notes or studying one of the thick tomes on neuropsychology, schizophrenia, brainwashing or multiple personalities that lay strewn around, although it was years since he had practised as anything but an occasional consultant.

Marc didn't wonder, either, why the light from the room with the fireplace was reaching him only now. Reflected by a mirror over the chest of drawers, it seemed to adorn the professor with a momentary halo. Then the old man stepped back and the effect vanished.

Marc sighed. Wearily, he leant his uninjured shoulder against the doorpost and raised his shattered hand.

'Please,' he implored. 'You've got to tell me.'

His tongue impinged on some loose front teeth as he spoke. He coughed, dislodging a little drop of blood from his nose.

'I don't know what's been happening to me.'

The psychiatrist nodded slowly, as if he found it hard to move his head. Most people would have recoiled at the sight of Marc and slammed the door in alarm, or at least summoned medical assistance. But Professor Niclas Haberland did nothing of the kind. He merely stepped aside and said, in a low, melancholy voice: 'I'm sorry, you're too late. I can't help you.'

Marc nodded. He'd expected this reply and was prepared for it.

'I'm afraid you've no choice,' he said, taking the automatic from his torn leather jacket.

# 2

The professor made his way along the passage to the living room. Marc followed close behind with the gun levelled at his back, but he was glad the old man didn't turn round and see how close to passing out he was. He'd felt faint as soon as he entered the house. The headache, the nausea, the sweating – all the symptoms intensified by his mental ordeal of the last few hours had suddenly returned. He was almost tempted to cling to Haberland's shoulders and let himself be towed along. He was tired, unbearably tired, and the passage seemed infinitely longer than it had on his first visit.

'Look, I'm sorry,' Haberland repeated as they entered the living room, whose most conspicuous feature was an open fireplace with a log fire slowly expiring on the hearth. His tone was calm, almost compassionate. 'I really wish you'd come sooner. Time's running out.'

Haberland's eyes were completely expressionless. If he was frightened, he managed to conceal it as effectively as the old dog asleep in a little wicker basket by the window. The buff-coloured ball of fur hadn't even raised its head when they came in.

Marc moved to the middle of the room and looked around irresolutely. 'What do you mean, time's running out?'

'Just look at yourself. You're in a worse state than this place of mine.'

Marc returned Haberland's smile, and even that hurt him. The decor of the house was as odd as its location in the forest. Not one piece of furniture matched any other. A grossly over-loaded Ikea bookcase rubbed shoulders with an elegant Biedermeier chest of drawers. The floor was almost entirely covered with carpets, one of them readily identifiable as a bathroom runner whose colour alone clashed with that of the hand-woven silk Chinese carpet beside it. Marc was invol-untarily reminded of a box room, yet nothing in this ensemble seemed to be there by chance. Every last object, from the gramophone on the tea trolley to the leather sofa, from the wing chair to the linen curtains, suggested a souvenir of times gone by. It was as if the professor feared he would lose a reminder of some crucial phase in his existence if he rid himself of any pieces of furniture. The ubiquitous medical textbooks and journals lying not only on the shelves and desk, but also on the windowsills, the floor, and even in the log basket beside the hearth, seemed to function as a link between the hetero-geneous junk.

'Do sit down,' said Haberland. He spoke as if Marc were still the welcome visitor he'd been that morning, when they deposited his unconscious form on the comfortable sofa whose plump cushions threatened to smother him. Now, though, he would sooner have sat right in front of the fire. He was feeling cold – colder than he had ever felt in his life.

'Shall I put some more wood on?' asked Haberland, who seemed to have read his thoughts.

Without waiting for an answer he went over to the basket of logs, extracted one and tossed it on to the embers. It caught at once, and Marc felt an almost irresistible urge to drive the cold from his body by plunging his hands into the flames.

'What happened to you?'

'I'm sorry?' It took him a moment to tear his eyes away from the fireplace and concentrate on Haberland once more.

The professor looked him up and down. 'Your injuries,' he said, 'who caused them?'

'I did.'

To Marc's surprise, the old psychiatrist merely nodded. 'I thought as much.'

'Why?'

'Because you're wondering if you exist at all.'

The truth seemed literally to pin Marc back against the cushions. That was just his problem. This morning the professor had confined himself to vague allusions, but now he wanted absolute clarity. That was why he was back on this squashy sofa.

'You want to know if you're real, that's another reason why you injured yourself. You wanted to make sure you were still capable of sensation.'

'How do you know?'

Haberland made a dismissive gesture. 'Experience. I myself was once in a similar situation.'

He glanced at his wristwatch. Marc wasn't sure, but he thought he detected some scars around the strap. They looked more like old burns than cuts.

'I may not practise officially any more, but my analytical flair hasn't deserted me. Far from it. May I ask what you're feeling at this moment?'

'Cold.'

'No pain?'

'It's bearable. I think I'm still too much in shock.'

'But don't you think you'd be better off in A and E? I haven't even an aspirin in the house.'

Marc shook his head. 'I don't want any pills. All I want is certainty.'

He put the pistol on the coffee table, with the muzzle pointing at Haberland, who was still standing in front of him.

'Prove that I really exist.'

The professor scratched the back of his head, where his grey hair was punctuated by a bald patch about the size of a beer mat. 'Do you know what is generally held to constitute the difference between man and beast?' He indicated the dog in the basket, which was restlessly whimpering in its sleep. 'Self-aware-ness. We reflect on why we exist, when we'll die and what happens after death, whereas an animal wastes no thought on whether it's on earth at all.'

Haberland had gone over to his dog while speaking. He knelt down and affectionately cupped its shaggy head in his hands.

'Tarzan here can't even recognize himself in a mirror.'

Marc rubbed some dried blood off his eyebrow. His gaze strayed to the window. For one brief moment he thought he'd glimpsed a light in the darkness outside. Then he realized it was only the reflection of the flickering firelight. It must have started raining again, because the outside of the window pane was spattered with droplets. After a while he discerned his own reflection far out in the darkness above the lake.

'Well,' he said, 'I can still see my reflection, but how can I be sure it isn't an illusion?'

'What leads you to assume you're suffering from hallucinations?' Haberland rejoined.

Marc concentrated once more on the droplets on the pane. His reflection seemed to be dissolving.

*Well, how about high-rise buildings that vanish into thin air just after I've left them? How about a man imprisoned in my cellar with a film script that describes what will happen to me in a few seconds' time? Oh yes, and how about the dead suddenly resurrecting themselves?*

'It's because there's no logical explanation for all that happened to me today,' he said in a low voice.

'Oh yes, there is.'

Marc spun round. 'What is it? Please tell me.'

'I'm afraid we don't have time for that.' Haberland glanced at his watch again. 'It won't be long before you have to leave here once and for all.'

'What are you talking about?' Marc took the gun from the coffee table and stood up. 'Are you another of them? Are you in this too?' He aimed the automatic at the psychiatrist's head.

Haberland put out his hands in a defensive gesture.

'It's not the way you think.'

'Really? How do you know?'

The professor shook his head sympathetically.

'Come on, out with it!' Marc shouted the words so loudly, the veins in his neck bulged. 'How much do you know about me?'

The answer took his breath away.

'Everything.'

The fire flared up. Marc had to avert his eyes, unable to endure the sudden glare.

'I know everything, Marc. And so do you. You refuse to believe it, that's all.'

'Then, then. . .' Marc's eyes started to water. 'Then tell me, I beg you. What's happening to me?'

'No, no, no.' Haberland clasped his hands together in entreaty. 'It doesn't work like that, believe me. Any realization is worthless unless it comes from within.'

'That's crap!' Marc yelled. He shut his eyes for a moment, the better to concentrate on the pain in his shoulder. Before going on he swallowed the blood that had collected in his mouth. 'Tell me right now what your game is, or I swear to God I'll kill you.'

He was no longer aiming at the professor's head, but straight at his liver. The bullet would destroy some vital organs even if he missed, and out here any medical assistance would arrive too late.

Haberland was unmoved.

'Very well,' he said eventually, after they had stared at each other in silence for a while. 'You want to know the truth?'

'Yes.'

Haberland slowly subsided into the wing chair and looked down at the fire, which was burning more and more brightly. His voice sank to an almost inaudible whisper. 'Have you ever listened to a story and wished you hadn't heard the ending?'

He turned to Marc with a compassionate expression.

'Don't say I didn't warn you.'

# 3

## ELEVEN DAYS EARLIER

Some people suffer from premonitions. They stand beside a road, see a car go by, and stop short. The car is inconspicuous, neither recently washed nor exceptionally dirty. The driver, too, is no different from all the other nameless faces that pass one every day. He's neither particularly old nor particularly young, isn't clutching the wheel too tightly or letting go of it in order to use his mobile phone or eat at the same time. Nor is he exceeding the speed limit by more than he needs to in order to keep up with the rest of the traffic. There are no portents of the disaster to come. Yet certain people turn to stare at the receding vehicle for some reason they cannot explain to the police after the event. They do so long before they see the nanny warning the vulnerable children in her care to hold hands when crossing at the lights.

Marc Lucas was another such 'Cassandra', as his wife Sandra had christened him, though his gift was less well developed than his brother's. Otherwise, he might have been able to prevent the tragedy of six weeks ago – a nightmare that seemed to be repeating itself at this moment.

'Stop, hang on a minute,' he called to the girl above him.

The thirteen-year-old was miserably cold. She stood poised on the extreme edge of the five-metre board with both arms hugging her ribs, which showed through the thin material of her swimsuit. Marc wasn't sure what was making her shiver, the cold or her fear of jumping. It was hard to tell from where he was, down here in the empty swimming pool.

'Fuck you, Luke!' Julia yelled into her mobile.

Marc wondered how the scrawny girl had been spotted up there at all. Neukölln's public baths had been closed for months. Some passer-by must have caught sight of her and called the emergency services.

'Fuck you and get lost!'

She leant over and looked down at the grubby tiles as if selecting a suitable spot to land on. Somewhere between that big puddle and the mound of dead leaves.

Marc shook his head and put his own mobile to his other ear. 'No, I'm staying. Wouldn't miss this for a pension, sweetheart.'

Hearing a murmur behind him, he glanced up at the fireman in charge, who had stationed himself on the edge of the pool with four colleagues and a jumping mat. The man looked as if he was already regretting having enlisted Marc's help.

They'd found his phone number in the pocket of Julia's jeans, which she had left neatly folded, together with the rest of her clothes, beside the ladder of the diving platform. It was no accident that she was wearing the swimsuit she'd had on when she ran away from home that summer day when her drug-addicted stepfather had been lurking beside the lake yet again, waiting for her.

Marc looked up once more. Unlike Julia, he had no hair left for the wind to ruffle. Not long after he left school his hair had already receded to such an extent that the barber had advised him to shave it off completely. That was thirteen years ago. Today, when his routine was governed by a hundred cups of coffee a week, it occasionally happened that some unknown woman smiled at him on the Underground – but only if she'd fallen for the lie peddled by men's magazines, which claimed that bags under the eyes, worry lines, stubbly chins and other signs of degeneration were marks of character.

'What the fuck are you talking about?' he heard her ask. Her breath steamed furiously. 'What wouldn't you miss?'

November in Berlin was notorious for its sudden cold spells, and Marc wondered which Julia would be more likely to die of, multiple injuries or pneumonia. He himself was quite unsuitably dressed. Not just for the weather, either. None of his friends went around in jeans full of holes and scuffed old trainers. But then, none of them did a job like his.

'If you jump I'll try to catch you,' he called.

'Then we'll both wind up dead.'

'Maybe. But it's more likely my body will cushion your fall.'

It was a good sign that Julia had allowed him to climb down into the grimy pool ten minutes ago. She'd threatened to jump at once if the firemen so much as threw a mat into the empty basin.

'You're still growing, your joints are very supple.'

He wasn't sure this was true, given her intake of drugs, but it sounded vaguely plausible.

'Don't talk crap!' she yelled back.

He could now hear her even without a phone.

'Land the wrong way, and you could spend the next forty years unable to move anything but your tongue. Until one of the tubes that drains your body fluids gets clogged up and you die of blood poisoning, thrombosis or a stroke. Is that what you want?'

'What about you? You want to die if I land on top of you?'

Julia's husky voice didn't sound like a thirteen-year-old's. It was as if the dirt of the streets had coated her vocal cords, which now betrayed her soul's true age.

'I don't know,' Marc replied honestly. An instant later he held his breath: Julia was caught by a gust of wind and swayed forwards. She retained her balance by flailing her arms.

*For the moment.*

This time Marc didn't turn to look as a groan went up from the crowd behind him. Judging by its volume, the police and the firemen had been joined by a number of interested spectators.

'Anyway,' he said, 'I've just as much of a reason to jump as you.'

'You're only talking crap to stop me.'

'Really? How long have you been coming to the "Beach", Julia?'

Marc liked the street kids' name for his Hasenheide office. *The Beach...* It sounded vaguely optimistic, but it suited the human flotsam washed up there daily by the billows of misfortune. Officially, of course, the centre had a different designation, but even local government records had long since ceased to refer to it as the 'Neukölln Juvenile Advice Bureau'.

'How long have we known each other?' he persisted.

'Search me.'

'Eighteen months, Julia. Have I ever bullshitted you in all that time?'

'I dunno.'

'Did I ever lie to you? Did I ever make an attempt to inform your parents or teachers?'

She shook her head. At least, he thought he saw her do so from down below. Her jet-black hair flopped around her shoulders.

'Have I ever told anyone where you get the stuff or where you crash?'

'No.'

Marc knew that, if Julia jumped, he would have to justify himself in that very respect. On the other hand, if he somehow managed to dissuade this crack-addicted teenager from committing suicide, it would be attributable simply and solely to his having gained her trust in the preceding months. He didn't blame people who failed to understand that – his friends, for example, who still couldn't grasp why he was wasting his law degree on 'anti-social elements', as they called them, instead of cashing in on it with some big law firm.

'You weren't there,' Julia said sulkily. 'Six weeks, you've been gone.'

'Look, we're two different people. I don't live in your world, but I've got problems of my own, and right now they're so bad, many other men would have topped themselves long ago.'

Julia flailed her arms again. From down below it looked as if her elbows were grimy, but Marc knew that the dark scabs were from self-inflicted cuts. It wouldn't be the first time a self-harmer turned serious. Youngsters who slashed themselves with a razor blade, so as at least to feel something, were among his most frequent customers at the 'Beach'.

'What happened?' she asked in a low voice.

Gingerly, he felt the sticking plaster on his neck. It would need changing in two days' time at most. 'It doesn't matter. My shit wouldn't make yours any better.'

'You can say that again.'

Marc smiled and glanced at his mobile, which was registering an incoming call. Turning, he caught sight of a woman in a black trench coat staring at him wide-eyed from the edge of the pool. It seemed that the police psychologist had just turned up and wasn't entirely happy with his approach. Standing behind her was an elderly gentleman in an expensive-looking pinstripe suit. He gave Marc a friendly wave.

He decided to ignore them both.

'Remember what I told you the first time you wanted to go back on the stuff because the pains were so bad? Sometimes it feels wrong—'

'—to do the right thing,' Julia broke in. 'Yeah, yeah, I've had that crap up to here! But you know something? You're crazy. Life doesn't just *feel* wrong. It *is* wrong, and your stupid bull-shit isn't going to stop me from. . .'

Julia took two steps back. All at once, her stance conveyed that she was about to jump.

The crowd behind Mark groaned again. He ignored another click on the line.

'Okay, okay. . . At least wait a moment, won't you? I've brought you something. . .'

He fished a tiny iPod out of his jacket pocket, turned it up full and held the earpiece against the microphone of his mobile.

'I hope you'll be able to hear it,' he called.

'What is it this time?' Julia demanded. Her voice had gone husky, as if she guessed what was coming.

'You know. . . The movie isn't over till the music starts.'

This time he'd quoted one of her own sayings. On the few occasions she'd attended his surgery voluntarily, she had always insisted on hearing a certain song before leaving. It had become a kind of ritual of theirs.

'Kid Rock,' he said. The opening was far too quiet and would be inaudible over the mobile in any case, thanks to the wind and the background noise. So Marc did something he'd last done as a teenager: he sang.

'Roll on, roll on, rollercoaster.'

Looking up, he saw Julia shut her eyes. Then she took a little step forwards.

'We're one day older and one step closer.'

The hysterical cries of alarm behind him increased in volume. Only a few centimetres now separated Julia from the edge of the diving board. Marc sang louder.

'Roll on, roll on, there's mountains to climb.'

The toes of Julia's right foot were already peeping over the edge. She still had her eyes shut and the mobile held to her ear.

'Roll on, we're. . .'

Marc stopped singing just as she was about to bring her left leg forward. In the middle of the chorus. A tremor ran through her body. She froze in mid-movement and opened her eyes in surprise.

'. . . we're on borrowed time,' she whispered after a long pause. A deathly hush had descended on the pool.

Marc put his mobile in the pocket of his jeans and caught her eye. 'You think it'll be better?' he called. 'Where you're going?'

'Everything'll be better,' she shouted back. 'Everything!'

She was weeping now.

'Really? I was just wondering if they play your song there too.'

'You're such an arsehole.' Julia's tearful voice had become a hoarse croak.

'Is that likely? I mean, what if you never hear it again?'

So saying, Marc turned and – to the horror of the spectators – strode uphill towards the shallow end.

'Are you mad?' he heard someone shout. Another furious comment was drowned by a collective outcry.

Marc was just hauling himself up the aluminium ladder when he heard the impact on the tiles.

He didn't turn to look until he'd climbed out of the basin.

Julia's mobile phone lay smashed on the spot where he'd just been standing.

'You're an arsehole!' she shouted down at him. 'Now I'm not only scared of living, I'm scared of dying as well!'

He nodded to her. She jabbed her middle finger at him. A deep sob shook her thin frame as she sat down on the diving board. Two paramedics were already on their way up to her.

'And you sing like shit!' she called after him, weeping.

Marc couldn't help smiling. He brushed a tear from his cheek.

'The end justifies the means,' he called back.

Elbowing his way through the electric storm created by the press hyenas' flashguns, he tried to evade the woman in the trench coat, who was barring his path. Having fully expected a reproachful tirade, he was surprised by her businesslike expression.

'My name is Leana Schmidt,' she said briskly, putting out her hand. Her shoulder-length brown hair was drawn back so tightly, it looked as if someone was tugging at her plait from behind.

Marc hesitated for a moment, fingering the plaster on his neck. 'Shouldn't you be seeing to Julia?'

He looked up at the diving board.

'That's not why I'm here.'

Their eyes met.

'So what's it about?'

'It's your brother. Benjamin was discharged from the psychiatric hospital two days ago.'

# 4

The shiny black Maybach parked at the mouth of the narrow cul-de-sac stood out like a sore thumb in this part of Berlin, and not only because of its exceptional size. Monsters of that order were generally to be seen cruising from one government ministry to another, not through the German capital's most crime-ridden district.

Marc had simply walked off when the woman accosted him about his brother and was trying to get away as fast as possible. For one thing, because he had enough on his plate without hearing news of Benny; for another, because he wanted to put some distance between himself and this cheerless place. Besides, it was growing steadily colder.

He turned up the collar of his leather jacket and rubbed his ears, the most weather-sensitive parts of his body. Their invariable reaction to sub-zero temperatures was a stabbing pain that swiftly spread to his temples if he didn't get into the warm in double-quick time.

He was just wondering whether to cross the street and head for the Underground when he heard the squeal of broad-gauge tyres behind him. The driver flashed his lights a couple of times, their halogen glare bouncing off the wet cobbles, but Marc kept to his side of the street and speeded up. If his work in the Berlin streets had taught him anything, it was to avoid responding to strangers for as long as possible.

The car caught him up and slowed to a walking pace, gliding almost silently along beside him.

The driver seemed unconcerned that he was on the wrong side of the street. The Maybach was so wide, an oncoming car couldn't have passed it in any case.

Marc heard the characteristic hum of an electric window. Then a breathy female voice softly called his name.

'Herr Lucas?'

The voice sounded friendly and rather feeble, so he risked a sidelong glance and was surprised to see that the speaker was an elderly man. He looked well over sixty, maybe even over seventy. Most voices tend to deepen with age. In his case the opposite had happened.

Marc was walking on even faster when he recognized the

man in the pinstripe suit, the one who had waved to him a few minutes ago from the edge of the pool.

*Fuck it, am I going to be pestered by nutters today?*

'Marc Lucas, thirty-two, of 67A Steinmetzstrasse, Schöneberg?'

The old man was sitting on a fawn leather bench seat with his back to the direction of travel. The limousine's interior was clearly spacious enough for half a dozen people to sit facing one another.

'Who wants to know?' Marc asked, without turning his head. He sensed that the stranger with the white hair and thick, bushy eyebrows represented no threat. Still, that didn't mean he couldn't be the bearer of bad news, and Marc had had more than enough of that in recent weeks.

The old man cleared his throat. Then, almost inaudibly, he said: 'The Marc Lucas who killed his pregnant wife?'

Marc froze, incapable of taking another step. The damp autumn air had transmuted itself into an impermeable glass wall.

He turned to the car as the rear door swung slowly open. There was a soft, rhythmical electronic beeping, the kind that warns you your seatbelt isn't secured.

'What do you want?' he asked when he'd recovered his voice. It sounded as hoarse as that of the stranger in the car.

'How long have Sandra and the baby been dead? Six weeks?'

Marc's eyes filled with tears. 'Why are you doing this to me?'

'Come on, get in.'

With an amiable smile, the old man patted the seat beside him.

'I'll take you to a place where you can turn the clock back.'

# 5

Seen through the Maybach's tinted windows, the buildings that slid silently past them looked unreal, like the façades of a film set. In the luxury limousine's sound-proofed interior it was hard to imagine that real people actually lived behind those grimy walls, and that the pedestrians on the pavements weren't extras – the old man searching dustbins for bottles with a deposit on them, or the gang of truants overturning a bag-woman's stolen supermarket trolley. There were also some wholly unremark-able individuals battling their way through the rain, of course, but even they seemed to be living in a lost, parallel world from which Marc had escaped since taking his place in the stranger's car.

'Who are you?' he asked, leaning forward. The hydraulic cushions of the ergonomically designed leather seat promptly adjusted themselves to his new position. In lieu of a reply, the elderly man handed him a business card. It was unusually thick, about as thick as a folded banknote. Marc could have sworn it would smell of some rare wood if he sniffed it.

'Don't you remember me?' the stranger asked with another good-natured smile.

'Professor Patrick Bleibtreu?' Marc murmured to himself, running a fingertip over the black engraved lettering on the linen card. 'Do we know each other?'

'You emailed my institute about two weeks ago.'

'Just a minute. . .' Turning the card over, Marc recognized the clinic's logo. Some ingenious commercial artist had woven the professor's initials into a figure eight lying on its side – the infinity symbol.

'That advert... the one in the *Spiegel*... it was yours?'

Bleibtreu inclined his head. He opened the armrest beside him and took out a magazine. 'We advertise in *Focus*, *Stern* and *Spiegel*. I think you replied to this one.'

Marc nodded as the old man handed him the open magazine. It was pure chance that the advertisement had caught his eye while he was leafing through it. He never read news magazines as a rule, let alone adverts. Ever since he'd had to have his dressing changed twice a week, however, he'd been obliged to kill a lot of time with the old illustrateds in the waiting area of his father-in-law's hospital.

'Learn to forget...' he read out. The headline had exerted a magnetic attraction on him.

*Have you experienced a severe trauma, and would you like to erase it from your memory? If so, email us. The Bleibtreu Psychiatric Clinic is seeking applicants to take part in a clinical trial under medical supervision.*

'Why didn't you respond to our calls?' the professor asked.

Marc briefly rubbed his ears, which were burning in that familiar, agonizing way as they gradually thawed out. So that accounted for all the calls from unknown numbers he'd left unanswered over the last few days.

'I never respond to unsolicited calls,' he said. 'And, to be frank, I never get into strangers' cars either.'

'Why make an exception this time?'

'It's drier in here.'

Marc sat back and pointed to the side window. The airstream was dragging plump raindrops across the water-repellent surface of the glass.

'Does the boss always attend to new patients in person?'

'Only when they're candidates as promising as yourself.'

'Promising in what respect?'

'Conducive to the success of our experiment.'

The professor retrieved the magazine and put it back in the central console.

'I'll be absolutely honest with you, Marc. May I call you that?' His gaze fastened on Marc's trainers and travelled upwards to the knee that was showing through his threadbare jeans. 'You don't look like someone who stands on ceremony.'

Marc shrugged. 'What does this experiment entail?'

'The Bleibtreu Clinic is a world leader in the field of personal memory research.'

The professor crossed his legs. His pinstriped trouser leg rode up over one sock to reveal the beginnings of a hairy shin.

'In recent decades, hundreds of millions in research funds have been invested in discovering how the human brain works. In simple terms, the main focus has been on questions relating to the subject of "learning". Hordes of researchers were and still are obsessed with the idea of using the brain's capacity more efficiently.'

Bleibtreu tapped his forehead.

'There has never been a finer high-powered computer than the one in here. Theoretically, anyone is capable of reeling off all the numbers in a telephone directory after a single reading. The ability to form synapses, thereby increasing our cerebral storage capacity to an almost infinite extent, is not a utopian dream. In my opinion, however, all these lines of research have been heading in the wrong direction.'

'And I suspect you're going to tell me why.'

The invisible chauffeur behind the opaque glass partition was negotiating a roundabout.

'Our problem is not that we learn too little. On the contrary, our problem is forgetting.'

Marc's hand strayed to the plaster on his neck. Becoming

aware of this involuntary movement, he quickly withdrew it.

'According to the latest statistics,' said Bleibtreu, 'one child in four is abused and one woman in three sexually harassed or raped in the course of their lives. There are few people on earth who have not been victims of crime at least once, and half of them have needed some form of psychological therapy there-after, at least in the short term. But irreparable scars are often inflicted on our mental "tissue", not only by crime but by numerous everyday experiences. From the psychological aspect, for instance, lovesickness possesses an almost greater negative intensity than the loss of a person close to us.'

'Sounds as if this isn't the first time you've delivered this lecture,' Marc interjected.

Bleibtreu removed a dark-blue signet ring from his finger and transferred it to the other hand. He smiled.

'Up to now,' he said, 'psychoanalysis has tended to unearth suppressed memories. Our research proceeds in the diametri-cally opposite direction.'

'You help people to forget.'

'Precisely. We erase negative thoughts from our patients' consciousness. Permanently.'

That sounds alarming, thought Marc. Having guessed that the experiment would amount to something of the kind, he'd felt annoyed by his tipsy response soon after sending off the email. He would never have replied to the Bleibtreu Clinic's dubious advertisement had he been sober, but that night he'd made a disastrous mistake and inadvertently told a cabby to take him to his old address. He had suddenly found himself back outside the little house that still looked as if the door would burst open at any moment and a barefoot, laughing Sandra come running out to meet him.

It was the 'For Sale' sign outside that had brought him face to face with his loss. He had turned away at once and run back down the street where local children played in the road in summer and pets dozed on dustbins because no one there, neither man nor beast, feared the advent of evil. He had run faster and faster, back into his new, worthless existence – back to the bachelor flat in Schöneberg into which he'd moved after being discharged from hospital. But he hadn't run fast enough to escape from all the memories pursuing him. Their first kiss at the age of seventeen; Sandra's laughter when she gave away the plot of a film before he guessed it himself; her look of disbelief when he told her how lovely she was; their tears when the pregnancy test turned out positive; and, finally, the advertisement he'd just reread.

# LEARN TO FORGET

He expelled a deep breath and strove to concentrate on the present.

'The advantages of deliberately induced amnesia are immense. A man who has accidentally run over a child will never again be haunted by terrible visions of the paramedics failing to resuscitate it. A mother won't spend the rest of her life waiting in vain for her eleven-year-old son to come home from swimming in the lake.'

Smoothly though the chauffeur braked, there was a faint clink from the cut-glass tumblers in the limo's walnut-veneered cocktail cabinet.

'The world's intelligence services are interested in our findings, I fully admit. From now on, there'll be no need to eliminate agents who threaten to defect to the enemy, taking all their knowledge with them. We'll simply erase the vital information from their minds.'

'Is that why you're rolling in money, because you're funded by the military?'

'It's a billion-dollar business, I grant you, and of unparalleled importance to the immediate future. But the pharmaceutical industry has always been like that. It may make a few people wealthy, but it also makes a lot of people healthy or even happy.'

Bleibtreu stared at Marc with the piercing intensity of an interrogator. 'We're still at the very beginning, Marc. We're pioneers – that's why we're looking for people like you. Guinea pigs who have had to cope with trauma as severe as yours.'

Marc swallowed hard. He was feeling just as he had six weeks ago, when his father-in-law brought the terrible news to his bedside.

*'She didn't make it, Luke. . .'*

'Just think,' Bleibtreu told him. 'Wouldn't it be nice if you could wake up in the mornings without your first thought being of your dead wife? Of the baby that never saw the light? You wouldn't feel guilty any more because you wouldn't know you'd driven the car into a tree. You'd be able to go back to work, socialize with friends and laugh your head off at some comedy film because the splinter in your neck wouldn't be a perpetual reminder that you escaped with a scratch whereas Sandra was hurled though the windscreen and bled to death at the crash scene.'

Marc ostentatiously unbuckled his seatbelt and reached for the door handle.

'Kindly let me out.'

'But Marc. . .'

'At once!'

Very gently, Bleibtreu put a hand on his knee. 'I wasn't being deliberately provocative. I was merely repeating what you yourself wrote in your email to us.'

'I was at the end of my tether.'

'You still are. I heard you at the swimming pool. You said you were contemplating suicide.'

Bleibtreu removed his hand, but Marc could still feel its weight on his knee.

'I can offer you something better.'

The glasses clinked again, like a couple of ghosts derisively toasting each other. Marc noticed only now that his back was wet with sweat despite the pleasant temperature in the car's air-conditioned interior. Nervously, he fingered the dressing on his neck. This time he left his hand on the plaster over the itching wound.

'Speaking purely hypothetically,' he said in a hoarse voice, 'this experiment of yours – what form would it take?'

# 6

Eddy Valka's shop smelt of cat's piss and roses. Not an unusual combination to anyone reasonably well acquainted with him. All that surprised Benny was that Valka had wanted to see him so soon. He'd only been out two days, and the ultimatum didn't expire until next week.

'What is this, a proposal of marriage?' He laughed and rubbed his left shoulder, which those two knuckleheads had almost dislocated when throwing him into the boot. He'd have got in of his own free will. You didn't object when Valka wanted a word with you. Not for long, anyway.

Valka threw him a quick glance, then devoted himself again to the long-stemmed roses lying on the counter in front of him. Picking them up one by one, he assessed their length, trimmed them with secateurs and placed them in a galvanized bucket.

'You'll have to ask my parents' permission first.'

'Your parents are dead,' Valka said in an expressionless voice, decapitating another rose. He evidently disliked its colour. 'Did you know that cut flowers should be dunked in boiling water when they droop?' He clicked the secateurs warningly at a Blue Chartreuse that was preparing to jump up on to the counter.

'Head first or stem first?' Benny quipped.

He watched the cat scamper off to join its siblings under a radiator. Nobody knew why Valka put up with them. He didn't like animals. He didn't like any living creatures, if the truth be told. He had opened the florist's only because he could hardly declare his true sources of income to the tax inspector. And also because he didn't want his tame rose-sellers – the poor devils who hawked their wares around the city's bars and pubs at night – to buy their stuff elsewhere. If Valka controlled a business, he controlled it a hundred per cent.

Benny looked around for somewhere to park himself, but the stuffy little shop wasn't equipped to accommodate waiting customers. In fact, it didn't seem interested in attracting customers at all, being far too remote from Köpenick's main shopping streets and bang next door to a boxing gym whose burly habitués weren't exactly a florist's preferred clientele.

'Great name, by the way,' said Benny, glancing at the grimy shop window, on which a semi-circle of self-adhesive letters spelt out the word ROSENKRIEG – 'Rose War' – in mirror writing. 'Very apt.'

Valka gave a gratified nod. 'You're the first person to notice.'

His was a Czech surname meaning 'war'. As the uncrowned king of East Berlin's nightclub-bouncer fraternity, Eddy Valka was inordinately proud of it. He wiped his hands on a green rubber apron and looked Benny in the eye for the first time.

'You're looking better than you used to. Not as flabby. Been working out?'

Benny nodded.

'Well, I'm damned, that funny farm seems to have done you good. How come they let you out so soon?'

'They reassess you every couple of months. It's regulations.'

'I see.'

Valka extracted an exceptionally long-stemmed rose from the bucket and sniffed it appreciatively.

'So the shrinks thought you'd ceased to be a danger to the public?'

'Yes, once my beloved brother had finally withdrawn his statement.' Benny fingered the frond of a yucca palm beside him. 'They released me after that.'

'They could always have consulted me,' said Valka.

Benny couldn't help grinning. 'To be honest, I'm not sure you'd make a trustworthy sponsor in the eyes of the law.'

The corners of Valka's mouth turned down. He looked affronted. 'Nobody's better qualified than me to testify that you wouldn't hurt a fly. How long have we known each other?'

'Getting on for twenty years,' Benny replied, wondering when Valka would get to the point. This meeting had to be more than just a chat about old times.

'Christ, my current girlfriend wasn't even born then.' Valka's smile went out like a light. 'We didn't want you in with us to start with, Benny. You were just too soft.'

Another rose lost its head.

'And that's precisely what I'd have told the shrinks who locked you up. I'd have told them that my former associate is an HSP.'

Benny smiled. It was very rare for someone to know the technical term for his disorder. But Eddy Valka was one of those people you couldn't judge by appearances. His bulldog features, bullet head and crooked teeth made him look like the archetypal roughneck. In reality, he had graduated from school and had even studied psychology for four terms before discovering that he wanted to be the cause of his fellow men's nightmares, not the solution to them.

'Who told you that?' Benny asked.

'Well, I often wondered what was wrong with you. Why you were so different from your brother, who never ducked a fight.'

Valka tugged at a jammed drawer beneath the counter and opened it with difficulty.

'I mean, I never saw you with a girl, so I thought you were gay or something. But then I came across this.'

He produced a newspaper article. 'HSP,' he read aloud. 'Highly Sensitive Person. Generally described as someone suffering from a pathological hypersensitive disorder. Such individuals are considerably more sensitive to their environment than normal test subjects. They sense, feel, see, taste and smell everything far more intensely.'

Benny made a dismissive gesture. 'That's all humbug.'

'Oh yeah? It says here that HSPs used to be sages and advisers at the royal courts of old. Or, thanks to their ability to empathize with the thoughts and emotional states of others, they became diplomats, artists, financial experts. . .' Valka glanced at Benny over the top of the paper. 'That would explain why you were always on at me to put mercy before justice, go easy on my enemies, and all that shit.' He snorted noisily. 'It also explains why I made you my bookkeeper.'

Benny's expression didn't change even now that Valka had finally came to the real reason for this meeting: money.

'But it also says' – Valka looked down at the article and clicked his tongue – 'that HSPs have a regrettable tendency to become depressive. Lots of them go insane and commit suicide.'

'I'm still alive.'

'Yes, thanks more to your brother than yourself.'

'*Must* we talk about Marc?'

Valka guffawed. 'Glad you reminded me of what I really wanted to show you. Come with me.'

Tossing his apron on to the counter, he picked up the secateurs and gave Benny an unmistakable signal to follow him into the back room.

Valka used the windowless room next door as a storeroom. Not for flowers, fertilizer or vases, but – as Benny was appalled to see – for garbage. Human garbage, and this specimen was still alive.

'It's time we cured you of this HSP disorder of yours,' said Valka, pointing to a naked man lashed to a St Andrew's cross. Jammed into his mouth was an orange ball gag with a central aperture the diameter of a drinking straw – his only means of breathing. He was on the verge of asphyxia, given that he couldn't inhale any air through his nose, which was broken.

'I want you to pay close attention,' said Valka. He turned on an inspection lamp dangling from the ceiling, rhythmically clicking the secateurs in his other hand as he did so. The gagged man's eyes widened at the sound. He couldn't see the blades because his head was imprisoned in a sort of clamp that prevented him from turning it. The retaining screws were inserted in his ears, and blood was already seeping from the left one.

Benny started to turn away.

'No, no, no.' Eddy clicked his tongue several times as though quietening a horse. 'Watch carefully.'

He went right up to the naked man and held the secateurs immediately in front of his face. The blades struck sparks from his victims' pupils, he was breathing more and more frantically.

'That article really opened my eyes, Benny. It said that HSPs are exceptionally sensitive to pain. Is that correct?'

Benny was speechless with horror.

'Many of them don't even respond to anaesthetics. Imagine the torture of going to the dentist!'

Valka thrust his victim's upper lip aside with the secateurs. The man had bad, nicotine-stained teeth.

'But what I found most interesting, Benny, was that people like you are said to be particularly sensitive to the sufferings of others. It seems they often feel other people's pain more intensely than their own.'

Valka raised the man's right eyelid with his thumb.

'Stop it,' Benny whimpered, although he knew it was futile. Valka wanted to demonstrate what would happen to him if he failed to repay the 90,000 euros he'd borrowed.

Valka turned to him one more time. 'That makes things simpler for me, my sensitive young friend. It means I can inflict pain on you without harming a hair of your head.'

Benny stared at the rhythmically heaving chest of the naked man, who couldn't have been more than twenty-five. Looking into those bulging eyes, he smelt the fear in which the dank little room was steeped. He could feel it on his skin and taste it under his tongue, and he knew that, in the next few seconds, he himself would be in excruciating pain – as if his own eyeball were being scooped from its socket and the optic nerve severed with a pair of rusty secateurs.

# 7

The Bleibtreu Clinic was situated in Französische Strasse, not far from the Gendarmenmarkt. An old building face-lifted with glass and steel, it immediately conveyed that the only national-health patients privileged to enter its portals were the cleaning women who worked there.

After the luxury of his preliminary car ride, which deposited him right outside the private elevators on Level 2 of the underground car park, Marc had been prepared for anything: for a koi carp pool in the reception area, Irish linen hand towels in the designer toilets and a waiting room fit to compete with a Singapore Airlines first-class lounge. But his expectations were surpassed when he found that the luxurious eleventh-floor men's room afforded a panoramic view of Friedrichstrasse. Those who got up this far might be suffering from some mental disorder, but they could still piss on the rank and file. His father would definitely have approved of this tasteful squandering of patients' fees. 'Money only feels at home in an expensive wallet' had always been a maxim of his.

Marc, on the other hand, felt like a vegetarian in an abattoir when he was prevailed on to sign a pledge of confidentiality and fill in a patient's questionnaire in the clinic's modernistic waiting room. Half an hour earlier he'd had to surrender his mobile phone, all metallic objects and even his wallet to the security guard in reception.

'Purely precautionary,' Bleibtreu had explained. 'You'd never believe the lengths our competitors would go to in order to steal the fruits of our research.'

He had then excused himself and handed Marc over to a swarthy-looking assistant who ushered him silently into a dimly lit consulting room and disappeared without a word.

The room reminded him at first sight of a dentist's surgery. Its central feature was a white, hydraulically adjustable couch connected to a computer console by numerous cables of different colours.

'Electroencephalography,' a woman's voice said softly. Marc gave a start and swung round as the heavy door behind him shut with a faint click. 'We'll be measuring your brainwaves with that.'

Part of the square room was partitioned off by a row of waist-high mandarin trees in tubs. He had failed to notice either the leather three-piece suite behind them or the woman doctor who now rose from one of the armchairs.

'My apologies, Dr Lucas, I didn't mean to startle you. I'm Patrizia Menardi, the inhouse neurologist here.'

She came over to him with her hand extended, managing to look simultaneously affable and dominant, partly because she had a gentle voice but didn't display even a hint of a smile. Marc detected a tiny groove in her upper lip, presumably the relic of an expertly performed cleft-palate operation. He felt pretty certain that her firm handshake and rather mannish demeanour formed part of a defensive barrier dating back to a time when she'd been teased at school because of her harelip.

'Actually, Dr Menardi, I only wanted to—'

'No, no "doctor". Just Menardi.'

'Okay, then please forget my label too. I only use it when booking hotel rooms, but it's never got me an upgrade yet.'

Her expression didn't change.

*Okay, so humour isn't her forte.*

'When do I see Professor Bleibtreu again?' he asked.

'In a few minutes. In the meantime, I'll prepare you for examination.'

'Hold on, I'm afraid you've got it wrong. I don't want to be examined. The professor was simply going to explain the nature of the experiment – purely hypothetically, because, from the look of things, I won't want to take part in it at all.'

'Really? I was told you're our next candidate for MME.'

'MME?'

'The memory experiment. The professor will familiarize you with it as soon as he's completed his rounds. Let's make the most of the interval by taking down your particulars.'

Marc sighed and looked at his watch.

'You're wasting your time,' he said, but he sat down facing the neurologist, who had returned to her armchair. She poured him a glass of water from a carafe and opened a slim folder lying on the coffee table between them.

'Marc Lucas, thirty-two, honours degree in jurisprudence.' She tapped the relevant section of the questionnaire in front of her. Marc had been meant to complete it at the same time as signing the pledge of confidentiality, but he'd lost interest halfway through and given up.

'You passed both examinations with distinction and gained your doctorate in juvenile law. Congratulations – very few people manage that, to the best of my knowledge.' She nodded admiringly.

'And you now work with socially disadvantaged children and young people in Neukölln?' she asked casually, her eyes straying to the watch on Marc's wrist.

'It's a fake from Thailand,' he lied, inserting a forefinger beneath the strap. He didn't feel like explaining how he could afford a luxury watch that cost as much as a family saloon car on a social worker's salary, even if it had been a birthday present from Sandra.

'Your father was a lawyer too.' She took a photo from her folder and held it so Marc couldn't see.

'You're very like him,' she said, and went on leafing through the file. Marc didn't react, despite his urge to snatch the questionnaire from her hand. His resemblance to his father was striking indeed, although outsiders didn't find it so noticeable because their similarities related mainly to character and outlook on life. Frank Lucas had also been a fighter. Like Marc, he had made up ground by going to evening classes and then devoted himself to representing the underprivileged. In the early days, when Frank still couldn't afford an office of his own and had set up shop in his living room, half the neighbourhood used to sit on his sofa and enlist his advice. Deceived wives, drink-drivers, petty criminals caught red-handed – they'd used Papa Lucas more as a pastor than a lawyer. He often gave his 'friends' time to pay or waived his fee altogether, even though Mama Lucas gave him stick because they themselves were behind with the rent.

In the course of time, however, some of the petty criminals whom he'd represented pro bono made a career for themselves – villains who could suddenly afford to pay cash and never asked for a receipt. As Frank's clients descended the ladder of criminality, so his practice gradually picked up, though not for long.

'Your father died young,' Menardi went on. 'Cirrhosis of the liver, undiagnosed. Your mother, a housewife, died not long afterwards.'

*How does she know all this?*

Unless his memory was playing tricks he hadn't completed those sections of the questionnaire, nor the ones that followed.

'You have a younger brother named Benjamin?' Menardi asked.

Marc's throat tightened. He reached for the glass of water. The neurologist had evidently wasted her time scouring the internet.

'Benny. At least, that's what he called himself the last time we spoke.'

'Which was when?'

'Let me think.' Marc took a sip and replaced the glass on the coffee table.

'It was, er. . . Monday, Tuesday, Wednesday. . .'

He counted off the days of the week on his fingers.

'At a rough guess, on a Thursday around eighteen months ago.'

'The day he was sectioned?' Menardi shut the folder and tapped her front teeth with her pencil. 'After another unsuccessful suicide attempt?'

The pressure on his throat increased again.

'Look, I don't know how you got hold of all this information, but I certainly didn't come here to chat about my family history.'

Marc started to get up, but she restrained him with a soothing gesture.

'Then please tell me about the traumatic experience that prompted you to contact us recently.'

He hesitated for a moment. Then, after another glance at his watch, he subsided on to the sofa once more.

'I hear voices,' he said.

'What sort of voices?'

'There they go again. Someone just said, "What sort of voices?"'

Menardi gave him a long look, then made a note in her folder.

'What's that you're writing?' he demanded.

'I'm making a note that you take refuge in humour. It's typical of creative and intelligent people, but it makes them harder to treat.'

'I don't want treatment of any kind.'

'You ought to consider it, though. Would you care to describe the accident for me?'

'Why ask me if you already know everything?'

'Because I'd like to hear it from your own lips. My concern is less what you tell me than how you tell it. For instance, your attempts to make a joke of everything are far more informative than the fact that your wife might still be alive if you'd sent for help at once.'

Marc felt as if the woman had opened a valve in his body and he was collapsing like an inflatable mattress. He could almost hear the hiss as all the strength leaked out of him.

'What do you mean? I couldn't summon help, I was unconscious.'

'Really?' Menardi frowned and opened the folder again. 'According to this accident report, you called the emergency services. But not until fourteen minutes after the crash.'

She handed him a printed form as thin and translucent as greaseproof paper. Looking up, he was doubly disconcerted to see the genuine concern on her face.

'One moment,' she said hesitantly. Her cheeks reddened and the sheet of paper in her hands developed a nervous tremor. 'Are you telling me you can't remember?'

# 8

This is impossible, Marc told himself. Quite impossible.

He couldn't have dialled 112. Not at that stage. True, it was his mobile number on the A & E report to which the clinic had gained access, God alone knew how. But it couldn't have been *him*. He'd lost consciousness at once after hitting his head on the door frame and steering wheel in quick succession. At once, not a quarter of an hour after the crash.

There was a knock at the door. Marc turned, expecting to see the neurologist reappear. She had left the room a few minutes earlier, looking worried. Instead, Bleibtreu materialized in the doorway, his face wreathed in an engaging smile that doubtless adorned many of the clinic's publicity brochures.

'What's the meaning of this?' Marc said sharply. 'I thought I came here to forget. As it is, I'll be leaving your clinic with a lot of my wounds reopened.'

'I must apologize for Frau Menardi's conduct, Dr Lucas. There's been a regrettable mistake.'

'A mistake?'

'She wasn't authorized to broach the subject.'

'Not authorized?' Marc clasped his hands behind his head. 'You mean I really did call the emergency services?'

'No.'

Bleibtreu made a gesture of invitation, but Marc preferred to remain standing by the window rather than resume his place on the sofa.

'It was a passer-by,' the professor explained. 'The man who was first at the crash scene had no mobile phone with him, so he reached through the shattered side window and took yours.'

Several motorists were performing a horn concerto in the street eleven floors below them. It was either a traffic jam or a wedding. Marc parted the beige lamellar blinds but couldn't see much. Immediately outside the window was some scaffolding swathed in plastic sheets.

'How do you know all this?'

Bleibtreu stared at him in surprise. 'There's a copy of the accident report in your file. Your email expressly granted us access to it.'

Marc dimly remembered clicking a box on the download form. He couldn't have cared less about anything that night.

'Have you never seen the report yourself?'

Marc shook his head. He'd never even asked about it. He could happily dispense with any more grisly details about the most terrible day in his life.

'I understand,' said Bleibtreu. 'You're still in the preliminary phase of the grieving process, of course.'

*1. Refusal to accept the truth. 2. Emotional turmoil. 3. Self-discovery and self-detachment. 4. A fresh attitude to oneself and the world in general.* Marc knew those categories because part of his job was to counsel the street kids who washed up at his office. Although that configuration had helped him to gain a better understanding of those who had lost a close companion, he didn't accept that it applied to himself.

'I'm not in denial about Sandra's death,' he insisted.

'But you're trying to suppress it.'

'I thought that was precisely your own recommended method, Professor. Forgetting!'

Bleibtreu had joined Marc at the window. The weather had turned stormy, and the tarpaulins over the scaffolding were being plastered against it by the wind.

'Well,' he said, 'paradoxical as it may sound, before forgetting comes remembering. I'm afraid we'll have to go over the circumstances of the accident together.'

Marc turned to him. 'Why?'

'In case we overlook any latent memories that may later sprout like weeds from the sediment of your subconscious.' Bleibtreu laid an age-freckled hand on Marc's shoulder, and for one brief moment this unexpected proximity breached his instinctive defence mechanism.

*The preliminary phase. Denial, suppression.*

# 9

They sat down again.

'There isn't much to tell. We were on our way back from a

little family celebration at her father's place when it happened.'

Bleibtreu leant forwards. 'What was the occasion?'

The wind was now buffeting the scaffolding so hard that its creaks and groans were audible even through the sound-proofed, double-glazed windows. Marc sighed.

'Sandra had just been commissioned to write a new film script. She was an actress and screenwriter – but you know that.'

Marc shuffled restlessly to and fro on the sofa as he spoke. Sandra had always laughed at him for being a fidget. He could scarcely sit still for five minutes in a cinema.

'It was to be her first screenplay for a feature film. The Americans were prepared to pay a vast amount of money for it, and we'd been celebrating the news with her father.'

'Professor Constantin Senner?'

'The surgeon, that's right. He's. . .' Marc hesitated. 'He was my father-in-law. Perhaps you've heard of the Senner Clinic?'

'We recommend it to any of our patients in need of surgery. Not that it happens often, I'm glad to say.'

Before going on, Marc adjusted his position yet again and plucked nervously at the skin beneath his chin. 'We were driving along a little-used road through the forest from Sakrow to Spandau.'

'Sakrow near Potsdam?'

'Then you know it. The Senner estate lies right beside the river, facing Pfaueninsel. Anyway, I was driving a bit too fast for a single-lane road. Sandra got angry with me – I think she threatened to get out.'

Shutting his eyes for a moment, Marc strove, as he had so often, to suppress his recollections of that fateful drive.

'What happened then?' Bleibtreu asked cautiously. The more quietly he spoke, the more feminine his voice sounded.

'To be totally honest, I don't know. My recollections of the last few hours before the accident are a blur. I can't remember any more than I've told you. My father-in-law attributes it to retrograde amnesia. Our little celebration and what we said on the drive home – it's all gone.' Marc gave a mirthless laugh. 'I only remember the outcome, alas. The rest is up to you.'

Bleibtreu folded his arms on his chest, a pose that underlined the note of suspicion in his next question. 'And your memory of those last few seconds in the car has never returned?'

'In part, but only very recently. However, I'm never sure what's a dream and what actually happened.'

'Interesting. What do you dream of?'

Marc shrugged. 'As a rule, all I can remember the following morning are disjointed snatches of conversation. Sandra is going on at me about something – begging me not to prevent it.'

*The end justifies the means – aren't you always saying so yourself? Isn't that your motto in life?*

*'You're crazy, Sandra. The end never justifies taking a human life.'*

'What did you want to prevent?'

'No idea. I suspect my subconscious is playing tricks on me and I'm talking about the accident itself.'

Marc was just wondering whether he should really acquaint the professor with every detail of their last conversation when Bleibtreu asked the most agonizing question of all.

'Why did she undo her seatbelt?'

Marc gulped. Once, then again, but the lump in his throat only seemed to increase in size.

'I don't know,' he said eventually. 'She reached back over her seat, probably for something to eat. She was in her sixth month – we always took something sweet with us in case she had a craving. And she often did, especially when she was in a bad mood.'

He wondered if someone had removed the bar of chocolate from the glove compartment before the wreck went into the crusher. The thought almost choked him.

'What happened then?' Bleibtreu asked quietly.

*I saw she was suddenly holding something in her hand. A photo? She showed it to me, but it was colourless and coarse-grained. I couldn't make anything out. In any case, I'm not sure the scene was real. I see it only in my dreams, though they're becoming steadily more distinct.*

Till now Marc had only told his father-in-law about this dream, and only in outline, because he thought it might be a side effect of the medication he had to take for the splinter in his neck.

'Then the tyre burst,' he went on. 'The car spun round twice before it. . .'

He tried to smile. For some absurd reason, he felt he had to play the tragedy down in a stranger's presence.

'I woke up in the Senner Clinic. You can read the rest.'

Bleibtreu nodded. 'How have you been feeling since then?'

Marc reached for his glass. It was nearly empty, but he didn't have the energy to refill it.

*How does anyone feel after killing his wife and unborn son?*

'I feel tired, limp. Every movement is an effort. My joints ache and so does my head.' He tried another smile. 'Stick me in an old folks' home and I'd have plenty to talk about.'

'Those are symptoms typical of severe depression.'

'Or of any other fatal disease. I Googled them, and the first things to pop up were banner ads for undertakers and coffin manufacturers.'

Bleibtreu cocked his left eyebrow, inadvertently evoking another memory of Sandra. Her eyebrows, which were naturally arched, had made her look permanently surprised.

'And you've only had these symptoms since the accident?'

Marc hesitated before answering. The truth was, there had been days before it when he felt wrung out and exhausted – hungover, too, even when he hadn't touched a drop of alcohol. Constantin, who was very concerned, had talked him into undergoing a thorough health check two weeks before Sandra's death, including blood tests and an MRI scan, but they'd failed to turn up anything untoward.

'Well, the accident hasn't exactly improved my condition, let's say.'

Marc heard a sudden high-pitched buzzing sound. It was a moment before he realized that his wristwatch alarm was reminding him to take his pills. He fished two out of the tiny pocket which for some reason is secreted in the right-hand pocket of most pairs of jeans. In the old days he'd kept sticks of chewing gum in there.

'You take those for the injury to your neck?' asked the professor as Marc washed them down with the rest of the water.

Marc nodded, instinctively touching his plaster. 'The surgeons won't risk operating. The splinter is only small, but it's right next to the cervical vertebrae. The pills I take are meant to help the foreign body knit with the muscular tissue so it doesn't cause inflammation or get rejected. If that doesn't work, they'll have to cut it out, though there's a chance I'll wake up paralysed from the neck down.'

'Does it hurt?'

'No, just itches.'

The real pain was more deep-seated. The ridiculous splinter was nothing compared to the axe-stroke that had cleft his soul.

'Well now. . .' said Bleibtreu, but Marc cut him short.

'No, that's enough. This medication makes me feel dog-tired.

I often feel queasy too, so I'll have to lie down soon if you don't want me to throw up all over your floor. Besides, I've had enough of this. You've been stringing me along ever since I got into your car. Instead of supplying me with answers, you and your colleague have given me the third degree. You've two alternatives: either I walk out of that door right now—'

'—or I let you into our little secret at last,' Bleibtreu interjected, flashing Marc another of his five-star, publicity-brochure grins. 'Very well.'

He heaved himself rather ponderously out of his armchair, but his smile didn't fade.

'Come with me. You may be only a few steps away from a new life.'

# 10

'The human brain isn't a filing cabinet,' Bleibtreu declared as he shut the leather-covered door of his study behind him. 'There aren't any drawers you can open and shut as you please, to deposit information or extract it.'

He seated himself behind a massive desk, but not before having to remove a stack of loose papers from the chair and add them to the other mounds of files and books on the floor. In the meantime, Marc sat down on an upright chair and gazed around him.

The room looked almost squalid compared to the antiseptic neatness elsewhere in the clinic. On the desk, dirty coffee cups and a half-eaten sandwich kept company with an untidy jumble of textbooks and patients' records. The harsh glare of the halogen ceiling lights showed up a gravy stain on the professor's tie which had escaped Marc's notice in the dimness of the limo and the examination room.

'I used to think the brain had a quite specific place for each and every memory. It isn't so, of course.'

Bleibtreu trundled his chair across the room on its castors, deftly avoiding the stacks of documents on the floor. He opened a laminated office cabinet and came back holding a model of a brain. This he deposited with difficulty between the telephone and a paperweight the size of a dumbbell, right on top of an open journal devoted to neuropsychology.

'Here, I'll give you a demonstration.'

Roughly the size of a child's football, the model was moulded out of synthetic grey sponge and mounted on a wooden rod inserted in a polished metal base.

By the time Marc had redirected his attention to Bleibtreu, the professor was holding a glass ampoule in each hand. The liquid in the one on the left was red, in the other colourless.

'A conjuring trick?'

'Something like that. Watch carefully.'

Bleibtreu snapped the top off the left-hand ampoule and tilted it over the spongy grey mass.

'A thought is like a drop of liquid.' He dripped about a millilitre of the blood-red fluid on to the part of the model representing the cortex. Instantly, it meandered its way through the sponge's capillary system.

'When an experience becomes a memory, it deposits itself in billions of nerve-cell junctions.'

'The synapses.'

'Quite so. Watch closely, Marc.' The professor picked up a ballpoint and tapped the model of the brain at various points, which were gradually turning red. 'Every memory becomes stored in countless interconnections. The sound of a car's engine, of people arguing, a smell, a certain song playing on the radio, an expanse of water, the rustle of leaves in a forest – all these things could reactivate your memory and summon up terrible recollections of the accident.'

'So how do you propose to erase them from my brain?' Marc asked.

'I don't.' Bleibtreu snapped the top off the other ampoule. 'Not separately, at least. I'm afraid we can only obliterate *all* your memories.'

'Just a minute.' Marc cleared his throat and tapped the last remaining grey area on the frontal lobe. 'Am I wrong, or did you just say you propose to deprive me of *all* my memories?'

'Total, artificially induced amnesia – yes, that's the only possibility. That's what we're researching.'

Bleibtreu turned the model towards Marc to give him a better view of the red fluid's continuing advance.

'Essentially, memory loss can be caused by three factors,' he said. 'Severe traumatic experiences which the human mind wants to forget, brain damage resulting from a blow, and active chemical substances such as anaesthetics.'

Bleibtreu now tipped some of the colourless liquid in the other ampoule over the sponge model. To his surprise, Marc saw that in some places the red coloration was quickly fading.

'Let me guess: you're betting on chemicals – you've developed an Alzheimer's pill and I'm supposed to swallow it, right?'

'More or less. It's a bit more complex than that, of course, but you're right in principle.'

'Purely as a matter of academic interest, what happens afterwards?'

By now, the sponge had almost entirely lost its reddish coloration.

'After we've induced total amnesia, you mean?'

'Yes.'

'That's easy: we reload you.'

'What?'

'But only, of course, with memories and experiences that you really want to regain. It's like reformatting a computer. If you can't locate a defect in the system, the best plan is to wipe everything and gradually reinstate the programmes that work. That's what we would do in your case. First, thorough questioning would elicit what you wanted to remember after undergoing artificial, retrogressive amnesia. Then, during the subsequent rehab phase, you'd be reintroduced to your past. Except, of course, for any experiences associated with your wife.'

'But what about my friends and acquaintances?' Marc objected. 'What about my father-in-law? I'd be reminded of Sandra's death as soon as I set eyes on him.'

'Not if you never saw him again.'

'Excuse me?'

Bleibtreu pushed his chair back with a smile, looking very much in his element and years younger than he had in the car. His voice, too, had gained strength.

'That's what makes you such an ideal subject. You're a social worker, but you don't have much of a social life. Your parents died young and you've lost touch with your brother. Your colleagues at work are forever changing and any contact you have with your clients is usually of brief duration.'

'But my friends would miss me.'

'The ones who work for big law firms and would forget your birthday if it wasn't stored in their Outlook file?'

'All the same, I don't live in a vacuum. What exactly do you envisage? Would I have to leave Berlin?'

To Marc's astonishment, the professor nodded. 'We would naturally take care of your new life. That, too, forms part of the experiment. We'd install you in another part of the country, find you a job and integrate you into your neighbourhood with an appropriate legend. We would even pay your removal expenses. We work with experts from the witness protection scheme, I might add.'

'Are you crazy?' said Marc. It was more a statement than a question.

'Our methods are extreme, it's true, but no one ever discovered a new world by sticking to the beaten track.'

The professor cocked his left eyebrow again. 'Consider the possibilities, Marc. You'd be one of the first people on this planet to start again from scratch, psychologically speaking. You'd be free from all mental ballast – as unencumbered as a newborn baby. I'm not just talking about the accident. We would make you forget *anything* that ever traumatized you.'

He pointed to the brain model, which was now as grey as it had been at the outset of his demonstration.

'Back to the default position?' said Marc. 'A total reset?'

'The choice is yours.'

Bleibtreu opened his desk drawer and took out a small but densely printed sheet of paper.

'You need only sign this application form and we can start at once.'

# 11

It was a mistake. Marc knew he shouldn't have let himself be talked into it, but he thought that submitting to the preliminary examinations and just never coming back would be easier than entering into a long discussion with Bleibtreu about the pros and cons of his wholly unacceptable experiment.

That was why he had only pretended to agree to be examined for any physical or mental condition that might preclude him from taking part.

*Who knows, perhaps you won't prove to be a suitable subject after all,* had been Bleibtreu's final argument.

An undetected mental illness, a serious infection or a weak heart would render him useless as a guinea pig. Even his rare blood group, AB negative, was something of a problem.

Another two and a half long hours elapsed before the Maybach dropped him outside his rented service flat in Schöneberg. A hundred and fifty minutes during which they'd taken his blood, tired him out on various pieces of gym equipment for an ECG, and electroencephalographed his brainwaves for abnormalities. He'd felt like a national service recruit when a doctor asked him for a urine sample and checked his heart-lung functions while he was waiting for the oculist to test his eyesight.

The doctors had shown no interest in the fact that many of these examinations had been carried out by his father-in-law only a few weeks earlier. The Bleibtreu Clinic was unwilling to rely on extraneous data, so he'd even had to undergo more CT and MRI scans.

But most of the time had been taken up with ingenious psychological questions. Unlike the personality tests in women's magazines, which Sandra had always been so fond of, those seemingly innocuous questions had left Marc wondering what on earth their purpose could be.

*If you had the choice, which would you rather do without, one eye or your sense of smell?*

*Which do you dream in more often, colour or black and white?*

*Complete the following sentence: 'I'm in favour of the death penalty for...'*

Marc had already forgotten what answers he'd given, he was so exhausted. Besides, his joints ached with every step he took. All he could think of was the sleeping pill and the hot bath he would soon be taking. He was so engrossed in his thoughts, it was no wonder he failed to see the dark figure lurking beside the entrance to the flats, where it had been waiting for him for a considerable time.

# 12

'Leana Schmidt?' He repeated the name she'd given him once before. That day, a few hours earlier, immediately after Julia's attempted suicide at the open-air baths in Neukölln. Her hair still looked as if it had been ironed flat at the back and he thought he glimpsed a plain, pale-grey trouser suit beneath her trench coat, which was buttoned up at the neck. The only thing that slightly dented the somewhat stern impression she made was a supermarket plastic bag overflowing with 'women's purchases' – the sort of goods which men ignore on principle, like bunches of radishes or sticks of celery. Sandra and he used to laugh at their disparate shopping habits. She would fill her supermarket trolley with fresh fruit, low-fat cottage cheese, fabric conditioner and parsley, whereas he lingered in front of promotion racks stacked with blank CDs and cordless drills, or bags of crisps.

'How on earth did you find me?'

The slim creature put her shopping down and kneaded her fingers where the handle of the bag had cut into them.

'I went to your office. They gave me your address.'

She spoke briskly, almost as if she expected him to apologize for keeping her waiting so long.

'Well, what do you want?'

'I'm. . . I was the nurse on your brother's ward.'

'Well?'

He took out his front-door key, not that he had to use it. Although the list of house rules he'd been handed when moving in exhorted tenants to lock the door to the street after eight at night, they observed it as seldom as they did the ban on dumping glass bottles in the communal refuse bin.

'I'm worried about Benny,' she said firmly, and Marc gained a pretty good idea of how this resolute woman treated her patients. Her tone was professional without being intimidating – a combination to prevent them from feeling patronized but authoritative enough to deter them from questioning her instructions. Leana Schmidt was probably not an ordinary nurse but the sister in charge of a ward, or at least on the way to becoming so.

The automatic light in the lobby came on as Marc went inside. She picked up her shopping bag and followed him in.

'He told me you saved his life once.'

'Really?' Marc said curtly.

Eighteen months ago he had found Benny in the bath with his wrists cut. They normally met only once a year – at Christmas beside their parents' grave – but that morning his mobile had registered three unanswered calls and his mailbox had recorded a message – almost unintelligible it was so broken up and overlaid with static – in what sounded like his brother's voice. When Benny didn't respond to his calls, Marc had obeyed a spontaneous impulse and driven to his place. There he received a drastic demonstration that the message on his mobile had been intended as a last farewell.

'I don't think you should have retracted your statement.' Leana blinked. 'To the judges and doctors, I mean.'

Marc still couldn't fathom where this odd conversation was

leading. When he'd saved Benny's life by calling the emergency services, he'd employed an old trick that always led to an attempted suicide being placed under immediate psychiatric supervision: he stated that Benny had previously threatened to kill him as well. This automatically branded his brother a danger to the public. It also constituted a criminal offence. Since Benny had already attempted suicide several times, an overall view of the circumstances warranted his temporary committal to a secure institution. Marc's lie had been a means to an end: getting his brother off the streets and out of an environment that was quite clearly dragging him ever deeper into the mire. Besides, Benny wouldn't find it as easy to get hold of a belt or a razor blade in a psychiatric ward. He would also be out of Eddy Valka's orbit at last.

'Look,' said Marc, 'I've had enough would-be suicides for one day. . .' He tried to open his letterbox, but some vandal seemed to have messed up the lock with a screwdriver.

*Not that on top of everything else!*

The key wouldn't fit, so the only post he could get at was a furniture brochure stuck in the slit.

'. . . so, if you've no objection, I'd like to call it a night and—'

'Your brother changed so suddenly,' she broke in. 'From one day to the next.'

She caught hold of his sleeve. He was tugging at it in an attempt to free himself when the light went off. The timer had run out, and since the antiquated switch in the hallway wasn't equipped with an LED in the usual way, he took a while to grope his way over to it. By the time the light came on again he was feeling utterly exhausted and incapable of putting an end to his conversation with this mysterious nurse.

'Of course Benny changed,' he said. 'He was in a loony bin.'

She shook her head. 'I don't mean that. He'd let himself go for months on end. Wouldn't shave, wouldn't eat, lay awake all night. He often refused to leave his room – became genuinely violent when asked to do so.'

Marc nodded resignedly. This was no news to him. It was why the doctors' prognosis had been so poor and Benny's temporary admission had turned into long-term confinement.

'But from one day to the next,' said Leana, narrowing her eyes in a way that rendered her gaze still more intense, 'about a month before his reassessment, he underwent a sudden change. He asked for fruit juice and vitamin pills, went jogging in the grounds under supervision – even took to reading the Bible.'

'The Bible?'

That really did sound unlike his kid brother.

'I'm not sure if it means anything,' she went on, 'but Benny's behaviour changed the day after he had an MRI scan.'

An *MRI scan*? Was Benny's mental disorder physical in origin?

'And here's another strange thing. We normally scan the brain for anomalies, but they only scanned the lower part of his body, although he'd never complained that anything was wrong. I got hold of the pictures.'

'And?'

'Nothing. He's perfectly fit.'

'You aren't a doctor, Leana.'

'But I've got a pair of eyes in my head. Several times after that scan I caught him trying to spit out his medication. When I spoke to him about it he said he didn't want his body absorbing any more poison.'

Marc turned and took a step towards her. 'What are you getting at?'

'I think he put on an act for the board of examiners.'

'Why would he do that? He knew I was withdrawing my statement.'

Marc had ceased to care about anything after his life was rent apart by tragedy and the accident had robbed him of what he loved most. Constantin had found it easy enough to persuade him to withdraw the false allegation that had consigned his brother to a mental institution, even though he himself would now be facing a charge of perjury.

'*Get your brother out of there,*' his father-in-law had urged him. '*You need him. He's the only family you've got left.*'

Although he had thought and worried about his unstable brother every day until Sandra's death, nothing had mattered to him afterwards. He no longer wondered whether Benny was better off in a secure unit than on the street; his own mental state had robbed him of the ability to distinguish between right decisions and wrong. Especially tonight, after a day on which he'd had to dissuade a girl from committing suicide and under-gone a marathon of a medical examination shortly afterwards.

Marc experienced a surge of anger. 'Look, I'm sorry, but you surely didn't ambush me just because Benny has suddenly discovered he's got a health-conscious streak?'

'No.'

'So why?'

'I'm very worried, as I said. You really ought to keep an eye on him. I don't think he's capable of surviving out here on his own.'

*No need to tell me that. After all, I found him in the bath that time.*

'What makes you say that?'

'This.'

Putting her bag down, she reached into the inside pocket of her coat and took out a bulging envelope.

'I found it in his room when I was changing the sheets an hour after he was discharged.'

She opened the envelope. Marc was at a loss for words.

'Fifteen thousand euros. The notes are genuine,' she said, sounding rather hesitant and helpless for the first time. 'I don't know what they mean, and I've no idea how your brother came by them in a secure unit.'

# 13

Marc had somehow managed to shake off the worried nurse by promising to keep an eye on his brother and clear up the mystery of the money. They'd agreed that she wouldn't touch the cash until he got in touch with her again – though when he would summon up the energy to do that, he couldn't imagine. For the moment, even climbing the stairs seemed an almost insurmountable obstacle.

Laboriously, he trudged upstairs, past the mounds of shoes outside each door, whose condition, size and smell were as informative about his fellow tenants as the stickers on their doors or the blare of the TV programmes that filled the passages. Although Marc had seldom come face to face with anyone in the short time he'd lived there, he had a very clear idea of the lives led by his new neighbours: the single mother who couldn't afford shoe repairs, the alcoholic who preferred to spend the mornings watching wrestling rather than taking his empties to the bottle bank, or the joker whose doormat said 'No Admittance'.

Marc reached the third floor at last and felt in his jeans for his keys, which he'd pocketed again while talking to Leana. In doing so he came across the application form for the memory experiment, which he'd naturally left unsigned at the end of his examinations.

*I need a bit more time to consider,* he'd lied to Bleibtreu when taking his leave. Theirs was an acquaintanceship that would never be renewed, that much was certain.

It was tempting, the thought of being able to forget the accident by swallowing a single pill, but not at the expense of his identity. He might just as well have contemplated living in a permanent, drug-induced stupor.

He fished out the bunch of keys, which the Bleibtreu Clinic's security guard had returned, together with his small change and mobile phone, when he left the building. The display had registered no calls in his absence.

A moth had somehow got beneath the plastic cover over the light above his door and was fluttering around inside it. With a sigh, Marc inserted the key in the lock.

*What on earth. . .*

He looked up to check that he hadn't made a mistake in his fatigue. No, there it was in black numerals on the green plaster: 317. His flat all right, but the key wouldn't turn so much as a millimetre.

*Damn it, that's all I needed.*

He withdrew the serrated security key from the lock and held it up to the light.

*All in order. No nicks, no dents.*

The moth emitted a menacing hum as he tried the key again. This time he jiggled it more violently. He even threw his weight against the door, but in vain. He was about to make a third attempt when he caught sight of the name on the card in the holder beside the bell.

He stopped short, dumbfounded.

*Who the hell did this?*

The bunch of keys in his hand started to tremble. He stared incredulously at the name. Someone had replaced his own card with another. Instead of *Lucas,* it read *Senner.* His dead wife's maiden name.

It took only a moment for his shock and horror to be succeeded by boundless anger at this cruel joke. He reinserted the key in the lock, rattled the door, even kicked it. Then he froze.

*Is someone in there?*

Yes, beyond a doubt. Clamping his ear to the door, he heard them loud and clear: footsteps coming straight for him. Inside his flat.

Rage gave way to stark fear.

He shrank back as the door opened. Only a crack – only as far as the brass security chain permitted. And then, just as he saw the sad-eyed, pale-faced, dishevelled figure staring out at him from inside his own flat, time stood still.

Marc blinked, unable to get a word out. He shut his eyes and opened them again to make sure, but he didn't need a second look. He had already recognized those arched eyebrows, that air of disbelief. It was as if he'd just told her how lovely she was.

She was standing there in front of him, close enough to touch.

Sandra.

The love of his life.

His heavily pregnant wife.

# 14

'W-what. . . You can't be. . . You're. . .'

Marc was incapable of thinking clearly. His stammer grew worse with every unfinished sentence.

'Yes?' said the woman in the doorway. She brushed a strand of hair out of her eyes, the honey scent of the French shampoo Sandra had liked so much instantly bombarding him with countless memories.

*It's her...*

'You're... here?' he said. His right leg started to tremble as if he'd just done the 400-metre hurdles. He reached through the crack, eager to satisfy himself that he wasn't talking to a ghost. The woman recoiled in alarm.

'What do you want?'

Instead of all the questions he'd meant to ask, he managed to articulate a single word. 'Sandra?'

'Do I know you?' The woman in the doorway stepped forwards again and raised her left eyebrow.

'Hah...' It was more an expulsion of breath than a laugh. 'Why are you...? I thought... How can you be...?'

'I'm sorry,' she said. 'I've got something on the stove.' She tried to shut the door, but Marc jammed his foot in the crack just in time. He felt the door squash his toes and welcomed the sensation because the pain told him he wasn't dreaming.

'I thought you were dead,' he blurted out, and the woman's features blurred. The blonde who looked like his wife, spoke in her melodious tone of voice, and was wearing the white tank top he'd bought her at the maternity shop only a few weeks ago, threw all her weight against the door and called for help.

'Please stop this!'

Marc pushed back. 'But it's me, Marc.'

'Please go.'

'Marc Lucas, your husband.'

'I don't know you.'

'*What?* Baby, you can't just reappear like this and then—'

'Go away!'

'But—'

'At once, or I'll call the police!'

She was shouting now, and Marc backed away – away from the cold expression in her eyes and the bitter realization that she meant it. His wife, who had been dead six weeks, had no idea who he was. She thought he was a stranger. Worse still, she was looking at him as if he were a stranger to be afraid of.

'Sandra, please tell me what. . .'

Marc failed to complete the sentence. He was addressing a closed door.

# 15

*Non-acceptance. Suppression. Denial.*

Tottering feebly down the stairs, he wondered whether hallucinations were yet another typical concomitant of the early phase of the grieving process. Then he remembered reading an article which stated that this phase was identical, surprisingly enough, to the process of dying. For the first few weeks, a terminally ill person resembles someone recently bereaved in refusing to accept the awful truth.

*Suppression. Denial. Oblivion. . .?*

Marc clung to the banisters. Not just because he felt faint, but because he wanted to feel the cool wood beneath his fingers. It felt damp at first, damp and rather unpleasant, like the touch of something dead, but at least he was feeling *something*.

*I'm alive. I may be losing my mind, but I'm alive.*

The pain in his side was another sure sign. He'd developed a stitch after only a few steps. But it didn't hurt half as much as the mental agony inflicted on him by Sandra's cold, apprehensive expression.

*She didn't recognize me.*

If it *was* her.

Still holding on to the banisters, Marc dragged himself further down the stairs. He wondered if his brain was playing tricks on him. Was he having a dream, from which he had only to wake up? If so, what did this dream signify? Why was there a different name on the door and why couldn't he get into his own flat? Why did his damned toes still hurt where Sandra had squashed them in the door?

He paused somewhere between the second and first floors. His eye had lighted on a pair of children's boots that looked as if they'd been left out for Santa Claus to fill. They belonged to the only person apart from the caretaker with whom he'd exchanged a few words since moving in. At weekends, whenever it wasn't raining, Emily would set up her little flea market in the yard and sell objects that had value only in the eyes of a six-year-old girl. Although Marc never needed any of them, he had quickly become her best customer. He simply couldn't walk past her stall without buying a marble, a Jungle Book pencil sharpener or a bunch of dried flowers. For a moment he wondered whether to ring her mother's doorbell.

'Sorry to trouble you. I know it sounds weird and you don't know me, but please could you wake Emily up? I'd like her to reassure my late wife that I really do live here, so she'll let me into my flat.'

He gave a wry laugh, realizing for the first time why so many people sit on park benches talking to themselves. Then his wristwatch buzzed another reminder to take his pills. Pills that were waiting for him in his bathroom cabinet, in a flat to which he was denied admission because the wife he'd thought dead had failed to recognize him and wouldn't let him in.

For the moment, he decided to make for his car. Since crashing

Sandra's car he'd driven the silver Mini only once, when going to have his dressing changed. His grief that day had been so overwhelming, he had been afraid of breaking down in the Underground. After that he'd kept a spare packet of pills in the glove compartment.

'That's what I'll do,' Marc said aloud, still talking to himself. As soon as he'd cured his headache he would make a plan. Perhaps he really was in the process of losing his mind. Perhaps grief had driven him mad. But as long as he could put one foot before the other, and as long as he was capable of reflecting on the absurdity of the situation, he wouldn't do anything rash.

His resolution was short-lived. It expired the moment he emerged from his block of flats into the rain-laden November wind and saw at a glance that his silver Mini was no longer in the parking bay. Nor were any of the other cars that were usually parked there. Flapping in the wind in their place were several rusty 'No Parking' signs he'd failed to notice earlier on, when talking to the nurse.

He sucked in lungfuls of cold air. It smelt of damp leaves and the rubbish regurgitated by flooded sewers. To calm his trembling fingers, he knelt beside the kerb and tied his shoelaces. At that moment a police van turned the corner and drove slowly along the cobbled street. Its uniformed occupants eyed him suspiciously as they crawled past at walking pace.

Marc rose to his feet. He wondered briefly whether to flag them down but missed his chance. The police van was already turning the corner.

He sprinted after it to the next intersection, running faster and faster. Having made one circuit of the block, although he knew for certain he hadn't parked his car in any of the side streets, he finally came to a breathless halt outside the entrance to the flats and looked up. On the third floor – where the room with all the boxes he still hadn't unpacked was situated, where his pictures were stacked on the laminated floor and his empty aquarium served as a rubbish bin – a figure dodged back behind the curtain. Someone with long fair hair.

*Okay, enough of this nonsense.*

Marc felt in his pocket and extracted his mobile from between the application form and an empty strip of pills. He hadn't often had to ask for help in his life, but he definitely couldn't cope on his own, not now.

*I'll call my flat first, to see if Sandra picks up. Then Constantin. Even the police, perhaps. . .*

'Shit, what's *this*?' Marc was talking to himself again. He shut the mobile and reopened it. He heard the familiar beep, ran his thumb over the familiar scratch on the display and saw his screensaver, with its familiar cloudy background. But the mobile felt odd for all that.

Nothing.

Not a single entry. He couldn't call a soul. His address book had been entirely deleted.

# 16

'No, Lucas is my surname. Lucas with a "c". Yes, both names with a "c", Marc *and* Lucas. Have you checked?'

He cupped his hand over the mobile and leant forward to speak to the driver of the Mercedes taxi he'd just hailed.

'Karl Marx Strasse, Höhe Hasenheide, please.'

The cabby's sole response to this statement of their destination was to snort and turn up the volume on the radio. Sitar music blared from the loudspeaker.

'Nothing? The licence number is B – YG 12. Okay, okay. So it wasn't towed away? Thanks.'

He hung up on the police pound he'd been put through to by his mobile-phone provider's helpline. The next moment he was flung back against the seat, which was covered in protective plastic sheeting, as the diesel cab accelerated away surprisingly fast. He groped for the seatbelt, but it had slipped down behind the folding rear seat.

'Problem?' asked the bald-headed cabby, glancing suspiciously in his rear-view mirror, which had a pair of felt poker dice dangling from it. He draped a steroid-enhanced arm over the headrest of the passenger seat. Stick a pipe in his mouth, and he'd have made an excellent Popeye impressionist.

*You can say that again. I've just seen my wife and I'd like to put my seatbelt on so as not to have to share her fate. She's dead, you see.*

'Everything's fine,' Marc replied. He would have preferred to sit on the other side, but Popeye looked as if he wouldn't like a passenger breathing down his neck. So he stayed where he was and stared out of the window sans seatbelt.

He had never, even when his grief was at its most intense, felt as alone as he did right now.

It was only five minutes since he had first stared at his mobile's blank display. Five minutes since he had become aware how utterly disconnected, in the truest sense of the word, he was from his life. In the past he had often debated with friends how far the world would come unstuck if all forms of power supply were cut off overnight. It had never occurred to him that the loss of his phone would constitute so drastic a turning point. In a society where the mobile phone was not only a means of communication but a computer with which people ran their entire social life, pinching someone's

SIM card was the surest way of isolating him from the outside world.

He had never dialled a number in recent years, just clicked on the name of the person he wanted to call in his digital address book. For Sandra, Constantin, his colleague Roswitha, his old university friend Thomas and his other intimates, all he'd needed to do was press a speed-dial key. The only phone number he still knew by heart was the one he now used the least: his own mobile number. He'd stored all the rest under their owners' names and forgotten them.

*Learn to forget.*

Marc ran another check on all his sub-menus: contacts, selected phone numbers, calls received in his absence, SMS and MMS. Nothing. Someone at the clinic must have changed his phone back to its default settings. Whether deliberately or inadvertently, the result was the same: he was cut off from the outside world. There was always directory enquiries, of course, but that was no use either – they wouldn't give him Constantin Senner's ex-directory number. If anyone could help him now, it was his father-in-law. For one thing, he was in the same boat, being as grief-stricken as himself; for another, he was a doctor. If he was in a delusional state, Constantin would know what to do. It was asking too much of his friend Thomas, who would shrug his shoulders and give him useless pieces of advice he'd already thought of himself: *Check the clinic you visited today, speak to the police, call a locksmith.*

Which wasn't so simple when you'd left your ID inside the flat and had yet to register your change of address officially. He had only moved in three weeks ago.

Besides, Thomas would keep looking at his watch and ask him to keep his voice down or he'd wake the baby and his wife would give him hell.

Marc wondered what it said about him that he hadn't kept up with his friends in recent years. He'd had only one really close friend in his life, and she had donated her body to science six weeks ago.

*Sandra.*

He hadn't been able to bring himself to pay her a last visit in Pathology, where her cadaver was now being dissected by medical students. That was why he still hadn't fixed a date for an official funeral.

'What's on tonight?' the cabby shouted over his shoulder. It didn't occur to him to turn the radio down.

Marc looked bewildered. 'What do you mean?'

'At Huxleys. Who's playing?'

*Do I look like someone on his way to a rock concert?*

'No idea. I've got to look in at my office, that's all.'

Popeye glanced in the rear-view mirror again and snorted, unmistakably conveying his opinion of a workplace in this district.

'I'm an Asian freak,' he volunteered. He seemed to expect to be congratulated on the fact that even a bodybuilder could have unusual taste in music. Marc tried to ignore him. He needed all his energy in order to solve the questions to which his brain had found no answers in the last few minutes. *Why can't I get into my flat? If Sandra is dead, how could she open the door? If she's still alive, why didn't she recognize me?*

'What kind of job do you do?' asked the cabby. He was now having to compete, not only with the strains of the sitar, but also with the unintelligible hiss and crackle of his call centre.

*No wonder I can't think straight.*

Marc's first thought had been to go straight to Constantin. Then it had occurred to him that his computer at the 'Beach' held a complete back-up of his phone database. Besides, the few euro notes in his wallet wouldn't cover the fare either to Constantin's house at Sakrow or to his private clinic in Heerstrasse.

*01621...?* Marc cudgelled his brains. Sandra's and Constantin's mobile numbers shared the same prefix. He also knew they both ended in 66.

'*The devil's digits,*' Sandra had quipped on one occasion. Unfortunately, she hadn't supplied him with a mnemonic for the missing four digits in the middle. He felt himself transported back to the days when he and Benny had tried to open cycle padlocks in the school playground. It would have been impossible to hit on the correct phone numbers by chance.

*Okay, one thing at a time. First go to the office, load your mobile and pick up some cash. Then get back into your life. Your identity.*

The meter clicked: €12,30. Marc had a sudden idea. Although he tried to suppress it, he instantly realized he had to pursue it if he wanted to find out what was going on. If someone had tampered with his mobile, the only way to find out was to use an outsider's phone.

'Excuse me?'

He held his mobile so the cabby couldn't see it and leant forwards.

'Mind doing me a favour?'

Popeye promptly took his foot off the gas and pulled into the kerb, although he was still 200 metres from their destination.

'You can't pay?' he asked suspiciously, turning round. Marc slipped the mobile under his thigh.

'No, no. I think I've lost my phone. Would you mind calling a number for me?'

He indicated the cabby's mobile, which sat in a plastic holder beside the meter. It also functioned as a satnav.

'Lost it? You were using it when you got in!'

*Shit.* Marc hadn't even thought of that, he was so befuddled.

'That's just my spare mobile,' he lied hastily. 'It's my BlackBerry that's gone.'

The cabby's scepticism was unmistakable. 'You gay?' he asked.

'What gives you that idea?'

'It's an old trick. I call you, you get my phone number. But I'm not one of those. I may like wearing leather, but that doesn't mean—'

'No, don't worry. I only want to know if I've lost my work mobile somewhere or left it at my girlfriend's place. I'd call her myself, but this thing has run out of juice.' He extracted the mobile from under his thigh.

The cabby still looked hesitant. 'My number's withheld in any case.'

'You see? There's no problem, then.'

Popeye flexed his biceps and snorted contemptuously, but then almost wrenched his mobile from its holder and keyed in the number Marc gave him.

'It's ringing,' he said after a while, taking the phone from his ear.

Marc heard it, faintly, although his own display registered no incoming call.

*So I was right, they simply swapped the SIM card. But why?*

The cabby broke in on his train of thought. 'Didn't you say you left it at a girlfriend's place?' he asked.

'Er, yes.'

'But there's a man on the line.'

'What?'

Popeye handed him the phone.

Marc held it to his ear. 'Hello?' he heard. The word was repeated several times in a deep male voice.

'Sorry, I must have misdialled.'

'No problem. Who did you want to speak to?'

Marc stated his full name and was about to hang up when the man gave a friendly chuckle. 'No, pal, you've got the right number. What can I do for you?'

'Huh?'

The mobile almost slipped through Marc's sweaty fingers and his pulse rate seemed to double.

'I'm Marc Lucas,' said the stranger at the other end. 'With two "c"s.' He gave another chuckle. 'Hang on, I'll be right back.'

There was a rustling sound. 'What is it, darling?' the man asked in a muffled voice.

Marc dropped the cabby's mobile – just after he heard the woman in the background laugh.

*Sandra...*

# 17

'Hey, you've forgotten your change!' the cabby called after him, but Marc didn't turn round. He had to get out of the taxi and into the fresh air although he knew it would do nothing to stop his urge to vomit. He was usually overcome by nausea shortly after he'd taken his medication, but now it was attributable solely to his phone conversation with the unknown man.

*A stranger who goes by my name? Lives my life?*

The taxi had pulled up on the wrong side of the street. In spite of his fatigue, Marc tried to run the last hundred metres to the lights he had to cross in order to reach his office, but he got a stitch after a few steps. He used to be able to jog for 10 kilometres without a problem, but since the accident his fitness level seemed comparable to that of a cancer patient.

And now, after all that had happened during the day, that was hardly surprising.

Constantin ascribed his general debility to the side effects of the immunosuppressants intended to prevent the splinter in his neck from being rejected, but not to them alone. '*Your soul is trying to run a marathon without any previous training,*' he'd said, and advised him to consult a psychoanalyst.

Marc clamped a hand to his side and tried to 'breathe into the pain' the way Benny had taught him when they were boys being chased by ticket inspectors on the Underground. That was long before mutual hatred had insinuated itself between them.

'I'm losing my mind,' Marc kept repeating. The rainy street was deserted save for a news vendor, a courting couple and an extended family of Turkish immigrants. None of them spared a second glance for the man shaking his head and muttering to himself. Not in Berlin. Not in this neck of the woods.

'Have I gone mad, or did they do something to me at the clinic?' he asked himself.

Just before the pedestrian crossing he passed a chemist's. The window grilles had been lowered but a light was still on inside. He looked at his watch. Three minutes to eleven. A flashing sign in the window said 'LATE-NIGHT SERVICE'. For the first time in ages, at least something seemed to be going his way.

He had three minutes to get some medication. He pressed the buzzer. The next moment, someone carrying a plastic bag came up behind him and lit a cigarette. Marc could see from the man's reflection in the glass shutter that his nose was bleeding. He was eighteen at most, probably younger. His reflection vanished as the weary chemist raised the shutter and nodded curtly. He was still holding the remote control he'd been using to zap through the TV channels until he was so rudely interrupted. Marc produced an empty strip of blister pack and handed it to the man, who, according to the ID on his smock, answered to the name *A. Steiner.*

A. Steiner peered at the back of the strip. 'Axemnosphalt?' he read out incredulously, as if Marc had asked for heroin. 'Got a prescription?'

Marc shook his head. He had always obtained the medication from the clinic's dispensary after having his dressing changed.

'Never heard of it,' said the chemist. He waddled around behind the counter in his orthopaedic shoes. Marc heard him open and shut several drawers of a metal cabinet.

'And bring me some aspirin and MCP drops while you're at it,' he called.

The youth behind him groaned impatiently and blew cigarette smoke at the back of his neck.

A. Steiner had abandoned his search. He returned to the hatch with a small paper bag.

'I checked. We don't stock it. If you come back tomorrow I could order some.'

*Hell, I can't wait till tomorrow.*

The chemist deposited the paper bag containing the other medication on the shelf inside the hatch and took Marc's Visa card. He had brought a point-of-sale machine to save himself a journey.

'No, there's some wanker ahead of me. Be right back, baby. . .'

Marc turned to look at the youth, who was evidently phoning his girlfriend.

'. . . then we can carry on where we left off.'

*Carry on doing what? What kind of foreplay entailed getting your nose busted?*

'Got another?' Marc heard the chemist ask. He peered through the hatch again.

'Why?'

A. Steiner showed him the POS display.

CARD INVALID

'That's impossible, it's brand new.' Marc handed over his American Express card, but the machine wouldn't accept that either. The chemist was growing impatient.

'In that case you'll have to pay cash, Dr Lucas. That'll be €14.95.'

'Or shift your butt and let me past,' the voice behind him said angrily. 'I'm in a hurry.'

But Marc reacted neither to A. Steiner nor to the youth with the bloody nose. He had just seen, reflected in the glass shutter, a light go out in a building across the street.

*In the 'Beach'! In his office!*

'Back in a tick,' he said, snatching the paper bag off the shelf.

'Hey!' cried the outraged chemist.

'Don't worry, I work over there. I'll just nip across and get some cash, okay?'

He couldn't waste time arguing, he had to get to the desk in his office. It contained all he needed to re-enter his life: cash in a locked drawer and his phone numbers in the computer.

So he shoved the youth aside and darted across Karl Marx Strasse. Although it was late, the traffic was still as thick as it might have been in the high street of some small provincial town.

'Hello?' he shouted when he reached the central island. A sports car deliberately drove through a puddle, soaking the legs of his jeans. Marc ignored this and called again to the man kneeling outside his office door. He had already lowered the steel grille and was securing it with a padlock.

The man was wearing a black raincoat with a hood that engulfed his head like a monk's cowl. His face was invisible even at close range.

'Hey, I'm talking to you!' Marc said when he finally reached the stranger's side. 'Who are you?'

'Oh, you mean me?' The man looked up.

A tall guy in his early thirties, he wore faded jeans and a pair of trainers Marc's feet could have fitted into sideways. He shielded his face with one hand to prevent the rain from falling into his eyes.

'What's up?' he asked, in a not unfriendly tone. He rose to his feet, towering over Marc by at least two heads.

'Who are you?'

'Who wants to know?'

'The manager of the establishment you've just locked up. I don't know you from Adam, so I'm wondering what you're doing here. Who gave you the key?'

The giant glanced in both directions as if in search of some witness to their exchange. Then he grinned down at Marc derisively.

'What's the date today?'

'November 12th. What's that got to do with it?'

'I thought it might be April 1st.'

Bemused, Marc watched the unknown man pick up a shoulder bag and walk off.

'Are you taking the piss?'

The man glanced over his shoulder. 'You started it.' It was all Marc could do to keep up with him.

'Hey, stop or I'll call the police!' he called, feeling rather ridiculous.

'And do what?'

'Report you for breaking into my office.'

'*Your* office?'

'Yes.'

The giant came to a halt.

'As if I hadn't had enough aggro for one day,' he said to himself, looking up at the dark sky. The raindrops falling on his unshaven cheeks didn't seem to bother him any more. Marc had a vague feeling he'd seen him before.

'*I'm* the manager of the "Beach", my friend, and I've no idea who *you* are.'

'This is absurd,' Marc protested, digging out his bunch of keys.

He ran back to the office while the unknown man stood there in the rain, shaking his head.

'My name is Marc Lucas and I. . .'

He broke off, staring at the new padlock in disbelief. There was no point in even trying – he didn't possess any key that would fit such a big lock – but he did it, one after another, until he heard the man's voice immediately behind him.

'Marc Lucas?'

He nodded.

'Never heard of you.'

Marc stood up.

'Okay, then call Rosi.'

'Rosi?'

'My secretary. She handles the paperwork.'

'You're mistaken. There's no Marc Lucas working here, and—'

'Look,' Marc cut in brusquely, 'I've had enough of this. I insist you call Roswitha Bernhard at once.'

'Okay, okay.' The man raised both hands in a conciliatory gesture and took out his mobile. He had evidently done a basic course in de-escalation techniques and was trying to pacify this unpredictable stranger by complying with an easily fulfillable request on his part.

'Just give me this Rosi's number,' he said.

Marc clutched his neck and blinked.

*Her number. Hell, I'm not even certain of my own.*

'I don't know it,' he conceded after a longish interval. The rain was subsiding. Everything seemed to be at a standstill: the weather, the traffic, time itself. Only the tide of pain flowed on inside him.

'Is something wrong with you?' The man's voice seemed to come from far away. All of a sudden, he sounded genuinely concerned.

'I... I don't know.'

'You really don't look well. Your eyes... Have you had them examined?'

'No, it's just the side effects...'

'You're on medication?' The stranger's tone conveyed a hint of comprehension.

Marc attempted to disabuse him. 'Yes, but that's not the problem.'

*I'm not psychotic. At least, I wasn't this morning.*

He gave a start. A hand had gripped his forearm.

The big man might look like a basketball player, but he was obviously a smoker as well. He was so close, Marc could smell the nicotine impregnating his clothes.

'Look,' the self-styled office manager said amiably, 'it's my job to sort out other people's problems and I've already failed once today. Maybe I can help *you*, at least. What say I keep my wife waiting another half-hour and see you home?'

*Home...*

Marc emitted a despairing laugh, but the stranger wouldn't give up.

'Is there anyone I can contact for you?' His eye fell on Marc's wedding ring. 'You're married?'

Marc laughed even louder, even more despairingly. Then he stopped abruptly and pointed to the door behind him.

'No, I'm not going anywhere. I need to go in there, that's all.'

The man's smile vanished. 'Sorry, can't be done. The "Beach" is closed to members of the public outside office hours, but I've another suggestion. I'll drive you to a hospital. . .'

*No, no hospital.*

'You can relax there and. . .'

*No, not again. Although. . .*

'. . . they'll check you over. . .'

*Well, why not? The clinic. . .*

Marc turned and looked across the street. The chemist had emerged and was shouting something unintelligible at him, presumably a demand to see the colour of his money. But he'd have to settle up later – the man had his credit cards, after all. He would pay him tomorrow. The remaining €15 in his pocket would be only just enough to dig him out of this hole.

*Damn it, why didn't I make a note of that nurse's number?*

Marc had listened with only half an ear when Leana Schmidt told him her number. It now seemed incomprehensible that he'd recently brushed off a woman who had €15,000 on her and could confirm his identity.

'Okay, come with me,' he said, grabbing the man by the sleeve.

'What? Where to?' He tried to free himself, but Marc had his raincoat in a vice-like grip.

'We're going to the police. Together.'

'Not on your life.'

'Oh yes, we are. That's precisely what we're going to do. We'll soon see which one of us needs medical attention.'

'No, I said! Not again.'

Marc was so taken aback he let go of the man's sleeve.

'Again?' he repeated.

'The cops were on at me all day long. It's a relief to be rid of them at last.'

'The police were here?' Marc indicated the door of the 'Beach'. 'At the office?'

'Of course. Take a closer look at my face.' The man pushed his hood back. 'Don't you recognize me?'

*Yes, but I don't know where from.*

'Haven't you seen the news?'

'No, why?'

'Lucky you. You missed the Julia business, then.'

'Julia?'

'The girl at the Neukölln baths.'

The man pulled the hood back over his head. Stooping a little, as tall people tend to do, he went over to a car parked beside the kerb.

Marc stayed where he was. Yet another part of his life seemed to be slipping from his grasp with the stranger's receding figure.

'What about her?' he called. 'What happened? Tell me!'

The man's hand was already on the door handle when he turned and looked at Marc for the last time. His weary eyes were expressive of a sadness almost unique in Marc's experience.

'I couldn't stop her, damn it,' he said, and aimed a furious kick at the nearest tyre. His voice was almost drowned by passing traffic.

'She jumped, that's all.'

# 18

A man's greatest source of strength – his family – is also his most vulnerable point. It is customary in some branches of the Mafia, and for good reason, to kill all who are dear to a traitor rather than the traitor himself. His parents, his friends, his wife – and, of course, his children. Children, in particular, are a man's

Achilles heel. Especially, as in Ken Sukowsky's case, when they're daughters.

Two of them, the five- and the seven-year-old, had spent the afternoon messing around with dead leaves in the front garden. They raked them together into a little heap and then showered each other with them, again and again. The youngest girl had had to watch her sisters playing from the window, muffled up in a thick dressing gown. She had a cold and so was staying in the warm. That, at least, was Benny's guess. He had been keeping watch on the Sukowskys' modest house since early that afternoon. It was dark now, but there were lights on upstairs and down.

*Can't be much longer now...*

Benny took a last look at the crumpled piece of paper in his hand: the list he'd made during his last few days at the psychiatric hospital, written in wax crayon because patients were forbidden to have sharp objects there. It was already falling to pieces, he'd unfolded and refolded it so often since the hearing at which his discharge had been approved. Although he'd only been out a few days, two of the ten names on it were already crossed off.

He replaced the thin slip of paper in the glove compartment. Then he flexed his head and shoulders until the vertebrae creaked. The stiffness could have been worse. The rented car Valka had provided him with was perfect for this stake-out. It was equipped with stationary heating and the seats folded back into a reclining position at the touch of a button. It also suited the Westend district, being neither so ritzy nor so cheap as to stand out among the wannabe limos and 4x4s.

Benny yawned. As ever, his mind refused to come to rest despite the long wait, and he found himself wondering how he and Valka could have come to this.

Their story was typical of Berlin, the city of adolescent dreams. Those who wanted to make a career for themselves in the German capital, the nation's poorhouse, had little chance of a job in high finance, industrial management or one of the big law firms. Well-paid jobs were as rare as streets devoid of dog-shit. Just occasionally, in the sea of lights on Potsdamer Platz or out here in the Grunewald, you got an inkling of what the city might look like if one person in four wasn't on the dole and 40 per cent of children didn't fall below the poverty line – children who could only dream, if at all, of a career in which you got rich without a graduation certificate, drove fast cars and picked up lots of skirt. A career on the football pitch or, as in Benny's case, in the music business.

He shut his eyes and thought back to the point in time that had determined his present situation. Marc hadn't wanted him in the band at first. On principle more than anything else, because Benny's inability to sing or play an instrument was no disqual-ification. It applied just as much to rest of the band, not that this deterred them from massacring hits by The Cure, Depeche Mode and the other groups they modelled themselves on. They styled themselves N.R., the New Romantics, wore make-up like Robert Smith and spent three nights a week rehearsing in the basement of a local undertaker's. The business belonged to Karl Valka, Eddy's father, who had placed a room beside his mortuary at their disposal. In return, they had to tolerate his overweight, irascible son as their drummer. Eddy would much rather have sung, but the place at the microphone had already been assigned to Marc, whose voice, though far from perfect, was more melo-dious than his. They played so badly the first year that Eddy's father jocularly declared they would wake the dead and put him out of business. Then came their first gigs at school, private parties and company shindigs. They didn't get any better, just better known, and that was when the trouble started. Berlin still didn't have any American-style gangs in those days. No one carried firearms and street fights were waged with fists, not knives, but N.R.'s rivalry with the other school bands intensified with every gig they played. Competition with the Psychs, whose sound was more reminiscent of a construction site than rockabilly, was particularly fierce. As Marc's popularity grew, so Benny became more and more of an outsider. He looked the perfect victim anyway, with his long lashes, curly hair and girlish features – someone who would have seemed more at home on a suburban tennis court than playing table football in an inner-city youth club. Marc did his best to protect him initially, accompanying him to school on the Underground even on days when their timetables didn't coincide. But he couldn't always be there for him, least of all when the band was rehearsing or away on a gig. So the inevitable happened. One night Benny was beaten up by two members of the Psychs. It was a week before he could walk and a fortnight before his dislocated jaw stopped hurting.

Marc was furious. The bastards had picked on the weakest link in the chain. He and Eddy Valka worked out two fateful plans that were bound to end in tragedy. For one thing, they made Benny a member of the band. He couldn't play an instrument – if he had any talent at all it was for drawing – but that was immaterial. It was Valka, of all people, who realized that Benny's sensitivity and intelligence could be better employed in organizing their gigs, looking after their finances and settling up with concert promoters. So Marc's sensitive young brother became the band's manager. He also wrote wistful lyrics for their original compositions – not, of course, that anyone listened to them. Marc and Valka also employed the toughest youngsters from their school as bouncers to maintain security during their concerts, both out front and backstage. That was the start of Eddy Valka's career in the bouncer business, where Benny would later become his bookkeeper.

Benny opened his eyes and gave a start: he had spotted movement inside the house.

*Okay, this is it.*

A tubby little man had got up from behind his desk in the conservatory, which was used as a study.

Benny took a newspaper from the passenger seat and turned it over.

The headline on the back page proclaimed,

**'DEATH'S DOORMAN'**

He could scarcely make out a word of the article, the car's interior was so dimly illuminated by the old-fashioned street lights, but he didn't have to. He knew it by heart and could well understand why Valka was so enraged. Although his name was never mentioned, it was quite clear who the investigative journalist had in his sights. Ken Sukowsky did his homework thoroughly. At this moment he was probably interrupting it only to give his nearest and dearest a quick goodnight kiss before settling down to write another exposé.

Benny laid the newspaper aside and waited another half-hour. Then, when all the lights except the one in Sukowsky's study had been extinguished, he got out.

He hesitated when he saw Sukowsky re-enter the conservatory with a glass of Scotch in his hand and return to his desk. Then he remembered what Valka had said and pulled himself together.

*'Ninety thousand euros, Benny. You called me a month ago and I did you a favour – smuggled half of it to you in that loony bin and transferred the rest to that lousy doctor's Czech bank account. Just the way you wanted.'*

He opened the garden gate and made his way past the little mound of dead leaves.

'*I warned you it wasn't kosher but you wouldn't listen. Now you've lost the lot.*'

He paused outside the front door.

'*You were taken for a ride at my expense. But I like you, Benny. You looked after my books for a long time, and you never ripped me off. That's why I'm giving you a chance to work off your debt.*'

He knocked gently. Once. Then, after a brief interval, a second time.

'*Make sure Sukowsky can't write any more shit about me.*'

He heard the chair in the conservatory being pushed back and took the secateurs from his breast pocket.

'*Do a job on him.*'

He counted slowly backwards from ten. The door opened at four.

'Ken Sukowsky?'

The man stared at him in surprise but didn't look unfriendly. 'Yes?'

'*And prove it by bringing me all the shitty fingers he uses to write his shitty articles about me.*'

'Have you broken down or something? Can I help you?'

'No.'

Benny shook his head and clicked the secateurs shut. Still adhering to one of the blades was the blood of Valka's most recent victim – the one in the back room of his florist's shop.

'*Look on it as a form of HSP therapy, my friend. Just let rip and it'll be all right.*'

'I'm sorry,' said Benny. 'I'm beyond help.'

And he shouldered his way inside.

# 19

Another taxi and another driver – a woman this time. Still the same nightmare, though. Marc lowered the window a little to let some fresh air in but promptly closed it again because he couldn't hear the woman on the other end of the line, whose number he'd got from directory enquiries.

'I'm sorry, I'm not authorized to do that.'

'But I'm his son-in-law.'

'I'm afraid I can't ascertain that on the phone.'

Marc groaned in annoyance, staring absently at the car that had pulled up beside them at the lights. The two children in the back stuck out their tongues and laughed when he turned away.

'Then please page him,' he said.

'No point, I'm afraid. Professor Senner is operating at present – and I've already told you more than I'm supposed to.'

*This can't be happening.*

He knew the hospital receptionist – he'd made her acquaintance when going to have his dressing changed. He knew she had a dog, painted each of the fingernails on her right hand a different colour, and doodled on her memo pad while she was on the phone. She had to know who he was, but she was treating him like a stranger, politely but distantly. And the more insistent he became, the more her voice lost its cheerful veneer.

'Okay. Can you at least tell him to call me as soon as he gets out of theatre? It's an emergency.'

He was about to hang up when he suddenly remembered something. 'Just a moment. Can you see my phone number on your display?'

'No. It's withheld.'

*Shit, he won't be able to reach me at my old number.*

'But if the professor really is your father-in-law he's bound to know your mobile number.' The scepticism in her voice was unmistakable now.

'Yes, of course.'

Marc hung up. He rested his forehead against the head restraint of the front seat and massaged his temples. Nothing relieved his headache, neither the cool imitation leather nor the gentle pressure of his thumbs. Why had he bought aspirin and codeine instead of some other painkiller that didn't need washing down with water?

'Everything okay back there?'

Marc laughed silently.

*Everything okay?*

Sure. Discounting the fact that a girl whose life he'd saved that morning was dead and his wife, who had until recently been lying in a mortuary, was still alive but failed to recognize him, everything was fine.

'Know those days when the earth seems to be turning in the opposite direction?' he said, taking note of the cabby for the first time. In a lonely hearts ad she would probably have described her figure as 'womanly, with curves in all the right places'. The truth was, she filled the seat from door to gearstick.

'Like in: "Stop the world, I want to get off?"' she said.

Her sympathetic chuckle went with the colourful material in which her ample form was swathed. Marc guessed that her wraparound dress was of African origin. That figured, to judge by the three Rasta plaits dangling from her neck.

'Sure, man, I know what you mean.'

*I wonder if you do.*

The taxi braked sharply to avoid a couple so intent on catching a bus across the street that they'd darted out in front of it.

'I picked up a grandad yesterday. Nice old guy. Late seventies, I guess. Halfway there he suddenly forgot where he wanted to go.'

*Okay, maybe you do have a rough idea.*

'Worst thing was, he forgot he was in a cab – thought I was kidnapping him or something.'

'What did you do?' Marc asked, looking out of the window again. The neon sign of a car-rental firm flashed past.

'If I've learnt one lesson in life, friend, it's this: when people go mad, stay sane.'

A fellow cabby was turning into Friedrichstrasse ahead of her. She tooted him twice in salutation.

'I just ignored grandad's hullabaloo and took him where he'd asked to go in the first place. His daughter was expecting him, luckily.'

She double-parked and looked in her rear-view mirror. 'Alzheimer's. You meet new people every day, huh?'

From the way she roared with laughter at her old chestnut of a joke, she might have just invented it. Then she peered out of the window dubiously. 'You did say No. 211 Französische Strasse?'

The taxi gave a lurch as she swung round in her seat.

'Yes, why?'

'I hope you've got a hard hat with you.'

Chuckling, she reached for her receipt pad, but Marc waved it away and gave her the last few notes in his wallet. Then he got out to make sure he wasn't suffering from an optical illusion. The view from the cab was so unbelievable, he had to take a closer look.

*A hole.*

The nearer he got to the fence, the slower and more hesitant his steps became. It was as if he were approaching a clifftop. Which, in a sense, he was.

Wind was blowing into his face and rain was blurring his vision, but not enough to prevent him from identifying the numbers of the commercial buildings to his right and left. He shivered.

*This is impossible.*

Left 209, right 213.

He advanced another step. The tip of his nose was now almost touching the sign that prohibited members of the public from entering the construction site.

He looked again at No. 209, the office building on his left, and then at the investment bank on his right. Finally, he looked down.

Seven metres down into the pit which had earlier that day been the site of No. 211, the Bleibtreu Clinic. It had vanished like the last remaining vestiges of normality in his shattered existence.

# 20

Before Marc's father died of liver failure at the age of fifty-seven he had been a business consultant, an artistes' manager, the owner of several hotel and casino complexes in South Africa, the father of two illegitimate children, an alcoholic, a composer, a cartoonist, a bodybuilder – even an international best-seller writer under various pseudonyms. All this in addition to his activities as an incompetent lawyer. And all in his imagination alone.

Frank Lucas had naturally told no one in the family of his experiences in this illusory world, any more than he had informed Marc, Benny or his wife that the small law office for which he daily set off with an empty briefcase had long been in the red because of his repeated legal blunders. In spite of his schizoid disorders, however, he had succeeded in keeping his head above water for another two and a half years, thanks to a few gullible clients. Even Anita, his secretary, had continued to work half-days for almost no pay until, shortly before his death, she realized that she would never benefit financially from his forthcoming construction project in Brazil because that, too, existed only in her debt-ridden employer's imagination.

None of these things – Frank's schizoid disorders and the family's disastrous financial position – had come to light until the day the police rang the doorbell and asked to interview Marc's sister about the rape she'd undergone. The family's reaction took them aback, for there was no sister and no rape. For the first time in his life, Frank had lied to the wrong people.

They'd all had their suspicions, of course. Neither his wife nor his children had failed to notice his mood swings, insomnia, recurrent bouts of sweating and penchant for self-dramatization. On the other hand, didn't they love him partly because he didn't take the truth too seriously? Because of the fanciful, incredible, picaresque stories with which he'd won his wife's heart and held Marc and Benny spellbound in their bunk beds? Besides, didn't a good lawyer have to lie occasionally in order to get his clients off the hook?

For fear of the truth, the whole family shrank from questioning Frank's Sunday-lunch accounts of the week's events. His wife sneaked off to the bottle bank with the empties more and more often to prevent the children and her neighbours from catching on, but she never believed her husband had a drink problem, and Marc himself was now no longer so convinced of it.

Although the doctors subsequently stated that Frank's delusions were the result of recurrent alcoholic binges, Marc thought the converse more likely. His father had never drunk himself into a world of illusion; having always lived in one, he'd resorted to the bottle only in his lucid moments, when the agonies of self-recognition became too much to bear. Marc had often wondered if anything could be more terrible than the moment when the veil of illusion is drawn aside to reveal the cruel actuality behind it; the moment when your dearest wish is a swift return to your accustomed world. Even when it doesn't exist.

*Did you go through this too, Dad?*

Marc breathed deeply, clinging to the construction site's wire-mesh fence like an exhausted long-distance runner. He had seldom felt as close to his father as he did now. Perhaps the doctors had been wrong to say that Frank's disorder wasn't hereditary. Perhaps he, Marc Lucas, wasn't the person he thought. Perhaps he had never been married, never fathered a baby and never visited this Bleibtreu Clinic. Perhaps the voice behind him existed only in his head. . .

'Excuse me?'

The woman sounded diffident, like a beggar who has been rebuffed too often to hope for even a modest handout. Turning his head, Marc saw at a glance that there was something wrong with the overweight creature. She was licking her upper lip and plucking nervously at her scabby fingers.

'What is it?' Marc said brusquely. He was in no mood to help out some vagrant.

She retreated a step, clinging to the wire-mesh fence like him. The dim light made it hard to tell how much of a down-and-out she was. Her dark, shoulder-length hair might have been greasy or simply wet with rain. The same applied to the white quilted jacket that made her corpulent figure look like a Michelin man.

'May I ask you a question?' she asked softly, as if she dreaded the answer. She stepped forwards into the glare of one of the lights mounted on the fence at two-metre intervals to warn of the abyss beyond it. The sight of her puffy face and scratched hands banished any doubts Marc might have had about her mental state. The woman with the double chin and the cheap glasses with sand-coloured frames was either heavily medicated or suffering from withdrawal symptoms.

'I'd rather you didn't.' Ostentatiously, Marc looked up as though interested in the crane overhead. A light was still on in the deserted cab. If he hadn't already been feeling dizzy, just gazing up at it would have made him feel queasy.

'Are you in the programme too?' asked the timid voice beside him.

*What?*

He didn't turn to face her until she repeated the question. She removed her glasses and rather clumsily wiped the misted lenses with her bare fingers.

'The programme,' she said again, looking straight at him for the first time. Her dark, beady little eyes lent her face a doll-like appearance. She might have been younger than him, although she looked older. Marc knew only too well what life on the streets could do to a person. He peered around suspiciously. The pavement was deserted. The shops and offices had been closed for hours.

'What are you talking about?'

'The trial. The experiment.'

Although his early warning system had been defective since the accident – it had failed him several times in the past few hours – what little remained of it was sufficient to put him on his guard. It was disconcerting enough to be accosted by a down-and-out while staring into a deserted construction site on a rainy night, but the subject she had just raised rendered the situation thoroughly unreal.

'Who are you?' he asked.

'Emma.' Her arm shot out like that of a child whose parents have told her to shake hands nicely with a guest. 'My name is Emma Ludwig, and...' Her good-natured expression reminded him of his mother. She used to give him the same kindly, rather wistful look in the kitchen at the end of a long, tiring day. He was about to shake hands when the rest of her sentence made him instinctively recoil. '... and I've been waiting for you for days.'

A car went speeding through a puddle behind her.

'For me?'

He swallowed hard. A plump raindrop landed on his bare scalp. He brushed it off before it could make its icy way down his neck. He couldn't remember when he'd last shaved his head, and the feel of the stubble beneath his fingertips made him even sadder. Sandra had liked it when his 'haircut' matched his three-day beard.

'You must be mistaking me for someone else,' he said at length, letting go of the wire-mesh fence. His jeans had become completely sodden in the short time he'd been standing there.

'No, wait,' she said. 'Why did you come here? To this hole in the ground, I mean?'

Marc retreated a step. His perception of some invisible threat intensified with every word this strange woman uttered.

'What's it to you?'

'I think I can help you.'

'Why should you think I'm in need of help?' he said dismissively.

Her reply took his breath away. 'Because I'm a patient too.'

*Too? Why 'too'?*

'I was in the Bleibtreu programme just like you.'

*Wrong. I didn't even sign the application form.*

'But then I got out. Since then I've spent every spare minute here.' She indicated the construction site and put her glasses on again. 'Here beside this hole, on the lookout for people who can't understand where No. 211 has got to.'

Marc turned to go. He was itching to get away from her even though he had no idea where he could go in the middle of the night, with no car, no money or medication.

'People like you.'

He wanted to go to Constantin or his old friend Thomas – even, perhaps, to Roswitha, whom he had never met outside office hours but who at least was a familiar face. In the end, however, he went nowhere. He stayed where he was, but not because the woman who called herself Emma Ludwig had offered to help him, nor because she wanted to show him a file that would, she claimed, be of interest to him.

'Please come with me, Dr Lucas. It's too dangerous for us to be seen together here.'

He stayed because this woman, if she really existed, knew his name and shared his belief that there used to be a clinic here. That meant there was an outside chance he hadn't lost his mind. Then at least he wouldn't be the only one.

# 21

The situation was ridiculous. Confronting him was an unknown woman who sounded like a paranoid conspiracy theorist. She imagined she was being dogged by unseen pursuers from whom they had to escape at once, yet he felt he had to talk to this creature because she was the first person in ages who appeared to recognize him.

'You know who I am?'

'Yes, come on.'

Emma pulled a snow-white hood over her bedraggled hair and set off. It was only now that Marc noticed that her knee-boots were, surprisingly, far from down-at-heel. She also seemed to be in better physical condition than her obesity suggested. It was an effort to keep up with her, and he soon broke out into a sweat.

'Do we know each other?' he asked. Emma strode along with her head down, looking like a boxer on his way to the ring. 'I mean,' he added rather breathlessly, 'have we ever met before?' He was suffering from the effects of lack of medication and felt even wearier and more wrung out than he usually did at this hour. At least his nausea had subsided a little, but that could be down to the MCP drops he'd taken at the beginning of his last taxi ride.

'No, we've never met.'

Emma's reply reassured and disturbed him in equal measure. On the one hand, it accorded with his own certainty that he'd never seen this woman before. On the other, it posed the question of how she knew who he was.

He caught hold of her sleeve and brought her to a stop. 'What do you know about me?'

'Please can we straighten that out on the way?'

'On the way to where?'

A car crawled past. Emma swiftly turned to face a shop window displaying women's shoes that cost more than a laptop – despite the 30 per cent price reduction emblazoned in bold lettering.

'He's only looking for a parking place,' said Marc, and she promptly lost interest in a pair of high-heeled Italian sandals.

'Quick, quick!'

She hurried across the street, taking a bunch of keys from her jacket pocket. When Marc saw what she was rushing towards, his original assumption about her was finally dispelled. Nobody who drove an old Volkswagen Beetle with a divided rear window could be an urban vagrant.

But he wasn't interested in going for a drive in this peculiar creature's car. He wanted some answers.

'Stop, wait.'

Although he hadn't raised his voice she must have sensed its latent threat. She turned and saw the mobile in his hand.

'What are you doing?'

'I'm going to call the police and—'

'No, don't!'

She came back with her hands outstretched defensively, stark panic in her eyes. Marc knew that look of desperation. He'd often seen it in his street kids when they were told their parents were waiting in the room next door.

'Oh yes, I should have done it before, at the "Beach".'

He dialled 110 and put his thumb on the key with the green telephone.

'The "Beach"? That's what you call your Hasenheide office, isn't it?'

*How does she know that?*

He removed his thumb from the key.

'What else do you know about me?'

Emma drew a deep breath.

'You're Dr Marc Lucas, lawyer and social worker, age thirty-two, of Steinmetzstrasse, Schöneberg. Widower, formerly married to Sandra Senner, thirty-three. She lost her life in a car crash. And...'

She opened the passenger door and went round to the driver's side.

'... and you mustn't call the police, not under any circumstances.'

The chill had spread from Marc's sodden trainers to his throbbing temples. He rubbed his ears, but they were as numb as his fingers.

'Why not?' he demanded.

'Not before I've explained what's happening to you.'

She opened the driver's door, got in and wound the window down. The eyes behind her glasses were blurred by raindrops.

Marc stared at her. 'Who the hell are you?'

She gave him a mournful look and started the engine. It wasn't loud enough to drown her mysterious and disconcerting reply: 'I can't remember.'

She backed out of the parking space with the passenger door open and pulled up right beside him.

'Please get in, Dr Lucas. We're in great danger.'

# 22

Benny knew he ought to answer Eddy Valka's call at once.

*At once. Without fail.*

He couldn't afford to ignore this muted call or his life would end sooner than he'd planned. Very probably tomorrow morning. By midday at the latest, but only if he was in luck and Valka felt like a lie-in.

He knew what was at stake. They had agreed that he would confirm that the job was done by eleven that night, and it was long past that.

But there were two reasons why it was impossible for him to put out his hand and take the mobile from the passenger seat.

The first reason was that an overwhelming fit of depression was paralysing him inwardly. The second wore a green peaked cap over her chin-length fair hair and was shining a flashlight in his eyes.

'Traffic control. Papers please.'

He nodded and leant towards the glove compartment, but his brain refused to transmit the requisite impulses to his muscles.

Many of the thugs he'd got to know through Valka poked fun at his fits of depression. They categorized them as a woman's disease, a luxury of affluent society peculiar to gays and chicks. He envied their ignorance of the truth. Genuine depression was like a sponge inside your chest that absorbed dark thoughts, getting heavier and heavier until you could physically feel its weight. It began by affecting your breathing and swallowing, but later it paralysed your every movement until you couldn't even extricate your head from under the bedclothes.

'A bit faster, if you can.' The young policewoman looked over at her colleague for help, but he was busy checking another car a few metres away.

Benny knew why she'd plucked him out of the stream of traffic on Brunnenstrasse. He'd been driving much too fast because the radio oracle had distracted him.

*Will I make it?*

He couldn't understand why he'd reverted to this silly game of Marc's, tonight of all nights. It had never brought them anything but aggro.

The rules of the oracle were simple but hard and fast. You asked a question, for instance: *Will I ever be rich and famous?* Or: *What do I have to do so Nicoletta from the tenth grade lets me feel her up at last?* Or, like today: *Will I make it?* Then you turned on the car radio and the lyrics of the first song you heard supplied the answer.

Many years ago they had let the radio oracle decide whether they should really dump their father's car in the flooded gravel pit.

Benny had been fifteen, Marc sixteen, and they should never, of course, have been driving Frank's estate. But nothing had ever gone wrong before on their nocturnal jaunts through Berlin. No accidents, no police checks, no stains on the seats. Everything went brilliantly. They crashed three parties a night and the girls let their 'heroes' paw them on the back seat because they were just the coolest in their gang: the only teenagers with wheels of their own.

Until one night, around four in the morning, they drove home to find their father's parking place outside the falafel restaurant occupied – a parking place reserved by local custom for 'the lawyer'. Unfortunately, some unwitting idiot with Hamburg licence plates had left his environmental hazard exactly where Lucas Sr. would be looking for his car in three hours' time.

Marc had consequently suggested dumping the Mercedes in the gravel pit before the shit hit the fan and they were packed off to boarding school. So they'd made one more circuit of the block and turned on the car radio just as 'Sailing' came on. This allowed only one possible interpretation, especially as they knew Rod Stewart was singing the song and it was an incontrovertible rule that the oracle counted only if you could identify the singer.

So they'd dumped the car.

'Here they are.'

Benny had somehow managed to hand his papers through the window without passing the policewoman the crumpled list of names that had also been in the glove compartment.

While she was suspiciously eyeing his driver's licence he picked up his vibrating mobile.

'Call you back right away, Eddy,' he said, but he earned himself an irritable frown for all that.

'Please get out,' she said.

Although surly, her voice was far more enthusiastic than Valka's at the other end of the line: 'Am I hearing you right?' His words were overlaid by loud dance music. He was probably propping up the bar in one of the discos or lap-dancing establishments he controlled. 'Like hell you will!'

Did this refer to him calling back or was Valka forbidding him to get out of the car? Benny wasn't sure.

'How long is this going to take?' he asked, loudly enough for Valka to hear him.

Valka was totally unimpressed. 'Done it?' he asked.

Benny gave an affirmative cough.

'That's entirely up to you,' the policewoman said briskly, and repeated her request that he get out. Valka went on talking too.

'Good, then bring me the proof.'

'Hang on a moment.'

'To hell with that!'

Benny laid the mobile aside without ringing off. Summoning up all his energy, he hoisted himself out of the car. The dark sponge inside him made every movement torture.

He shut his eyes and blew into the breathalyser, long and hard.

'You wait here,' the policewoman said curtly. She went over to the police van, doubtless to run a check on his papers.

Benny put the mobile to his ear again. 'Eddy?'

'Are you crazy, you dickhead, keeping me hanging on like this?'

'Listen, there are cops here. I can't speak now.'

Valka yelled something unintelligible and the background music faded abruptly. Then he came back on the line. 'I want proof that you've done the job.'

'It's in my boot.'

'Which brings us to job number two. Get rid of the garbage.'

'No worries, I'll do that as soon as I'm past this traffic control point.'

The door of the police van slid back and the blonde police-woman emerged.

'And then get out of town.'

'Doing a John Wayne, are you?' asked Benny.

'I mean it. That's job number three: Beat it. I never want to see your face in Berlin again.'

The policewoman came marching over.

'Okay, give me a couple of days.'

Benny thought of the list. Only two names had been crossed off. Two out of ten.

'You've got two hours.'

'That's not enough.'

'Shit, I think my mobile's playing up.' Valka laughed. 'I thought I heard you say no.'

'I need a bit more time.'

'What for? To pack your sports bag?'

'I. . .' Benny gulped. He couldn't possibly tell Valka the truth. 'I've got to say my goodbyes.'

'Who to?' Valka laughed again, more derisively this time. 'Don't mess me about, amigo. I can't afford to let people think I've gone soft. Get that consignment out of Berlin and never come back, understand?'

Benny pocketed his mobile just as he caught a whiff of the policewoman's perfume behind him. 'Escape' by Calvin Klein.

*Escape. . .*

He couldn't help smiling at the irony.

'Your reading was zero,' the policewoman said, sounding almost disappointed, and returned his papers.

'You haven't been out long, have you?'

His smile vanished. 'Is that it?'

She gave him a lingering stare. Then she did the thing he'd been dreading most: she pointed to the boot.

'Just the breakdown triangle and the first-aid kit, please. Then we're through.'

# 23

It's easy to spot a mistake after the event. But as long as you haven't reached the eye of the storm and are still on the edge of the vortex of insanity, you're subject to its irresistible attraction. While the set pieces of your own life are whirling about your ears, you lose your perspective and make one wrong decision after another. Marc guessed he was making a mistake the moment he got into Emma's car. He also guessed that he would be making an even bigger one by following her into the cheap commercial travellers' hotel near the airport.

If he'd been watching a biopic of his own life, he would doubtless have been able to ply the wretched hero on the screen with sensible pieces of advice. *Call the police. Go to Constantin's hospital. Enlist some impartial assistance. But don't go anywhere with this woman, least of all to a seedy hotel in Tegel!*

He wasn't relaxing in a comfortable cinema seat, however, but sitting on the edge of a worn-out hotel mattress. Nor was his brain functioning normally, in a way that would have enabled him to come to a rational decision. Within the space of a few hours Marc had lost everything he'd believed in up to then: the authenticity of his memories and his own existence.

During the drive Emma had silently handed him a sheet of paper that looked as if it had been ripped out of a binder by someone in a rage. Out of a CV, to be precise, because closer inspection by the car's dim courtesy light revealed it to be the first page of a three-page résumé. It seemed even less consistent with Emma's outward appearance than his initial assumption that she begged for a living.

Apparently born in Dresden, she had fled to France with her parents before the reunification of Germany and studied at the Sorbonne. Medicine to begin with, then German, Spanish and French. Thereafter she had worked as a simultaneous interpreter at trade conferences, mainly for the pharmaceutical industry, for which her discontinued medical studies particularly fitted her.

Marc made another attempt to breach the wall of silence. 'Well, what did you want to show me that's so important?' Since reaching the hotel she had confined her conversation to bare essentials. She signalled to him to wait a moment.

Having so far limited himself to watching her get out a holdall and extract several batches of old newspapers, he made a leisurely survey of her hotel room. Its neglected, gloomy appearance matched that of the night porter who had handed them the key at the reception desk. It was also probable that the stale, over-heated air smelt like his armpits. Emma had presumably left the 'Please Don't Disturb' sign on her door for days. She had spent the interval transforming her quarters into a cross between a box room and a second-hand bookshop.

Half of the double bed was strewn with press cuttings, sheets of paper written on both sides and medical textbooks, more of which could be seen on the small desk beside the TV cabinet. Emma had taken off her boots and her white hooded jacket, which was lying in a heap on the threadbare carpet. All she wore now was a baggy woollen dress that reached to her ankles.

While Marc was debating how much longer to give her before

he finally cut and run, Emma sat down on a precariously creaking upright chair with her left leg draped over her massive right thigh, massaging the ball of her foot.

He got up and went over to the window.

'Don't. They might see you.'

'Who?' He lowered the blind.

'Bleibtreu's people.'

She fiddled nervously with her glasses, then took them off and chewed the end of one arm.

'Bleibtreu?' said Marc.

'Yes.'

'So the clinic really exists?'

*Great. You're seeking reassurance from a nutter.*

He opened the window without raising the blind.

'Of course.'

Emma had to speak up to make herself heard above the patter of the raindrops, which were hitting the pane like bullets. The wind blew an occasional ricochet into the room. 'Of course the clinic exists. I was there myself.'

She pushed the glasses up over her forehead like an Alice band, nervously licking her lips again. All at once, as if something had occurred to her, she rose with a jerk and stomped over to the wardrobe.

'So where, tell me, has the building gone?' Marc demanded.

Emma keyed a six-digit code into a safe the size of a shoebox secured to one corner of the wardrobe.

'It hasn't gone anywhere, Marc. You just didn't see it.'

His sarcastic laugh was rather shriller than he'd intended. 'Look, I've had one hell of a tiring day. My powers of comprehension are roughly equal to those of someone emerging from a general anaesthetic. Just for once, could you possibly say something that doesn't raise more questions than it answers?'

Emma took out a slim folder folded in half to enable it to fit into the safe. It trembled in her clumsy-looking hands.

'It's all part of their plan. They want to rattle us, confuse us, traumatize us.'

Studying her face closely for signs of the insanity he suspected in himself, Marc could detect nothing but the residue of long-vanished good looks. He guessed that Emma must once have been extremely attractive – until something happened to throw her out of kilter, first mentally, then physically. Today, only the regularity of her features recalled a time preceding the medication that had left such visible traces behind, or so he surmised. Cortisone, for example, which often resulted in a moon face like hers. Psychiatric drugs perhaps, or worse.

*Drugs?*

'All right,' he said, 'let me try a different approach.' He resumed his place on the edge of the bed. 'This morning, a little old man in a very expensive car offered to delete all my unpleasant memories for ever.'

'MME. The amnesia experiment.'

'You took part in it yourself?'

'Till I broke it off a week ago.'

'Really?' Marc frowned. 'Okay, be that as it may. My problem is – well, how can I put it? – at the moment I'm undergoing experiences that would knock any mystic sideways but which can't have any connection with the Bleibtreu Clinic.'

'Why not?'

'Because those people wanted to blot out my memories, but they're all still in here.' Marc tapped his head. 'Unaltered. It's just that they don't add up any more. To be quite honest, the professor and his associates may be a bunch of lunatics, but I've no idea how they could have completely brainwashed me in such a short time without my noticing.'

Emma stared at him in bewilderment. 'A short time?'

'I was only there five or six hours. I swallowed no pills, wasn't given any injections and drank a couple of glasses of water.'

'You're wrong.'

'Are you disputing what I remember?'

'No. All I meant was, today wasn't your first day as part of the trial.'

'Huh?'

'That's why I wanted you to come with me. To show you this.'

She opened the folder and took out a sheet of paper printed on both sides. Marc had seen it once before. A few hours ago. At the clinic.

'See this?'

She held out the form and tapped the handwritten box in the top-right corner.

'This is. . .'

. . . *impossible.*

Marc took the sheet from her.

*Quite impossible.*

'Now do you see why it's so important for us to have a talk?'

He nodded without taking his eyes off the application form, which had been completed and bore his signature. What startled him most of all was the date.

October 1st. The date of the accident.

Four weeks *before* he answered the Bleibtreu Clinic's advertisement.

# 24

It looked like an original, but before he could satisfy himself that he was holding a forgery in his hands there was a knock at the door: three short, two long. Although it sounded like a prearranged signal, Emma didn't seem to be expecting anyone. She glanced nervously at the door, then at Marc. Then she snatched the application form back.

'*Who?*' she breathed. The right-hand corner of her mouth was quivering.

Marc shrugged. He'd never heard of the Tegel Inn Hotel until a quarter of an hour ago. How should he know who was standing outside her door, which wasn't, unfortunately, fitted with a spyhole? They would have to open it to discover who wanted them so late. It could hardly be a member of the staff. This seedy hotel boasted neither room service nor a minibar in need of topping up.

'I'll go and see,' he whispered when the knock was repeated. The same rhythm, the same knuckles tapping on laminated wood.

'No!' Emma shook her head fiercely and grabbed his arm, pulling him so close that the tip of her nose brushed his ear. 'Don't you see what's going on here?'

'No.' He tried to free himself.

'They're after us.'

'Who? Bleibtreu?'

Her hair tickled his cheek as she shook her head again. 'He doesn't do his own dirty work. He's got people for that.'

Her eyelids flickered violently and her massive bosom heaved at every breath. 'That's just why I need you,' she said in a low, shaky voice. 'I need a witness who'll confirm what they're doing to us. . .'

She put a finger to his lips just as he opened his mouth to speak and touched his tongue. Unlike him, she seemed not to notice this involuntarily intimate contact.

'This is getting ridiculous,' he whispered.

'. . . a witness who'll document the results of the experiment. No one will believe my word alone.'

He shook his head vigorously and freed himself from her grasp. Before she could protest he strode swiftly to the door, undid the chain, and opened it.

Too late.

# 25

The narrow but surprisingly well-lit corridor was deserted. There was nothing to be seen apart from a trolley overflowing with dirty sheets and a soft-drinks dispenser at the far end.

Marc came back into the room. For one brief moment he was afraid that Emma, too, had disappeared. Then he heard her voice.

'We must get out of here.'

She was tugging a holdall from under the bed. It looked far too small to contain all the papers strewn around the room.

'Look, calm down.'

'No, I won't!' She almost shouted the words. 'You don't understand the situation we're in.'

'You're right, I don't understand any of it, but you're making no attempt to enlighten me.'

Emma slammed the holdall down on the clear side of the bed and brushed a thin film of sweat off her forehead with her forearm. Then she glanced at her watch. 'All right, here's the short answer: you're in the amnesia programme because there's something you've got to forget.'

'Yes, I know.'

He started to tell her about the accident that had robbed him of his wife and unborn son, but she interrupted him after only a sentence or two.

'No, that can't be so.'

'Why not?'

'They wouldn't go to these lengths if it was only a question of heartache.'

*Heartache?*

'Hey, I'm not just talking about a broken date. My pregnant wife and unborn son are dead and *I'm* to blame.'

'I'm sorry, I didn't mean to hurt your feelings, but there's far more involved here than a personal tragedy.'

'What makes you say that?'

She struggled with the holdall's zip, which had jammed. Marc came to her aid.

'Have you any idea what this series of experiments is costing? Implementation, supervision, evaluation? Add in a new identity and it'll run to seven figures. No, it's quite out of the question.'

'But why would they publicly advertise for guinea pigs if it's so damned expensive?'

'They don't.'

She went over to the desk and opened a drawer. It was filled to the brim with old magazines.

'When did you send that email?'

'Two weeks ago.'

She pulled out one magazine after another and tossed them carelessly on the floor until she found what she was looking for.

'Here.'

She handed him a news magazine. It was the issue in which he'd come across the Bleibtreu Clinic's advertisement on page 211. The page number had lodged in his memory only because Clause 211 of the penal code related to murder. The habit of using mnemonics to remember telephone and room numbers was a lawyer's disease you could never shake off, even if you didn't practise as an attorney or judge.

'Take a good look,' Emma told him. 'Go through it from beginning to end. You won't find the advertisement there.'

It was true. On page 211 Marc found a puff for an internet bank, not a psychiatric clinic's slogan.

*Learn to forget.*

The article at the top of the page, a report on the unutterable cruelty of transporting livestock over long distances, was still there.

*Either there were two different editions of the same issue in Constantin's waiting room...*

He lowered the magazine and stared at it blankly.

*... or the edition in Constantin's waiting room was a fake. But that would mean...*

He leant against the wall because he felt the room tilting beneath his feet.

'What about you?' he asked with his eyes shut. 'What was your reason for taking part in the experiment?' He heard Emma clear her throat.

'It was about a year ago. I received a job offer that didn't come via my translation agency. It sounded vaguely suspect but involved a great deal of money. Cash I now need to make good my escape.'

'What was the job?' Marc opened his eyes.

'Routine, really. Simultaneous translation on a flight to Barcelona in a pharmaceutical company's private jet.'

'A flight during which matters were discussed which you'd have done better not to hear?'

'Correct.'

'What were they?'

'No idea. That's just my problem, I broke off the experiment too late. I can't remember.' She ran her fingers nervously through her hair. 'I've only a patchy recollection of my identity and my life before the amnesia experiment. All I know is what I've gleaned from the papers I stole from the records before I escaped.'

*So that's how she got hold of her CV. From the clinic.*

'Why did you escape?' he asked.

'Because of you.'

'Me?'

'I'm sure they explained the methodology of the experiment. In phase one your memories are deleted. In phase two you're fed with memories of pleasant experiences you never wanted to forget. Last of all, you're provided with a new identity.'

'Yes, that I *do* remember.' Marc laughed derisively. 'But how come *you* know it if your memory has such big gaps in it?'

Emma gripped her Adam's apple and cleared her throat again. 'I've done some research on the internet since I escaped. There are a number of blog entries describing such amnesia experiments.' Marc raised his eyebrows incredulously, but she pressed on undaunted. 'Well, I was just starting on phase two when I overheard a conversation between Professor Bleibtreu and another man.'

'What was it about?'

'You.'

'Me?'

Emma nodded. 'Bleibtreu was arguing fiercely. He'd been asked to treat someone named Marc Lucas, but he was dead against it.'

*Bleibtreu didn't want to treat me? Then why did he pick me up in his car?*

'Who was the other man?' Marc asked.

'I've no idea. They were behind the frosted-glass door that separated the consulting room from my examination room. A nurse had brought me along too early – they didn't know I was waiting next door.'

'What else did they discuss?'

'They talked about the bogus advertisement that had lured you there. So you could undergo further treatment.'

'Further treatment?'

'Yes, but this time it was to be done properly.'

*What? What was to be done? And why?*

Emma gave him no opportunity to pursue this train of thought. 'Bleibtreu was startled out of his wits when he saw me,' she went on. 'He stepped in front of the other man, quick as a flash, so I never got a chance to see his face. After that I knew there was something fishy going on.'

'And you escaped?'

'An opportunity arose the very next day. I stole an overall from one of the cleaning staff.' Emma looked down at herself with a disparaging expression. 'I look more like a charwoman than an interpreter in any case. It was child's play.'

'But first you took your file?'

She nodded. 'Yes, from the patients' records. It was a fortunate coincidence our surnames are so close together. Ludwig, Lucas. My folder still contained my car keys and a parking card, but there was nothing in yours except this application form.'

She pointed to the form she'd taken back from him, which was now lying at the foot of the bed beside a textbook on neuropsychology.

Marc felt the back of his neck. 'But why? I still don't understand any of this. Who has designs on my memories? Why are they trying to drive me insane?'

Emma's eyes widened. She gazed at him expectantly, like a teacher waiting for her pupil to come up with the right answer. 'That's just what I'm asking you. What deadly secret – one you can't remember – are you carrying around with you?'

'Deadly?'

She expelled a deep breath. 'Yes. Why do you think I'm on the run? We're in the greatest danger. We're both in possession of some secret we want to forget. Our enemies are more powerful than us, that's for sure, but together we may manage it.'

'Manage what?'

'To find out what they're doing or have done to us. Then we document it and put it on the internet. We publicize the awful truth.'

Marc looked at his watch. Not for the first time, he wondered whether the alarm would go off at some point and extricate him from this nightmare. 'Have you any idea how crazy you sound?'

'Not half as crazy as the man who was giving Bleibtreu an earful.'

'What do you mean?' Marc felt his stomach fill with bile. 'What else did he say?'

Emma's hands started to tremble. She put them to her lips as if to lessen the impact of her words. 'He said: "Marc Lucas mustn't remember, or there'll be more deaths."'

# 26

The hot-water tap wasn't working. The other gushed like diesel from a pump for HGVs, but the water was too cold to dissolve the aspirin tablet Marc had dropped into the tooth mug. The hotel bathroom was a windowless cubbyhole partitioned off from the bedroom by thin plasterboard walls that provided optical privacy at most, but certainly not acoustic. He could even hear Emma tossing more papers into her holdall.

*What deadly secret are you carrying around with you?*

He wondered whether to tell her about the last few minutes before the accident. About the moment when Sandra undid her seatbelt in order to get something from the back seat.

*That coarse-grained, monochrome photo. The one I couldn't make out.*

But what did that sequence, which seemed to him more like a dream than a genuine memory, have to do with the shock waves whose turbulence now engulfed him? Who was so anxious to brainwash him? He could scarcely recall the last few minutes before the crash in any case. There was no need to expunge his memory of them; it had dissipated of its own accord, thanks to the painkillers they'd given him at the scene of the accident.

He opened the bathroom cabinet in search of a nail file or some other implement with which to break up the aspirin, but the hotel's complimentaries were limited to a two-pack of condoms past its use-by date. Shutting the cabinet again, he flinched at his own reflection in the mirror. His face looked as if a seismic shock had sent its individual features into free-fall. His sunken eyes surmounted two pendulous pouches, and even the corners of his mouth seem to be sagging under the effect of gravity. It was a long time since he'd coerced them into a smile.

Dusty though it was, the overhead light shed a glare that accentuated his look of general ill health. The colour of his eyes and skin was reminiscent of someone suffering from jaundice.

He held his wrists under the icy jet. Its chill helped him to sort out his thoughts. If the Bleibtreu Clinic and the amnesia experiment really existed, he hadn't gone mad but had become the victim of a conspiracy.

That was the good news. The bad news: if she wasn't dead, his wife must be actively involved in that conspiracy.

*But why? To what end?*

Why would Sandra want to subject him to such unutterable torment? Why would she have faked her death and come to life a short while later, only to traumatize him still further by pretending not to know him? Was she capable of such cruelty?

True, she was an actress. She found it easy to take people in. Marc remembered their first date only too well. She had invited him to a performance at her drama school, introduced him to her fellow students as her brother, and then shocked them by kissing him passionately on the lips two minutes later. After that they had made a game out of putting each other in embarrassing situations. His revenge for the incestuous kiss had been to stand up in the middle of her next public appearance and clap so frenetically that she burst out laughing and forgot her lines. They were both proficient in swapping roles, but never in order to wound each other. Sandra's acting ability and her sense of fun had formed a bond between them, never a rift. Besides, there was no reason for her to want to destroy what they had built up together.

*Unless. . .*

Marc stirred the aspirin with his forefinger. Only a third of it had dissolved.

*Unless this really is a matter of life and death.*

He took a swallow, although the tablet wasn't even frothing on the surface. On a scale between white- and red-hot, his headache was entering the incandescent zone.

*Or. . .*

The thin disposable cup crumpled in his hand as a possible explanation occurred to him.

*What if it's Sandra who is in the Bleibtreu programme, not me? What if she genuinely can't remember me any more?*

Throwing the broken cup on to the floor, he opened the bathroom door and headed back to the bedroom along the narrow passage flanked by the wardrobe. He must ask Emma what she knew about his wife. Perhaps she'd gathered that Sandra had also been part of the experimental programme. Although that would raise a myriad new questions, it would at least account for her whereabouts during the last few weeks, not to mention her recent behaviour.

The premises were so cramped that the open wardrobe door was barring his route back to the bedroom. He was about to shut it when the sound of his own name abruptly froze him to the spot.

'Marc Lucas,' Emma was saying in a low voice. 'I've found him. We're now at the Tegel Inn Hotel on Bernauer Strasse.'

Holding his breath, Marc peered through the narrow crack between the wardrobe door and the outer wall of the bathroom.

*What the hell's going on?*

No doubt about it: Emma was on the phone to someone.

'It's now one minute to midnight,' she said. 'I'm not sure if I can persuade him to come with me.'

He drew back. In an even lower voice, she said: 'It'll be hard to gain his trust. He's very suspicious.'

The last words were like a starting pistol. Heedless of what he might be leaving behind in the room, he quietly opened the main door and stole out into the corridor. The overhead light had gone out. The corridor was in darkness, so he had to find his way by means of the thin slivers of light escaping from under some of the doors.

*Who was Emma talking to? What was her role in this crazy affair?*

He didn't dare put on speed till he reached the stairs, which he raced down two at a time. He almost lost his footing when he reached the ground floor and slalomed around the reception desk.

'Oh, you were in all the time. . .' the night porter called after him.

Marc continued on his way to the exit, walking backwards. 'Was it you who knocked earlier on?'

'Yes. There's a problem with the hot water, and. . .'

He didn't hear the rest. It was swallowed up by the revolving door that propelled him out of the hotel and into the street.

*What now? Where to?*

The traffic was noticeably sparser. There was no one in sight but a shift worker walking his cocker spaniel.

*Where shall I go? Without money, without a car, without a home. . . without any memories?*

He stood beside the kerb at some temporary traffic lights, looking first left and then right like some well-trained schoolboy. Behind him, the hotel's neon sign deluded potential guests with three stick-on stars.

His wristwatch vibrated, reminding him of another vital necessity he lacked: the pills for the splinter in his neck.

The man with the cocker spaniel was coming towards him, far too engrossed in his mobile phone to notice that his dog had been wanting to relieve itself for a considerable time.

Marc looked up at the third floor, where light showing through cracks in the blind denoted Emma's probable location. He wondered if he'd left his mobile up there but found it in his jacket pocket.

He opened the phone and decided to go right, guessing that a busier intersection lay in that direction – possibly an Underground station as well. He seemed to have inadvertently turned off his mobile after that last call in the taxi, because the display was dead. It couldn't be for lack of juice, because when he turned it on he was asked for his PIN number. The first time it beeped a warning he thought he must have mistyped the number. The second beep reminded him of the strange man who had answered his own number – and called himself Marc Lucas! After the third attempt he felt sure he didn't know the code for the swapped SIM card. He came to a halt, satisfied himself that no one had been following him, and wiped a raindrop off the display.

*Input incorrect.*

Utterly exhausted, he read the second line of the automated error message.

*Phoned locked.*

And suddenly knew what he had to do.

# 27

The man looked less like a hunter than a hunted beast. His eyes swivelled to and fro as he spoke, incapable of focusing on any particular feature of the office. Not that it contained much that was worth a second glance. Neither the walls plastered with 'Wanted' notices and street maps, nor the battered regulation filing cabinets, nor the yellowish washbasin on the right of the door, nor the anonymous utensils on the cramped little desk – one of three – at which they sat facing one another. Marc had often wondered if members of the municipal administration were selected for their colour-blindness – those of them, at least, who were privileged to choose the interior decoration of public buildings. The police station was done up in shades of brown and ochre never to be found in nature. It looked as unhealthy as the policemen working there, whose pallid complexions had changed as little in recent years as the surrounding décor.

Marc knew Wedding police station of old. As boys, he and Benny had tried to steer clear of the place, not always with success. He now discovered that it made a considerable difference, when you were waiting to make a statement in these airless rooms, whether you were a perpetrator or a victim. He had never felt as bad in the old days, when they were called to account because one of their gigs had ended in a punch-up. He had always got off with a caution, fortunately – a criminal record would have put paid to his law studies.

'Let's get one thing straight,' said the policeman who had just entered the office trailing a cloud of cigarette smoke and introduced himself as Detective Inspector Stoya. 'We've had enough nutters waltzing in here and wasting our time today, so kindly get to the point. What do you know about this kidnapping?'

Bewildered, Marc watched him vandalize a half-empty mug of coffee with several artificial sweeteners from a dispenser.

'Kidnapping?' he said. That made Stoya look him in the face for the first time. For one brief moment he felt he was staring into a mirror that reflected negative features only. Tired eyes, sunken cheeks, pouches that looked heavy enough to drag the whole head earthwards. Marc knew just how tense the policeman's neck muscles would feel if he touched them. His own ached whenever he moved.

Stoya slid a newspaper from under his mug and pointed to the front page.

Over the photographs of two children, yesterday's headline screamed –

**'THE EYE COLLECTOR STRIKES AGAIN!'**

Marc recalled having heard something about a serial kidnapper on the radio – a psycho who abducted children aged between seven and twelve and gave the parents seventy-two hours to find their hiding place before he killed them and cut out their left eyes. No child had yet been rescued alive from the clutches of the 'Eye Collector', and his latest ultimatum was due to run out in a few hours' time.

'No, I'm not here about that,' said Marc. He now realized why the 35th Precinct was so busy at this time of night. The corridors were teeming with uniformed officers and plain-clothes men, numerous telephones were ringing simultaneously, and the waiting room was full to overflowing. If he and Stoya had this three-desk office to themselves, it was presumably because the other two occupants were out on the manhunt.

Stoya sighed and glanced at the clock above the door. 'Sorry, I was misinformed. So what do you want?'

*I want to report a crime. To be more precise, a conspiracy.*

Marc had spent the long wait trying to think of some suitable preamble, but without success. He had eventually decided to answer any questions off the cuff – a mistake, as it turned out, because what he had to say sounded ludicrous even to his own ears. He could almost predict how the conversation would go.

'*You can't get into your flat?*'

'*That's right.*'

'*Why come to the police? Why not call a locksmith?*'

'*Because someone's holding the door shut from the inside.*'

'Who?'

'My late wife...'

Stoya eyed the clock impatiently. He looked as if he might jump to his feet at any moment, so Marc broke the silence. 'I want to report a crime.'

He went on to summarize the inexplicable events that had overtaken him, speaking faster and faster the more often the policeman's facial expressions changed. They ranged from impatience and boredom to astonished incredulity and undisguised scepticism. There were even times when Marc wasn't sure Stoya was listening to him at all. He had pulled his computer keyboard towards him and spent the last couple of minutes staring at the antiquated box monitor with one hand on his mouse.

'Okay...' he drawled when Marc was finished at last. 'In that case, I've only one question for you.'

'Which is?'

'Got any left?'

'Any what?'

'Any of the stuff you've been taking.'

Stoya rose and signalled to a young uniformed cop who had just come in.

'Look, I know it sounds absurd...' Marc began, but the inspector raised his hand with an indulgent smile.

'No, no, don't worry, I hear this sort of thing every day.'

Marc got up too. 'Please, can't you send an officer to my place to check it out?'

The young cop was now standing just behind him, awaiting instructions. He smelt of warm sleep and cheap cologne. He'd probably been taking a nap in a broom cupboard and freshened himself up with aftershave.

'I don't have time for this nonsense, not now of all times.'

'Okay, then at least check my identity. Then I'll know if I'm really insane or the victim of a criminal offence.'

Stoya picked up his mug and walked to the door. 'I've already done that.'

'Done what?'

The young cop tried, overzealously, to hustle him towards the door. Marc could feel his warm breath on the back of his neck.

'I checked your statement. My colleague here will attend to you from now on.'

Stoya opened the door to the passage. A babble of voices drifted into the room. 'I have to save the lives of two children. Afraid I don't have time for shoplifters.'

'Shoplifters?' Marc repeated in bewilderment. He shook off the young cop's hand.

'Chemists don't like it when people fail to pay for their medication.'

'No, that was a misunderstanding. I made a point of leaving the man my credit card.'

'Which was invalid.'

'But I'm not here about that, damn it!'

'All right, I'll give it to you straight: I know what medication you're taking. The complainant says you asked for a psychiatric drug of the strongest possible kind.'

'What?' Marc's hand went to his neck. 'No, no, no. I needed something for a splinter in my neck. I'm not crazy.'

'The splinter you acquired in a car crash?'

'Yes.'

'A car crash that killed your wife?'

Marc groaned aloud.

'Who now refuses to let you into your flat?'

Marc fell silent. They'd come to the end of the conversation he'd previously conducted with himself.

'And you're telling me you *aren't* crazy?' Stoya nodded to his colleague and strode off without a backward glance.

'Okay, let's go.'

This time Marc didn't have the energy to shake off the young cop's hand as he was steered along the passage – away from the senior officers' ground-floor offices and upstairs to the rooms he had so often seen from the inside as a youth.

He bowed his head, wondering where else the billows of insanity would wash him up tonight, now that they had already swept away his car, his pills, his personal contacts and his money. He had even forfeited the trust of the police. He longed for a trapdoor to open and swallow him up – send him plummeting down, away from this unreal reality and into a black hole of oblivion.

But that happened only in dreams. In cruel actuality there were no secret passages to a better world, no heaven-sent rope ladders to a tree-house in which you could hide from the devil and come to rest. Miracles didn't happen in the harsh, neon-lit reality of a big-city police station.

*Or did they?*

Just as he had a few hours ago, when staring into the crater of the building site, Marc couldn't believe his eyes as he was shepherded through the reception area.

*How was it possible?*

He had told no one where he wanted to go, yet barring his path was the one person he'd longed to have at his side here and now, in this hopeless situation.

# 28

Before his first encounter with Constantin at the Senner family home, Sandra had warned him against the impulse to salute which her father evoked in most of his fellow men. 'He walks into a room, and 50 per cent of those present stop talking. The other 50 per cent resist an urge to jump up and break into spontaneous applause.'

She'd had to shout those few words, which characterized Constantin so aptly, to make herself heard above the rock music blaring from the car radio. She was eighteen, exactly seven months older than Marc, and already in possession of a driving licence.

His memories of that sweltering summer's day were shrouded in a pale-blue haze but as vivid as if he'd had to memorize every detail for an exam. It was the day on which she proposed to introduce him to her parents for the first time. *Him*, a good-for-nothing youth whom she'd met at a New Romantics concert in Zehlendorf. Marc would never normally have strayed into such an upmarket district, but the school authorities had instituted a competition for best band, and one of the venues was the assembly hall of Sandra's Westend high school. They'd all thought at first that the blonde, pony-tailed girl in trainers was making fun of him, but after the concert she'd left her place in the front row and gone backstage to talk shop with him. She not only knew all the bands they imitated, she even went to their concerts and listened to heavier music than Marc himself. What he found far more surprising was her boyish behaviour. She drank beer from the bottle, belched after taking a long swig and borrowed his lipsalve heedless of the risk of infection, although he couldn't detect any cold sores on her lips.

They ended up arranging to meet the following weekend at the Koma, a heavy-metal disco in Reinickendorf. Although Marc didn't believe the 'Westend dolly bird' would really turn up, he bought fifty Labellos in every available flavour just in case – just to see the look on her face if she asked to borrow a lipsalve again and he produced his assortment all at once. It didn't come to that because he'd forgotten about the body search at the door. The Koma's tattooed bouncer looked nauseated as he fished one 'lipstick' after another out of Marc's jacket pockets. He eventually – and disgustedly – let 'the little queer' in, but without his Labellos.

Marc did get his first kiss, but not until much later. Sandra kept him dangling for so long he was worried she had another secret admirer. But then, from one day to the next, she seized the initiative and, on his birthday, 'had it off' with him – as she put it, smirking – in his parents' bedroom.

'Your father's going to loathe me,' he prophesied three months later during the drive to Sandra's family home in Sakrow. 'One look at the knot and he'll know I never wear a tie. One question and he'll discover why he's never met my dad at a Bar Association ball: because he only represents petty criminals and antisocial elements, not stockbrokers or surgeons. And—'

'—and he'll shave your nuts with a Bunsen burner if he finds out you've been banging Daddy's little darling for the last month,' Sandra amplified, flashing him a saucy grin that exposed her anterior molars. So saying, she yanked at the handbrake and jumped out of the car in her bare feet. That was just what Marc had fallen in love with: the antithesis between her angelic face and upper-class background and the bawdy remarks which, coming from her, sounded so enchanting.

'I wouldn't put it past you to tell him.'

'I won't have to,' she retorted with a laugh. 'He's like you: a very perceptive person. He'll sense what we were up to in the shower half an hour ago.'

Back then, as they strolled hand in hand up the neatly raked gravel drive, he could never have imagined that Sandra's father would one day loom so large in his life. There had certainly been no indication of it after their first chilly encounter that summer evening.

'How did you find me?' Marc asked, looking around for the first time. The ground plan of the police station reminded him of a modern polytechnic. They were standing in a low-ceilinged entrance hall flanked by two massive staircases that led to the upper floors, though these harboured more offices, interview rooms and a number of spacious assembly areas, not class-rooms.

'Are you all right?' Constantin's air of concern was that of a man who didn't expect an affirmative answer. As ever, he was wearing a dark suit with a snow-white handkerchief in the breast pocket. And, as ever, he gave no sign of having just put in a twelve-hour stint in the operating theatre.

Marc felt the hand of the young cop who had been taking him away for questioning detach itself from his shoulder. The instinctive urge to salute was taking effect.

'What's going on here? What does he want with you?' Constantin demanded, as if the man wasn't there. He looked around in search of some superior officer competent enough to answer his questions. At that moment, Stoya emerged from the men's room. He stopped short and stared at the trio in surprise.

'And who might you be?' the young cop demanded, trying to inject some authority into his voice. Constantin didn't deign to answer him, still less stand aside.

'How did you find me?' Marc repeated. He hadn't the remotest idea how his father-in-law could have run him to earth.

'How do you think? I had you in my mailbox.'

*Huh?*

'But that's impossible.' Rather awkwardly, Marc extracted his mobile from the pocket of his jeans. 'I don't have your number any more.'

'Are you joking? We spoke together only yesterday.'

'Yes, but someone swiped my SIM card. I don't know your mobile number by heart and your receptionist at the clinic wouldn't put me through.' Marc showed him the blank display. 'Anyway, the thing doesn't work.'

'Your SIM card was stolen?' Constantin asked, sounding puzzled, and took the mobile from him.

Just then Stoya walked over to them. 'Is there a problem?'

Like Constantin, Stoya ignored his colleague and directed the question straight at the senior figure of the three. As in the animal world, so in a police station, alpha males seemed to recognize each other instinctively.

'There is indeed. I'm Professor Constantin Senner, and I wish to know, this instant, what gave you the right to haul my son-in-law into this police station.'

'In the first place, we didn't haul Herr Lucas—'

'Dr Lucas,' Constantin broke in.

'Very well, we didn't haul *Dr* Lucas in here. He came on a voluntary basis, and—'

'Is that correct?' Constantin cut the inspector short again. He gave Marc a searching look.

'Yes.'

'But why?'

*Because someone has stolen my identity. Because the miserable remnants of my life have been smashed to smithereens and I need someone to gather up the pieces.*

'I needed assistance from someone impartial,' Marc said, sensing how cryptic that sounded.

'Are you in some kind of trouble?' Constantin's leather soles squeaked as he took a step towards him. Unconsciously, Marc ran his forefingers over the cracked skin around his thumbnails.

'I'll explain when we get out of here.'

'Which may take some time.' The young cop had summoned up the courage to open his mouth again. 'We still have to question him about a theft.'

'A theft?'

Marc fingered the plaster on his neck and sighed. 'I needed some medication and the chemist wouldn't accept my credit cards, but that's immaterial now.'

'Just a minute,' said Constantin. 'You mean you actually took the stuff without paying?'

'Yes, but not deliberately. I simply forgot.'

'You *forgot* to pay?'

'You'd understand if you knew what's happened to me today.'

'Then kindly explain. I'm rather confused, to put it mildly, and—'

'Could I have a quick word with you?' This time it was Stoya who cut in on the surgeon. He indicated a massive concrete column adorned with not one but two 'No Smoking' signs. Constantin hesitated for a moment, then followed him, glancing back at Marc twice before he disappeared from view behind the column.

The inspector and his father-in-law were only three metres away, but the ground-floor acoustics were so bad Marc could only pick up a few scraps of their conversation. Furthermore, the young cop was trying to repair his damaged authority by enlightening Marc on the serious consequences of his theft, which might even constitute credit-card fraud. He was all the more taken aback a minute or two later when Stoya reappeared with Constantin and instructed him to release Marc at once.

Thirty seconds later Marc was standing outside the precinct gates in the pouring rain, wondering yet again what had happened to him.

'What about the charge?' he asked his father-in-law.

'I fixed it.'

'How?'

'Stoya's a sensible fellow. He's also got more important things on his plate tonight. I undertook to settle the bill and he understood your circumstances.'

'My circumstances?'

'He now knows what you've been through these last few weeks. It's no wonder you're a bit forgetful.'

'Forgetful? I saw Sandra today.'

Marc faced away from the wind. Raindrops drummed on the back of his head. They seemed to have no effect on his father-in-law's immaculately wavy hair.

'I know, I see her myself. All the time.' Constantin pressed the remote control on his car key and opened the central locking of a Mercedes saloon double-parked right outside the police station. There were two faint beeps and the warning lights flickered, but he continued to stand on the pavement, brushing away several raindrops that had lodged in his bushy eyebrows.

'I even ran after a woman in the park the other day. She looked like Sandra from behind.'

He fingered his prominent Adam's apple and massaged his neck. His voice developed a tremor.

'And yesterday, when a young woman was sitting in my consulting room, I wept, despite myself. She didn't even resemble her. It was just that she looked at her fingernails while speaking, the way Sandra did when she was nervous.'

Marc shook his head and drew back. 'No, you don't understand. She was real.'

He stepped out into the road and heard the central locking click shut because too much time had elapsed without anyone getting into the car. Going up to it, he rested both arms on the roof and shut his eyes.

'Grief is driving me mad too, Marc, but it won't get us anywhere.'

Marc didn't look up, didn't speak. Not even when he felt an arm drape itself around his shoulders.

'You're probably suffering from post-traumatic shock. Let's go to the clinic and I'll give you something.'

A fat raindrop burst right on Marc's forehead.

'I know what I saw,' he whispered, more to himself than to Constantin.

'The way you know your mobile isn't working?'

Marc opened his eyes and spun round. For the second time that night he stared incredulously at his phone, which Constantin was holding up for him to see.

'How did you do it?'

He wiped his wet hands on his jeans and opened the contacts menu.

*This is impossible.*

All the entries were complete.

'You switched it to flight mode by mistake, that's all. That's why you couldn't call anyone.'

Marc's hands started trembling. He felt suddenly hypoglycaemic, as if he'd just completed a mental forced march.

*Can this really be? Am I so deranged I can't operate my own phone?*

'Let's go to the clinic,' Constantin repeated. He unlocked the car again.

*But why did a strange man answer my landline?*

Marc raised his head and watched an ambulance with dirty headlights coming slowly down the street past the police station. He couldn't see inside, as the side windows were reflecting the street lights.

'Okay,' he said at length, when the ambulance had driven past. 'Let's go. Not to the clinic, though.'

'What do you have in mind?'

'I want to see if I've really lost my mind. And for that I need your help.'

# 29

*No Admittance.*

The same doormat, the same old block of flats pervaded by the same stale smells of food, the same sisal runner on the scuffed wooden stairs and the overflowing metal letter boxes in the entrance hall.

All that had changed in the last few hours was Marc's general condition. His physical and mental states seemed to be becoming more and more similar – heading for rock bottom. He wondered, as he accompanied his father-in-law up the stairs to his flat, whether his physical discomfort was just a painful concomitant of his hallucinations, or whether the exact opposite applied and his hallucinations were being caused by the steadily worsening pains in his head and limbs.

'Do you *have* to live in this area?' asked Constantin, who

appeared to be taking the stairs with ease. The surgeon worked out for an hour and a half every other day in the basement of his art nouveau villa, the only part of the house devoid of air-conditioning. He took the view that a workout wasn't a workout unless you wound up sweating like a pig.

'I can well understand why you didn't want to go on living in your old home, not after. . .' he said thoughtfully.

*After. . .*

Marc turned to his father-in-law, who was distastefully eyeing a baby buggy parked outside someone's door.

'But *here?*' Constantin shook his head. Even his housekeeper lived in a more exclusive residential area.

Marc clasped his side to combat the stitch that had suddenly hampered his breathing. 'There are worse places,' he panted, and trudged on up the stairs.

For instance, the Berlin district in which he himself had been raised. Where their neighbour on the balcony below fired his Kalashnikov in the air whenever Galatasaray scored a goal back home in his native Turkey. Marc had seriously considered moving back there after Sandra's death – back to his roots. Then it struck him that his roots had been severed long ago, the first of them by the death of his father, whose sudden demise had aroused wild speculation in the neighbourhood. *'Frank Lucas drank himself to death – must have been in debt, and no wonder, with those good-for-nothing sons of his. His old woman probably lifts her elbow as well.'*

At first his mother had tried to enlighten their neighbours on the true circumstances of her husband's death and tell them about his congenital liver trouble, which had been diagnosed far too late because the doctors had concentrated on his mental state. In a healthy person the amount of alcohol Frank had been drinking towards the end would not have been lethal, but he'd never been healthy. As for Marc's mother, she never regained her own health. Only a few months after her husband's death she died of heart failure – in every sense of the term.

'Why are you here?' Marc asked wearily as he continued to drag himself up the stairs.

Behind him, Constantin sighed. 'I thought we'd been through all that. You called me, I went to the police station, and –

'No, I don't mean that. You're still speaking to me. I wonder why.'

'Oh, so that's it.' His father-in-law was far too intelligent a man for Marc to have to say more.

Constantin had become the most important person in Marc's life after his father died, a mentor who had urged him to make the most of his abilities instead of wasting them. It had never been a question of money. All Constantin had done was motivate Marc by introducing him to people who had made something of their lives. But it hadn't been like that at first.

'You think I should be angry with you?' Constantin asked, catching him up. 'You think I should wash my hands of you?'

'You tried to once.'

Constantin grimaced, and Marc promptly apologized for hitting him below the belt. Six months after their first meeting at the villa, Constantin had taken him aside and shepherded him into the drawing room, leaving Sandra and her mother in the kitchen. Marc thought at first that the ice had finally broken, because Constantin's manner towards him was friendly for the first time. He even chuckled as he handed Marc an envelope containing the equivalent of €20,000 in crisp new 100-mark notes. Sandra had told Constantin about his father's financial problems. Frank Lucas's law firm was already in the red at that stage, so the family's debts would have been cleared at a stroke.

*'Break it off with my daughter and the money's yours.'*

Marc hadn't turned a hair. He thanked Constantin politely for his generous offer. Then he went over to the fireplace and, without a moment's hesitation, tossed the envelope into the flames.

'I thought you'd finally forgiven me for that.'

'I have,' said Marc. He nodded, leaning against the banisters.

Back then, Marc had gathered from the hint of a smile on Constantin's lips that he'd been put to the test. He had passed it with flying colours, even though Constantin hadn't reckoned on his future son-in-law's impulsive reaction. From that moment on, the Senner family had been poorer by €20,000 but richer by one new member of the family.

'You were afraid I was only interested in your money.'

'Worse than that. I thought you'd break Sandra's heart.'

'Well, now I've even managed to kill her.'

By now, they had reached the third floor and were only a few metres away from what Marc had until recently thought of as his own flat.

'Tell me, are you still taking your pills?' Constantin asked in a worried voice. He had just noticed Marc nervously feeling the back of his neck.

'The immunosuppressants?' Marc shook his head. Constantin looked more worried still.

'But you were given enough to last until your check-up next week.'

'I know, but they're in there.'

Marc indicated the door of the flat. The overhead light in which the moth had been fluttering around had given up the ghost completely.

'Fine, so let's go in and get them. Then I'll take you to the clinic for observation.'

'I'm only too happy to go, but...'

'What's the problem?'

'Take a look at that.' Marc pointed to the door. 'I knew it! I'm not completely deranged.'

Although the light from the stairwell was dim, he'd seen it at a glance.

'What do you mean?'

'The name on the card. It's still wrong.'

Constantin went right up to the door. He took his reading glasses from his coat pocket and held them up to his eyes without putting them on.

'Semmler,' he read slowly.

*What?!*

'No, no...'

Marc peered at the card too.

*Shit, what is it this time?*

Constantin struck a match, but Marc already knew his father-in-law was right.

*Semmler. Not Senner.*

'But this is... this is...' He blinked nervously. Then he laughed despite himself. The situation was just too absurd. He had definitely seen the name 'Senner', Sandra's maiden name, beside the doorbell. Who on earth would have taken the trouble to substitute a second, even less appropriate surname?

'Was that the name of the previous tenant?' Constantin hazarded.

'No, and my eyes didn't deceive me the first time.' Marc extinguished the match, he spat out the words so fiercely. 'There's something fishy going on, and I'll prove it to you.'

He produced the serrated security key from the pocket of his jeans. His hand was trembling so much he had to pause for a moment before he could insert it in the lock.

'Shall I?' Constantin asked solicitously.

'No, no problem.' Marc's tone was almost curt. And then, to his utter consternation, not the slightest problem presented itself. The key slid into the lock with a faint click, and he turned it with his thumb and forefinger as easily as if the mechanism had just been oiled.

# 30

Once, when Marc was twelve years old, he had staggered his mother by announcing that tidying his room would be contrary to the laws of nature. A Michael Crichton thriller had just, for the first time, confronted him with the phenomenon of entropy, a term from thermodynamics from which it can be deduced, inter alia, that everything in nature tends towards a state of the utmost disorder. Just as a car tyre loses its pressure and tread, or a T-shirt fades in the wash and becomes frayed, or roof tiles sometimes need replacing, so human beings eventually disintegrate into their component parts and lose the energy that binds their extremely complex anatomy together. They become old and ill and die. So why waste a brief human lifetime tidying things when all your efforts are bound to be nullified by a force of nature?

His mother's response to this lecture had been to plant her hands – which in Marc's recollection were usually encased in yellow rubber washing-up gloves – on her ample hips. Then she threw back her head and roared with laughter. 'All right,' she said, 'in that case I won't give you any more pocket money because you'll only spend it.'

Today, more than two decades later, one might have gained the impression that Marc had gone along with that deal. His flat still looked like a chaos theorist's ideal object of study.

'Good God!' As he walked in, Constantin gave a noisy sniff as if he expected such a pigsty to give off an awful stench as well. In fact, the place was redolent only of freshly sanded floorboards, freshly applied emulsion paint, and the other smells typical of redecoration that had been lingering in the air since Marc moved in.

'What happened here?' Constantin asked, doing his best not to tread on any of the numerous objects strewn across the floor of the little hallway.

'Nothing.' Marc shoved a stack of CDs aside with his foot. 'I dropped a box, that's all.'

'Only one?'

Lying on the floor, surrounded by remote controls, income tax files, two multiple sockets, an overturned lamp, three photo albums and numerous books, were several overturned pot plants. All had dried out, even the cactuses.

Marc stepped over the box whose contents lay strewn across the lobby. He'd left it out in the rain for too long, and the cardboard bottom had become so sodden it couldn't support the higgledy-piggledy contents and gave way. It was the very last box, which he'd meant to leave out for the dustmen in any case. He was so furious with himself he'd deliberately hurled the box full of house plants at the front door.

*Sudden rages...*

Another new trait laid bare by the scalpel of grief.

'What on earth has happened to me?' he muttered to himself as he went into the living room to turn on the standard lamp, which doubled as a DVD rack.

This, the largest room in his two-room flat, made a better impression, although the numerous unopened boxes littering the floor resembled aid packages jettisoned from a helicopter. There were no shelves or cupboards that could accommodate

Marc's few possessions, so he lived out of a suitcase like a commercial traveller. He took anything he needed straight from the box – if he could find it. Sandra had always been the practical one of the two. She would have neatly labelled the boxes with their contents.

Marc heard a cupboard door being opened in the adjoining room. He slowly subsided on to a black leather sofa which the removals men had deposited in the middle of the room facing the window. The raindrops that were lashing the panes at irregular intervals created an inappropriately snug atmosphere in the gloomy, rather overheated living room.

'Nobody here.'

Marc swung round. Constantin had somehow contrived to enter the room silently in spite of his leather soles.

'I've checked the kitchen and the bathroom. I even looked under the bed. There's nobody here.'

# 31

'There must be,' Marc said wearily, although he knew his father-in-law was telling the truth. He'd known it the moment his key fitted and the door swung open. Just as it did here in the living room, everything looked exactly the way he'd left it that morning.

Sandra had never been fussy, that was for sure. She was quite as capable as he was of turning a tidy room into a shambles in no time at all. But her love of plants was so great that she would never have carelessly uprooted her favourite bonsai and left it lying beside its own potting compost. And that fact allowed of only one conclusion.

*Sandra wasn't here – never had been.*

Marc felt Constantin sit down beside him. 'I'm losing my mind,' he whispered with his eyes shut.

'No, you aren't.'

'I am.' Marc kneaded his temples. The soothing pressure did nothing to relieve the nausea constantly simmering away inside him. 'I saw her. I could have put out my hand and touched her.'

'Here, take this.'

He looked up. His father-in-law must have found a plastic mug in the kitchen and was holding it out. He himself had appropriated a cut-glass tumbler with a slightly chipped rim.

'Drink up, it's only water. You need plenty of fluid when you're in shock.'

The white mug's thin, fluted sides made a crackling sound as Marc grasped it. Its contents gleamed like the surface of a dark lake in the dim light. He raised it to his lips but stopped short.

'Just water?'

'What else?'

Constantin deposited his glass on the coffee table. Then he took Marc's plastic mug and drained it in one. 'Satisfied?'

He looked down at Marc with a paternal expression.

'I'm sorry.'

Constantin nodded and picked up his glass again. It left a ring of moisture behind on the coffee table. 'But I ought to give you something to relax you soon. I'm genuinely worried about you, Marc.'

'That makes two of us.'

*I feel like someone who's swallowed a magnet that attracts insanity, not metal, and I'm very much afraid its effects are getting stronger by the minute.*

'Come on, it's getting late. Let's go to the clinic.' Constantin put his empty glass down, plumb on the wet ring. He held out his hand, but Marc had shut his eyes again. He had learnt, even as a boy, that he could think better when not all his senses were activated. When he opened them again his father-in-law was standing at the window, tracing the course of a raindrop trickling down the pane like a teardrop.

'How often do you think of that day in May? How long ago was it exactly?' Constantin's voice had gone husky all of a sudden.

*That day in May.*

They had never referred to it as anything else. In their conversations it had never been 'the day Sandra was attacked' or 'the day they gagged her and tied her to the kitchen stove with a wire noose'. Nor was it 'the day Sandra should really have accompanied him to a lecture but stayed behind at her father's house because of morning sickness'.

'Christian would be three now,' Marc replied.

'Exactly. It was three years ago.'

Constantin sighed, as if an eternity had gone by since then. And it had, in a sense. Sandra had been pregnant once before. The burglars came just as she had settled down with a family pack of crème brûlée ice cream on her lap to watch an old *King of Queens* DVD. It was six hours before Constantin came home. By then the two thugs in ski masks had forced the safe, stripped the walls of valuable originals and gone off with cash, a collection of antique clocks, all the family silver and an old laptop.

*Six hours.*

The bleeding had started three-quarters of an hour before.

'Is that why you didn't want to choose a name for your second baby?'

Marc nodded. 'Yes. That day destroyed so many things. We thought she could never have another child. When she became pregnant after all, we didn't want to tempt providence. Pure superstition.' He gave a mirthless laugh. 'Ironical, isn't it?'

Constantin turned round. He looked infinitely old all of a sudden. 'You're wrong, you know.'

Marc stared at him. 'What do you mean?

'You said that day destroyed a lot of things. It's true, of course. Cruel as it may sound, though, it granted you another three years of happiness together.'

'I don't understand.'

'Sandra was going to leave you, Marc.'

'What?'

Marc shivered, hunching his shoulders like someone expecting an ice cube to land on the back of his neck at any moment.

'I'm not sure, but I think that was why she was staying with us out at Sakrow. She wanted a word with me as soon as I came home from the clinic.' Constantin was breathing heavily now. 'She called me – said it was about your relationship and another man she'd met recently.'

'That can't be so,' said Marc, although he had every reason to believe his father-in-law. Dismal old memories elbowed their way into the forefront of his mind. He had tried to suppress them back then, attributing Sandra's behaviour to hormonally governed mood swings during pregnancy. At first she had simply been distrait and silent, but she became steadily more withdrawn until it seemed that her self-absorption had given way to depression. He offered to cancel all his commitments and stay at home with her until the birth, but Sandra wouldn't have it. She went walking by herself for hours, even in neighbourhoods she normally steered clear of. One day, when he had been visiting the parents of a notorious truant in Neukölln, he caught sight of her emerging from a seedy café and getting into a taxi, lost in thought. When he raised the subject that evening she flew off the handle and 'refused to testify, Counsellor'.

'Who was the other man?' Marc asked. It was the question that had tormented him at the time.

Constantin shrugged. 'I really have no idea. We never got a chance to clear the air. When she came round after the emergency op she wouldn't say another word on the subject. All she wanted was to see you.'

Marc felt a touch of cramp in his calf and struggled to his feet. For some strange reason he was involuntarily reminded, at this of all times, of a tired old joke his father had told him: You can always recognize men of fifty or over by the way they groan whenever they sit down or get to their feet. By that measure he himself had aged eighteen years in a single day.

'Why tell me this *now*?' Marc demanded. He picked up the empty plastic mug Constantin had drained and deposited on the coffee table. He had to go to the bathroom, dunk his head in the basin and take some medication at last.

Constantin didn't reply until he'd already shut the bathroom door behind him. 'Because you asked me just now why I still regard you as my son. A tragedy can form a tremendous bond between people who love each other.'

'Fine, then let me know when you can't stand me any more and I'll kill someone else. . .'

Marc propped both forearms on the washbasin, staring at the place on the wall that should really have been occupied by a mirror. He was glad he hadn't bothered to put one up. It spared him the sight of his own haggard face.

'Stop hiding behind your sense of humour,' Constantin called, his voice muffled by the door between them. 'It's just self-pity.'

'That's the second time in twenty-four hours I've been told something of the kind,' Marc muttered, reaching for the tap. He was about to turn it on and run cold water over the inside of his wrists when his eye lighted on the crack between the plug and the plughole.

*What on earth...?*

He bent down and extracted the chrome-plated plug. It came away with a faint plop.

*It can't be...*

Dangling from the black rubber gasket was a single human hair. It was about fifteen centimetres long and curly at the lower end like a treble clef. Involuntarily, he clutched the back of his head, which he hadn't shaved for four days.

'Constantin,' he called hoarsely. No answer, so he called again, louder this time.

*So I was right after all.*

He stared as if mesmerized at the blonde hair draped over his forefinger, which certainly wasn't his. His hand trembled as he put it to his nose. He couldn't smell anything, of course, but he was quite sure.

*Sandra...*

The flat had been renovated before he took it over. The wash-basin was brand new and he'd had no guests.

*This proves it. She was here.*

He shut his eyes, clasped one trembling hand with the other and drew a deep breath. Then, clutching the hair in his fist like a child clutching a coin en route to the sweet shop, he hurried out of the bathroom.

'Constantin? I haven't gone mad, this proves it!' he called. On his way back to the living room he barked his shin on the leg of a metal stool protruding from a half-open packing case, but the pain was blotted out by sheer consternation when he came hobbling in. The window was wide open.

The living room in which he'd just been sitting on the sofa with his father-in-law was deserted. Constantin had vanished. So had the tumbler and the ring of moisture on the coffee table.

# 32

'Hello?'

Marc had lost all sense of time. He didn't know how long he'd stood staring out into the dark, rainy night. Up here on the third floor there was no fire escape or ledge, no scaffolding or window-cleaner's cradle anyone could have used to leave the flat.

'Constantin?'

His father-in-law had disappeared into thin air.

He shut the window, tottered out into the hallway and tried to turn the overhead light on, but nothing happened. He saw, when he looked again, that the bulb was missing.

'Hey, where are you?'

His voice re-echoed from the pictureless walls of the small hallway.

*Please let me wake up. Please let this all be just a dream.*

Turning to look at the front door, he flinched when he saw that the safety chain was on.

'Where have you got to?' he whispered to himself, as if he already guessed what he would find in the bedroom after checking the kitchen: *nothing.*

Nothing apart from a double mattress and another box with a cheap bedside light standing on it. He left this on every morning so he didn't have to fumble around in the pitch black for the little switch when he came home at night.

But he was wrong – so wrong that it redoubled his doubts about his sanity: the bedside light had disappeared.

*Like Constantin. Like Sandra. Like my life.*

Yet the room wasn't dark, because faint rays of pale-blue light were seeping through the cracks in the box.

*This is impossible.*

He went over to the mattress, suddenly overcome by an almost irresistible urge to flop down on it, pull the bedclothes over his head and sink into an everlasting, dreamless sleep. But the dim light exerted a hypnotic attraction on him. At the same time, he remembered a conversation he'd had with Sandra years ago.

*'Hey, what's the matter? Why are you looking at me like that?'*

*'Promise me...'*

*'What?'*

*'Promise you'll always leave a light on?'*

He opened the box, parted the flaps with trembling hands... and found his surreal vision confirmed.

*'What do you think?'*

*'Hm... I'd call it, well... an acquired taste?'*

*'Utterly hideous, more like.'*

He shut his eyes, but the memories refused to fade.

*'What is it? Are you crying?'*

*'Look, I know it sounds a bit weird, but I'd like us to make a deal.'*

*'Okay.'*

'If one of us dies – no, please hear me out – the first of us to go must give the other one a sign.'

When he opened his eyes the hideous, battery-powered, baby-blue dolphin bedside light was still in the box.

And it was on for the first time in its existence.

I'm coming to find you if it takes me all night
Can't stand here like this any more
For always and ever is always for you
I want it to be perfect like before.
Ohohoho... I want to change it all.

'A Night Like This', The Cure


Nothing sounds as good as I remember that

'I Remember That', Prefab Sprout

# 33

A distracting noise that ultimately unnerved him even more than the self-illuminated dolphin lamp, it resembled the menacing hum of a hornet trapped between a blind and a window pane and becoming steadily more aggressive in its desperate attempts to escape. Except that the sound was coming from the hallway, where there were no windows, and was far too rhythmical to be made by a maddened, struggling insect.

Marc turned towards the bedroom door and the humming in his ears abruptly ceased. The sudden silence was so complete that he could hear the faint click of the electricity meter and the liquid gurgle of the central heating.

'Anyone there?' he called, dry-throated, only to flinch in alarm the instant he crossed the threshold of the darkened hallway.

The hornet was back. It sounded even louder now. Louder and more infuriated.

Marc's heartbeat speeded up as he crept along in search of some object with which to defend himself. But then, just before the humming noise became continuous, he realized the absurdity of his behaviour. He looked up at the little grey box above and to the right of the door frame.

'Shit, I'm afraid of my own doorbell,' he whispered. He made another attempt to laugh at himself, but his efforts to master his fear misfired.

*Like a hornet. It sounds like a trapped, infuriated hornet.*

No one knew his new address except the men from the removals firm and Roswitha.

*So who can it be?*

His eye fell again on the door chain, which someone must have replaced from the inside *after* his father-in-law disappeared. He shivered.

'Constantin?'

Goose pimples broke out all over his body as he put his eye to the spyhole. He peered through it and groaned aloud. Although the continuous hum had changed to a rhythmical staccato, he couldn't see anybody with their finger on the button.

*What's going on here? Perhaps it's all in my head. Perhaps there isn't any bell at all. No door, no flat, no Sandra.*

He really did laugh now, albeit with a touch of hysteria.

*Perhaps there isn't even any me?*

In a sudden access of fatalism he removed the chain and wrenched the door open.

*Nobody.*

Neither right outside the door nor in the passage. No Constantin, no neighbour, no stranger. He was alone, and that was how he felt – alone – as he slowly pushed the door shut and rested his head against it.

The infuriated buzzing of the bell stopped for a moment, then adopted a different rhythm.

Three short, three long, three short.

*SOS?*

He fingered the sweat-sodden plaster on his neck, the only part of his body unaffected by the icy stranglehold that was steadily tightening its grip on him.

*A ghostly doorbell signalling in Morse. Even my hallucinations show a sense of humour, you've got to grant me that.*

He backed into the living room without taking his eyes off the little buzzing box above the door. From it, a length of flex ran down the wall, dividing at the level of the door handle. One half ran down to the skirting board, the other ran parallel to the floor and disappeared behind his overcoat, which was hanging on a rail that had been there when he moved in.

*Three short. Three long.*

Of course!

*I'm so exhausted I can't think straight.*

He pulled the coat aside, recalling the rapturous sales talk of the estate agent, who had implied that a simple intercom was NASA's latest technical achievement and more than justified the exorbitant rent.

The intercom emitted a beep as he picked up the receiver. Instantly, the hornet stopped humming.

'Yes?' he croaked. He was almost relieved to get an answer, even if the voice belonged to the person he'd recently run away from.

'Can you talk?'

*Emma.* Her diffident, submissive tone was unmistakable.

He stared at the displayless intercom, incapable of replying.

'Hello? Is he still with you?'

There was a click. Marc finally regained the power of speech.

'Who do you mean? How did you know where I live?'

'I followed you,' she said, and coughed.

'You followed me?' he repeated stupidly.

'Yes, to the police station. Then here. I saw you go inside with him.'

'Constantin?'

'I don't know his name. He's one of them, that's all I know.'

*One of them?*

'Come down here before it's too late.'

He shook his head, as if Emma could see him from down in the street below. 'So you can trap me again?'

'What do you mean, trap you? What are you talking about? I'm the one who's being hunted.'

*Hunted?*

'Listen. . .' His voice was shaking. 'I don't know who you're working for, but—'

'Working for? What on earth do you mean? I'm on the run like you. I'm all on my own.'

'Oh yeah? So who were you talking to about me on the phone? Back at the hotel, I mean?'

Emma sighed. 'Oh, so that's it. I'll explain later.'

'No, now. Who were you calling?'

There was another click on the line and the static grew louder.

'My mobile.'

'What?'

She hesitated. 'I call myself once every hour and tell my mobile where I am, who I'm with and what I'm going to do next. It's just a precaution, in case something happens to me or they wipe my memory again.'

'And I'm supposed to believe that?'

'Why should I lie to you? I'm in need of help myself, even though you're now in greater danger than I am. So hurry up and come down here.'

'I'm sure I'm safer up here in my flat than I would be down there with you.'

'Nonsense. I've been here for half an hour and I haven't seen anyone leave the building. That means he must still be with you. And that, in turn, means that you're. . .'

'I'm alone,' he broke in.

'. . . in great danger, because the programme is still in operation.'

'I'm not *in* any programme!' Marc bellowed into the receiver.

'You are, and I'll prove it to you.'

'How?' he demanded. He felt a sudden breath of air on the back of his neck, as if someone were coming up behind him. He swung round, wide-eyed with fear.

'She's still alive,' he heard Emma whisper. 'Come down here and I'll prove it to you.' Her voice was almost inaudible.

*It can't be true. It mustn't be.*

He didn't hear himself utter the words aloud, but he saw that he had by his breath. The all-embracing chill was no delusion; it was streaming into the flat like liquid oxygen. Through the wide-open window in the living room. The window he'd only just firmly secured.

# 34

Marc locked the front door from the outside although he knew he wouldn't leave the unseen threat behind. Whatever was pursuing him seemed undeterred by physical barriers. Insanity resembled a mist that was seeping through the cracks of normality into his shattered life. If he wasn't to lose his bearings still further in its murky depths, flight was his sole recourse.

He emerged into the street convinced that he was alone again, so he was almost startled to see Emma waiting for him in her car. Her old VW Beetle was double-parked, and it took him a moment to realize that the car she was obstructing was his own. It was parked exactly where he'd looked for it only a few hours earlier.

'Come on,' she called, looking in her rear-view mirror. The car, which had been puttering away until now, emitted a sort of death rattle as she underlined her impatience by gunning the engine, but Marc was still nonplussed by the reappearance of his car. He made his way round Emma's Beetle like a man in a trance, staring at the Mini as if he'd never seen one before.

'What is it?' The engine gave another death rattle.

'Just a minute,' he called without turning round. He patted

his pockets in search of his car key, then remembered that he'd removed it from the bunch a long time ago.

Cupping his face in his hands, blinker fashion, he peered through the rain-streaked window. Sure enough, it was his car that had materialized here in the last few minutes. The sports bag he hadn't used since the accident was lying crumpled up in the footwell behind the driver's seat, the back seat was littered with old newspapers, an empty McDonald's carton and numerous returnable bottles, and the tangled charging cable for his mobile was plugged into the cigar lighter.

'Come on, damn it!' Emma called angrily, turning off the ignition. Marc heard the door creak open as she got out behind him. He looked around for something to smash the window with.

'What are you doing? We have to go.'

'Where to?'

He bent down and tried to dislodge a cobblestone protruding from the pavement, but his fingers kept slipping off the wet edges.

'Lost something?'

*Yes, my mind.*

He could see her boots under the car. She was standing beside a puddle in the road, shifting impatiently from foot to foot.

'I've just got to get something from my car, then we can go.'

'So why are you crawling around on the ground?' she demanded. He heard a click and the car's interior light came on.

*How on earth had she done that so quickly?*

He straightened up, blinking in bewilderment, then opened the driver's door as easily as the one Emma had already opened. He stared at her suspiciously.

'How did you know—'

'Look!' She shrugged and pointed to the ignition lock beside the steering wheel. 'The key's in there. You must have forgotten it.'

*No way. I haven't had it on me for days.*

He propped one knee on the driver's seat and reached for the glove compartment. The light hadn't worked for ages, but he found what he was looking for as soon as he opened the flap and shoved a stack of CDs aside.

Emma gripped his wrist just as he was removing the strip of blister pack.

'What sort of pills are those?'

'Mind your own business,' he said, rather more sharply than he had intended, but his tone of voice had the desired effect. She retreated several steps, pulled the white hood over her head and turned away.

He was bending over the rear seat when he heard her get back into her Beetle and start the engine again. Just as he was reaching under the seat to fish out a bottle of Coke, intending to wash his first pill down with it, he heard the low hum of a diesel engine. His first thought was that Emma had driven off in a huff, and that alarmed him. After all, she'd promised to provide him with proof that his wife was still alive.

But, when he raised his head and looked out at the street, which seemed to be lit by stroboscopic flashes, he could scarcely believe his eyes. Emma had been right: he ought to have got a move on. He was so startled, he dropped the Coke bottle. The pills, too, slipped through his fingers. From the look of it, they really were in the programme.

# 35

The roaring in Benny's ears was growing louder at every step. Quite faint at first, it had started the moment he drove away from the police checkpoint. The policewoman had never got round to examining the contents of his boot. Before he could open it, her assistance had been requested by a colleague in need of back-up, who was having trouble persuading a recalcitrant Mercedes driver to undergo a breath test. Benny's pulse rate hadn't dropped since then, and he was sweating as he climbed the stairs to his flat.

'Know why none of your attempts at suicide has ever succeeded, Benny?'

Valka didn't call him often. That he'd done so twice today was an ominous sign.

'No,' Benny replied truthfully, breathing hard. He didn't trouble to ponder the point of the question. Valka loved staging set pieces. Whether out to impress a woman, kill an opponent or simply chew the fat, he devoted a lot of prior thought to making the greatest impact possible. His opening gambits were thus of a purely rhetorical nature.

'Because you're a wimp, that's why. I still remember the first time, when that Yoko Ono slut destroyed our band. Laughable, it was.'

Valka never referred to Sandra by her real name and regularly compared her to the woman who had split up the Beatles. It was true that Marc had had no time for rehearsals and gigs once he and she were a couple.

'The bunch who'd protected you suddenly weren't there any more. Your best friend, your brother, was busy screwing his new girlfriend while you, you sensitive soul, were all on your lonesome. Christ, I've never understood how anyone could be such a mummy's boy. But you couldn't even do the job properly. I mean, the few pills you swallowed wouldn't have put a cat to sleep.' His laugh was so hearty it sounded as if he was about to slap his thigh.

Benny came to a halt. Although he was only wearing a thin T-shirt under his green bomber jacket and the janitor had turned off all the radiators because of rocketing oil prices, he felt as if he were in the tropics.

'I know you've never really liked me, Benny, but I've always been there for you, you've got to admit. I looked out for you – I gave you a new life.'

'Oh yeah?' Benny muttered, already feeling in his pocket for the key to his flat. Only another two floors to go. The final flight of stairs to the converted roof space was carpeted in burgundy sisal that muffled his footsteps.

'And today, if I let you leave town, I'll be giving you another present.'

'I thought we were quits, Eddy. The job's done.'

'I know, my boys just confirmed it. They say that lousy hack's house looks like a football pitch there are so many green uniforms milling around inside.'

Valka was evidently using a satellite phone. Either that or he assumed his conversations weren't being monitored.

Or he was simply suffering from delusions of grandeur.

*Probably both,* thought Benny.

'Okay, now pin your ears back. . .' Valka had abandoned his spuriously jovial tone of voice. It was like a light going out. 'That shit in your boot – get rid of it.'

Benny nodded, distracted by the realization that the key in his hand was redundant. The door to his flat was ajar, though only just. Gingerly, he shoved it open with his foot. It was dark inside.

'Where are you now?' asked Valka, who must have heard the door creak.

'My place.'

An almost imperceptible, sweetish smell greeted Benny as he entered the little hallway.

'Good. Then pack up your things, get into your lousy car and take that garbage to Holland tonight.' He gave Benny an address in Amsterdam and a contact. 'If Vincent doesn't call me back by midnight and confirm that the goods have arrived, I'll come looking for you.'

Benny came to a halt and switched the phone from one ear to the other. 'Midnight? No dice, I need more time.' He turned on the overhead light. The smell was becoming stronger.

'Tell me something, Benny. Do I sound like a hooker?'

'No.'

'That's a relief, I thought you wanted to fuck me. I'm doing you a favour, letting you pay off your debts instead of perforating your balls with a nail gun, and you say you need more time? Who do you think you are?'

'Look, Eddy, please give me a day to say goodbye to everyone.'

'Like who, you moron? Your parents are dead, your brother hates you and your pals are in the nuthouse.' Valka chuckled. 'Still, I thought you'd say something like that, so I've laid on a little surprise for you. One that'll underline the gravity of the situation.'

Benny shut his eyes. He had grasped the grisly significance of the smell.

# 36

Survivors of a plane crash, terrorist bomb, road accident or some other life-threatening occurrence are often unanimous in stating that they perceived the instant of the disaster in slow motion. It's as if the explosion, fireball or collision has torn a hole in time or even brought it to a stop. Marc instantly grasped the reason for this perceptual phenomenon: the moment a lethal threat presents itself, the human brain is incapable of absorbing multiple impressions simultaneously, still less of sorting out the sequence of events.

Marc saw the brightly lit ambulance, its dirty headlights, the silently flashing lights on its roof, and the rear doors, open to reveal the loading space within. He registered the bearded male nurse in the white smock, who was holding something in one hand as he strove to drag Emma out of her Beetle with the other. He even noted insignificant details such as the blood-red fluorescent stripes on the vehicle's sides and the rosary-like chain suspended from its rear-view mirror which seemed to dangle in time to the flashing lights. He also heard the bubbling of its diesel engine, which mingled with that of the Beetle, and wondered why Emma didn't utter a sound until she started to scream for help. It was highly probable that he took in all these things at once, or separated only by fractions of a second, after the bearded nurse had slapped Emma's face and sent her glasses spinning across the asphalt.

At this point another figure appeared on the scene. A woman, or so Marc thought at first, because she was rather lightly built and had a ponytail. Then he recognized her as a young man.

'Hey!' Marc yelled, squeezing out of his car backwards. 'Let go of her!'

The rubber soles of his trainers slipped on a little mound of wet leaves as he tried to go to Emma's aid. In the meantime, the bearded nurse had managed to haul Emma's bulky body out of the driver's seat with such force that she reeled around beside the car, still half dazed by his original blow. In a trice, Beardie grabbed her by the arm and pinned her, bosom first, against the ambulance.

'Over here!' he shouted to the man with the ponytail, who seemed undecided as to whom to tackle first. Emma's captor bellowed his order twice as loud and jerked his head at the ground. Whatever he had dropped during the struggle, he evidently needed it in order to subdue Emma, who had recovered her wits and was struggling fiercely. It was all he could do to restrain her, despite his muscular build.

'What do you want with her?' Marc yelled. He noticed out of the corner of his eye that a light on the third floor of his block of flats had just come on. The flashing lights and the sound of engines and shouting would sooner or later prompt one of the residents to call the police. Later rather than sooner, though, because nocturnal brawls weren't uncommon in Schöneberg, and most of its inhabitants relied on their neighbours' ability to settle their differences without the help of the authorities. Besides, the ambulance would make onlookers feel that everything was under control.

'No, please don't!' gasped Emma. Ponytail had just picked up a longish, cigar-shaped object and handed it to his confederate.

'Now for you,' he said. Having satisfied himself that Beardie had regained control of the situation by twisting Emma's wrist behind her back until it was on a level with her shoulder blades – her cries of pain merged into a long-drawn-out howl – he took a step towards Marc.

Marc's immediate inclination was to hurl himself at Beardie, who was now struggling to apply the cigar-shaped object to Emma's upper arm.

But in order to do that he would have to get past Ponytail, who at first glance seemed far less muscular than his colleague. This was deceptive, however. Marc was familiar with the type and knew how dangerous such scrawny youngsters could be. You tended to underestimate them because they looked like victims themselves but they compensated for their lack of muscle with self-destructive fanaticism, lashing out at anyone and anything within range, even when seriously hurt.

'Don't give me any aggro,' said Ponytail. He took a step closer, crushing Emma's glasses underfoot.

*Kneecap!* The word flashed through Marc's mind. He raised his arms in a gesture of surrender – he even smiled faintly, just as he'd been advised to by Khaled, the sixteen-year-old half-Tunisian who proudly came to the 'Beach' after every street fight to show off his latest war wounds.

Khaled was right. There really was no better target than the kneecap for felling an opponent and putting him out of action. But you had to follow it up at once, while he was still being transfixed by dazzling yellow shafts of agony. Three or four kicks aimed at the jaw and temples. If you got the angle right you might even be able to drive your quivering victim's nasal bone into his brain.

*Go down and you're a goner. Stay on your feet and you walk away* was Khaled's first rule of the street. It was a rule that had governed the lives of Marc and his brother years ago, long before they went their separate ways. And now Marc was about to discover whether it was still valid after all this time.

# 37

The attack was over as quickly as it had begun. Ponytail's eyes widened in disbelief, like those of a comic-book character registering boundless amazement. To Marc, though, the fact that his adversary had gone down so easily came as almost more of a surprise than it did to the man himself. He hadn't laid a finger on him; Emma had. Before he could ask her how she had escaped from her captor's armlock, she tossed him her car keys.

'Quick, you'll have to drive.'

Still rather dazed by Beardie's blow across her face, she tottered round to the passenger side and flopped down inside the Beetle. 'I can't see too well without my glasses.'

Marc stared down in bewilderment at the limp forms of the two male nurses, but not for long this time. He shook off his inertia, and a few heartbeats later he was turning on to a deserted Bülowstrasse. Glancing feverishly in the rear-view mirror, he floored the old banger across the intersection into Nollendorfplatz.

For a while neither of them spoke. Then he couldn't restrain himself any longer. 'What did they want with you?'

Emma felt absent-mindedly for her safety belt. She didn't reply until her trembling hands had clipped it together. 'Bleibtreu...' she said breathlessly, wiping a skein of saliva off her lower lip. 'Those were Bleibtreu's boys... They were meant to take me back... Back to the clinic... to delete the rest of my memories...'

*The clinic? But it doesn't exist any more. No. 211 Französische Strasse is just a hole in the ground.*

Emma pinched the bridge of her nose, gasping for breath. Every sentence she uttered was punctuated by a pause during which she sucked air noisily into her lungs. 'They were out to get you too – believe me now? We're both in the same programme... Alone we don't stand a chance, but together we may shake them off.'

Marc glanced at her. She was looking utterly exhausted but seemed quite lucid, even if she did sound like a deranged conspiracy theorist.

*But why is all this happening?*

If the programme really existed, what memories of his did they want to obliterate? *Or had they already done so?*

Even attempting to find answers to these absurd questions verged on insanity, so he changed the subject. 'How did you do it?'

'What?'

'Those men. How did you do it?'

Emma's snow-white teeth flashed in a smile – partly, no doubt, to relieve the tension. 'I bit him,' she said. 'That made him drop his... What would you call this?' She handed him the cigar-shaped cylinder Beardie had threatened her with. 'Is it a vaccination gun?'

Marc glanced at it briefly, drove through an amber light on Kurfürstenstrasse, and nodded. *Anaesthetic.* She had neutralized their attackers with their own weapon.

'I hope they're still breathing,' she said quietly. Judging by the sudden note of uncertainty in her voice, she wanted him to say she'd done the right thing. 'After all, I was only defending myself.'

He nodded.

*The end justifies the means. Sometimes you have to do the wrong thing to get the right result.*

Marc slowed as they entered the 30-kph zone on the bend

by the Esplanade Hotel. He hadn't a clue where they were going or who his uninvited companion was. The impression she made on him was not only increasingly mysterious but ever more ominous.

'Who exactly are you?' he demanded.

She looked at him and hesitated for a moment, then lowered her eyes again. 'I've already told you all I know about myself. They've already deprived me of the rest of my memories.'

'Crap!'

Emma flinched as he thumped the Beetle's plastic steering wheel. 'We didn't meet today by chance.'

She drew a deep breath. 'No, not by chance. I was waiting for you at the building site, don't you remember? I've never made any secret of it.' She stared angrily out of the window. 'I'm on your side – how much more proof do you need? Should I have let Bleibtreu's people kill me?'

Once Marc had turned into Potsdamer Strasse, Emma unzipped her jacket and took a mobile phone from the inside pocket.

'Who are you calling now?' he demanded as he sent the Beetle speeding into the Tiergarten Tunnel. A red X warned him to change lanes.

'No one.'

She kneaded her forehead with one hand and used the other to press the same key on the mobile repeatedly until she found what she was looking for.

'Here.'

She switched on the dirty old interior light above their heads and held out the display for Marc to see. He was just over-taking a lone garbage truck, so he could only take a fleeting glance.

'What is it?'

'I promised you some proof. See for yourself: she's alive.'

'Sandra?'

He stamped on the brake and the Beetle went into a skid. It lurched twice and the suspension creaked alarmingly as he overran a kerb and slithered to a halt in the middle of the tunnel, just opposite an emergency exit.

'You think this is wise?' said Emma, who had dropped the phone. She had to wipe some mud off the keyboard before handing it to him.

'Where did you take this?' he demanded.

'I told you: I followed you after you ditched me at the hotel.' She scratched her peeling hand. 'I took this outside the police station.'

'Sandra was at the police station?'

Marc held the phone at an angle because the plastic display was reflecting the light, but he still couldn't see much. The yellow Volvo Constantin was standing beside might have been photographed any night anywhere. The digital time code was registering the hour at which Marc had been inside the police station, but altering a mobile's electronic calendar was the easiest thing in the world.

'That is her, isn't it?' said Emma, tapping the phone. Marc couldn't take his eyes off the figure he saw there. The profile, the blonde hair, the slender finger pointing to something off-screen – they all looked so familiar. On the other hand, every-thing was so indistinct and ill lit, despite the street light beneath which the car was parked, that he couldn't be absolutely certain.

'I got there a bit too late, just as your father-in-law was saying goodbye to her.'

*Sandra followed Constantin to the police station? None of it makes any sense.*

What reason could there be for father and daughter to play such a cruel trick on him? In a cheap soap opera it would all prove to have been a plot designed to discredit him in the eyes of a court and place him and his assets under legal supervision.

*Except that I'm the poverty-stricken wretch. It's Sandra who'll inherit a lot of money one day.*

A chill ran down his spine and his jaw developed a tremor.

*Revenge,* he thought, feeling colder still. *If they're really trying to destroy me, their only possible motive is revenge.*

But what was he supposed to have done to them? What inadvertent, unremembered act on his part would justify the unimaginable nightmares to which they were subjecting him?

*Have I done something so heinous that Sandra wants to drive me insane? Something for which she may once have wanted to leave me just before she miscarried?*

He was about to restart the engine when another equally alarming thought occurred to him. He leant over, grabbed Emma by the shoulder and looked at her searchingly. 'That file on me you found at the clinic. . .'

'Yes?'

'Did it also contain a photo of my wife?'

'No.'

'Was she in the Bleibtreu programme too?'

'Not to my knowledge.'

'Really? So how did you know it was her?' He squeezed her shoulder harder.

'You're hurting me.'

He merely nodded. 'What makes you so sure it's Sandra in the photo?'

Emma squirmed in his grasp. 'You told me about her, and the man kept calling her Sandra.'

'Constantin?'

'If that's what he's called.'

She put her hand, which felt pleasantly warm, on his. He relaxed his grip at once.

'What did he say?'

'They were arguing, the two of them, that's the only reason I took the picture. I couldn't catch what your wife was saying because she didn't get out and she left the engine running.'

*That doesn't sound like her,* Marc said to himself. *Sandra was so eco-friendly, she even turned off her engine at the lights.* He couldn't help smiling ruefully. For one thing, because he'd often teased her when the drivers behind them tooted her for not pulling away fast enough; for another, because he realized he'd just been questioning the behaviour of a dead woman.

'And my father-in-law?'

'I already told you. He kept repeating the same thing.'

'Which was?'

Emma stroked her cheek in agitation. The skin around her eyes was somewhat darker than the rest of her face, he noticed. 'He said something like: "Calm down, Sandra, it'll all be over in another few hours."'

*All what?*

Two motorbikes roared past them in quick succession, using the deserted tunnel as a racetrack. Marc scanned Emma's face. Even though her eyelids were flickering nervously, he couldn't detect any sign of insincerity. She was simply on edge.

'That's what he said, Marc. Then she drove off in a rage and he climbed the steps – went inside the police station to get you.'

*I don't believe that, it doesn't make sense – any of it. Why would Sandra and Constantin gang up on me? Why were they arguing? And what will soon be over?*

The more Emma said, the more his jigsaw puzzle of a life disintegrated and the harder he found it to tell who was suffering from severe psychotic delusions, himself or the people around him.

He took another look at the photo of Constantin and his wife. 'Too bad the licence plate isn't on it.'

'Yes, I was in too much of a rush.'

'Oh, naturally.' He gave a sarcastic laugh and started the engine.

'But. . .' Emma delved into her inside pocket again. This time she brought out a small notepad with the remains of some torn-out pages protruding from the edges '. . . maybe this will help.' She turned the pad over and tapped some numerals scrawled on the cardboard back.

B – Q 1371

'I made a note of it instead.'

# 38

'What sort of surprise?' Benny asked quietly, and this time it was he who expected no answer from Valka as he walked slowly along the passage. The way his ear was burning, he might have been on the phone for two hours.

'She's waiting for you in the bathroom.'

Benny's terrible presentiment hardened into certainty. There was someone in his flat.

The bathroom door was ajar. He pushed it open and peered in.

'Jesus Christ.' His instinctive reaction was to look away, but he overcame his initial shock and hurried inside.

She was naked, fourteen years old at most, and lying motion-less in his bathtub. Her arms were folded behind her head and her wrists imprisoned in the far too tight handcuffs with which she'd been manacled to the shower pipe. Her small breasts were dappled with discoloured patches, some of which looked like bruises, others like burns. Issuing from between her legs, which were shackled together by the ankles, a red stain was spreading across the white enamel.

'That's Magda. She comes from Bulgaria.'

'You filthy, fucking psychopath.'

'I'll take that as a compliment.'

Benny felt her pulse but could detect nothing.

'Why? Why did you do it?' he demanded over the sound of Valka's laughter.

'Come, come! I had nothing to do with it. It was an accident. These things happen when my friends indulge in a little horseplay.'

'Why?' Benny yelled the word louder still.

He touched her thin face and began to weep, ran his forefinger over her split lips and sensed, with every fibre of his being, the mental and physical torment this girl must have endured in the last few days of her wretched existence.

Valka, by contrast, sounded quite unconcerned.

'She's my insurance, just in case you imagine you can somehow pin that muckraking journalist's death on me. It won't be so easy when they find the girl at your place. That is, unless you think the public prosecutor condones serial murder?'

Benny buried his face in his hands, breathing spasmodically. His fingers – the fingers that had just touched Magda – seemed to smell of death. The fact that he knew her name made everything even worse.

'In half an hour I'm going to call the police,' Valka went on, 'so you'd better hit the road as soon as possible. Because, believe me, even if you managed to dispose of the girl in time, you certainly couldn't get rid of the traces of DNA that have trickled down your plughole.'

With that he hung up, leaving Benny in a mental torment for which there was no relief. He sat down on the edge of the bath and started to tremble all over. Afterwards he couldn't remember how long he'd sat there. Although it felt like an eternity, only a few minutes might have elapsed before he heard footsteps in the passage.

# 39

*B – Q 1371.*

There was only one person he knew who could identify the owner of a car without access to a police computer. Marc felt sure that person wouldn't be inclined to be helpful, for understandable reasons, and certainly not at this hour, but he had no alternative. He could hardly pay a second visit to the police, least of all armed with a request that would only reinforce their suspicion that he was suffering from a progressive mental disorder.

'Hello?'

He slowly made his way towards the light issuing into the narrow passage from the bathroom door, which was ajar. Every step intensified his sense of déjà vu, leaving no room for any thought of the real reason he was there.

It had been just the same on his last, unheralded visit. He had walked along the same passage and, a few seconds later, discovered his brother's motionless form in the bathtub. Except that the front door hadn't been wide open the way it was now.

'Benny?' he heard himself call, and was relieved to detect a sign of life. A shadowy figure loomed up behind the frosted-glass door. It grew bigger, and a moment later it opened.

Marc felt as if an unseen hand had turned over the brittle

page of an old photo album. The face he saw seemed simultaneously familiar yet unfamiliar, like a long-forgotten photograph that bears only a vestigial resemblance to one's transfigured memory of the past. He had managed to avoid meeting his younger brother when he had testified to the board of examiners. Now, for the first time in years, he was face to face with him.

'Hello, kid,' Marc said in a voice he didn't recognize, hesitant and nervous but striving to sound confident. Rather than replying, Benny stared at him in consternation like the woman who had refused to let him into his own flat a few hours earlier. The woman he still thought was Sandra.

Benny reached blindly behind him and, without taking his eyes off Marc, pulled the bathroom door shut. He didn't raise a hand in greeting, didn't even brush aside the dark hair plastered to his forehead with sweat. The hair Marc had envied even as a boy.

Instead, Benny thrust his fists into the pockets of his metallic-green bomber jacket and stared at Marc with an inscrutable expression.

*Despair? Concern? Anger?*

Marc was suddenly struck by a horrible thought. It seared his innermost self like a stinging nettle on bare skin.

*What if he doesn't recognize me? Like Sandra?*

*What if none of this is real? What if it's all in my imagination: my brother, the passage, the bathroom behind him?*

He was involuntarily reminded of a short article in a psychology magazine he'd started to read in his dentist's waiting room. It was about a patient who consulted a psychiatrist, whom he took to be a product of his own diseased imagination because he firmly believed himself to be the sole survivor of a viral pandemic; the last man on earth, who had taken refuge in an illusory world so as not to die of loneliness. This confronted the psychiatrist with an utterly insoluble problem. How did you convince a patient that he *wasn't* suffering from hallucinations – that all he could see and feel actually existed, not only in his self-made imaginary world but in reality?

Marc's name had been called before he could finish the article. He had never regretted not knowing how a story ended as much as he did at this moment.

'*Do you know who I am?*' That was what he really wanted to ask, but Benny got in first.

'This is a bad time, Marc.'

The use of his name, the familiar tone of voice reserved for people one doesn't have to make an effort for, and the twitch of the eyebrows – a mannerism with which they'd always greeted each other in the past – all these helped to banish Marc's direst fears. He wasn't an anonymous stranger after all.

'You know who I am,' he blurted out in relief, heedless of how absurd this must sound. Benny seemed even more exhausted than Marc himself, although he looked to be in better shape physically. He had filled out, like an athlete whose training has improved his posture. But for all that, he was looking drained – wrapped in an air of melancholy fatigue that had nothing in common with the warm, dreamy look of someone roused from sleep in the middle of the night. His shoulders seemed bowed beneath an invisible burden that rendered it impossible for him to take a step towards his brother.

'I need your help,' said Marc.

'I can't.'

Although he'd anticipated this reply, it surprised him nonetheless. On the one hand, it was curt and dismissive. On the other, Benny's tone was far milder than he'd expected. Marc was responsible for his enforced confinement in a psychiatric hospital, after all, yet there was nothing hostile about his younger brother's manner – indeed, he seemed in urgent need of help himself.

'I'm afraid you'll have to go. . .' Benny stopped short. Somewhere on the stairs, a board had creaked as loudly as if someone had crushed a nutshell underfoot.

Benny froze.

Marc was about to explain that he hadn't come alone, but Benny motioned him to be silent. There was another creak, and although it sounded this time like the creak of a decrepit beam in an old building, Marc sensed that his brother was becoming more nervous still.

'Were you followed?' Benny asked in a whisper.

'Not exactly.'

At that moment the front door swung open and Benny whipped something out of his jacket pocket – something Marc had never seen him holding before: a cocked automatic pistol.

# 40

Two minutes later, after Emma had narrowly escaped being shot because she hadn't wanted to wait outside the door any longer, and after all three had calmed down a little, they were standing in the living room beside a long, hand-crafted oak dining table. The fruit bowl on it was piled high with bananas, apples and grapes. Marc could detect no dust or glass rings on the freshly polished surface. Leana, the psychiatric nurse, had been telling the truth: Benny really had turned over a new leaf. His kid brother, who had been permanently broke and given to sleeping amid a clutter of pizza boxes and empty cans of Red Bull, seemed to have adopted a vitamin-rich diet and acquired a cleaning woman. Or a girlfriend, which was even more inconceivable. The only reminder of his former lifestyle was the stale air pervading his top-floor flat. It harboured a curious, rather cloying smell suggestive of windows long unopened or garbage that urgently needed taking outside.

Benny, who had pocketed the pistol, glanced nervously at his watch. 'What do you want?' he asked uncertainly, blinking as if someone had thrown sand in his eyes. The lids were puffy and he seemed totally stressed.

'I need some information, Benny.'

'What sort of information?'

'You've got to check a licence-plate number for me.'

Benny blew out his lips incredulously and gave a forced laugh.

'In the middle of the night? Are you crazy?'

Marc nodded. 'Believe it or not, that's precisely why I'm here: to find out if I am.'

He helped himself to an apple. Although he hadn't eaten all day, he didn't feel hungry in the least and put it back.

'Well. . .' Benny glanced at the window. 'If you want my honest opinion, your fat girlfriend over there certainly has a screw loose.'

Emma had left them and gone over to the living-room window, where she was feeling the heavy linen curtain with one hand as if checking the quality of the material. The other hand was holding her mobile, into which she was whispering. The brothers could only catch snatches of what she was saying.

'I'm now. . . Benjamin Lucas's flat. . . near Kollwitz. . . fifth floor. . .'

'What on earth is she doing?'

'Leaving a message on her mobile.'

'Huh?'

'Forget it. It isn't important.'

Marc prefaced his summary of the previous few hours by asking if Benny had heard about the car accident. Benny's only response was an indifferent shrug. His resentment showed through for the first time, although he seemed to find it an effort to inject some indignation into his voice. 'I'm sorry. As you're probably aware, I was in a psychiatric hospital until recently. You don't get to hear much about the outside world in there.'

He pulled up a chair. His reproachful undertone had gone the next time he spoke. 'Look, I'm really sorry about Sandra, but I knew nothing about her death – I didn't even know she was pregnant. It must be hell for you, Marc, but right now I've got other worries, honestly.'

'Lovely,' they heard Emma mutter to herself, and turned to look.

She had left the window and was examining an unframed canvas hanging just above the leather sofa.

'I'd like to be there too.' She went closer and bent over with her hands clasped behind her back like someone in a gallery trying to decipher an artist's signature.

*I'd like to be there too? Where?*

The picture was a big white expanse with isolated patches of beige, coarse-grained canvas showing through it. From a distance it looked as if it had been sprayed with frothy milk.

'Let me give you a brief account of all that's happened to me today,' Marc began, only to be interrupted once more.

'Did you paint this?' Emma asked.

To his boundless surprise, those few words of hers seemed to monopolize his brother's attention. Benny went over to her. 'Yes,' he said, nodding wearily.

*Yes?* Marc was familiar with his brother's passion for art. In the old days, Benny had even ventured to produce some roughs for the sleeve of their demo CD, though they'd had been far less abstract than this.

'It's wonderful. That house...' Emma indicated the pallid expanse. 'The deserted forest...'

*House? Forest?* thought Marc. He went over and peered at it. True, there seemed to be something indistinct in the background. The picture was on two planes, but he couldn't make out a building of any kind. An ice-bound, snowy wasteland or a cloudscape at most, and even then with a lot of imagination.

'Benny,' Marc said, trying to pick up the thread again, 'will you listen a minute?'

Although his brother nodded, he seemed to be as wholly engrossed in the painting as Emma. Marc launched into his account of the traumatic experiences he'd undergone in the last few hours, uncertain whether anyone in the room was listening to him. He was all the more surprised when Benny, having torn himself away from his handiwork, produced a complete and accurate summary of what he'd been told.

'Well, if I've understood you correctly, it's like this: having got me committed to that loony bin, you turn up here and announce that Sandra and her baby have died in a car crash. Someone has wiped your memory of the event and your wife has resurrected herself, the only evidence of that being a fuzzy photograph of a blonde sitting in a yellow Volvo. And now you need the address that matches the licence plate, right?'

Marc nodded. 'B – Q 1371.'

Benny was about to go on when they heard a rhythmical humming sound that vaguely reminded Marc of his doorbell. Benny took his mobile from his jeans pocket, checked the incoming text message and grimaced as if he'd just extracted a filling with some chewing gum.

'What is it?'

Puzzled, Marc watched his brother go over to a TV cabinet. He opened it and took out a brand-new, half-open sports bag.

Marc wasn't sure, but he thought he glimpsed a wad of banknotes before Benny zipped it up.

'Who's texting you at this time of night?'

Benny stared at him blankly and put the bag on his shoulder. 'We have to go,' he said. He stopped short. 'Where's she gone?'

Marc didn't know what he meant for a moment. Then he, too, saw that Emma wasn't standing in front of the picture any more.

She wasn't in the room at all.

'No idea,' he said, glancing at the living-room door.

*Hadn't it been ajar just now?*

He knew the answer even before Emma started screaming outside in the passage.

# 41

'We've got to get out of here!'

Panic-stricken, Emma was tugging at the front door, which Benny had locked before they went into the living room. Something must have scared her so much she hadn't even noticed the key in the deadlock with the massive bolt running right across the door.

'What's the matter?' Marc demanded.

'Let me out!' she cried shrilly, tears trickling down her red-veined cheeks. She kicked the door with each foot in turn.

'Hey, take it easy,' said Marc, but when he touched her shoulder she swung round with unexpected violence and dealt his jaw an inadvertent karate chop with the heel of her hand.

'What's the matter, for Christ's sake?' He was now shouting as loudly as Emma, who appeared to have choked on her own saliva, because she started coughing violently.

'She's. . .' she gasped between two paroxysms '. . . dead.'
*She's dead?*
'Who's dead? What's she talking about?'

Marc looked at Benny, who was standing in the passage a couple of metres behind him, roughly on a level with the bathroom door. Benny just shrugged, so he addressed himself again to Emma, who was being shaken by another fit of coughing. Her breath started to rattle in her throat. He tried to open her quilted jacket but couldn't because she had slid to the floor with her back against the wall and was cowering beside the door like a beaten dog.

'Don't touch me,' she whimpered, fending off imaginary blows with both hands, and started to hyperventilate.

'Dead. . .' she repeated, gasping like a drowning woman who'd surfaced in the nick of time. Although her massive bosom heaved at every breath, her oxygen intake seemed to be steadily diminishing. Eventually, after a last, desperate gasp, her eyes rolled upwards and she passed out.

'Jesus,' said Benny, 'she belongs in a funny farm.'

'That's where she's come from.' Marc bent down and checked Emma's pulse, though her double chin made it hard to find the jugular.

'She's okay. Passed out, that's all.' Marc looked helplessly at Benny. 'What now?'

'Search me. She can't stay here, anyway.' Benny quickly released the deadlock that had just defeated Emma and opened the door. He pressed a switch on the landing and the stairwell was bathed in yellowish, energy-saving twilight. 'Come on, we'd better take her to A and E.'

They lugged Emma outside, each with an arm around her shoulders. Marc could hardly support her weight. The last few hours had weakened his already debilitated body, and he wondered if it was wise to manhandle an overweight woman down five flights of stairs with a splinter in his neck. Constantin had even forbidden him to tote boxes around when he was moving house.

'I'll help you get her to the car,' Benny said when they reached the third floor. 'After that, you'll have to manage by yourself.'

'Where are you off to so late?' Marc panted. He would have liked to take a breather, but Benny seemed to be in a hurry and even put on speed.

'Sorry, I can't tell you.'

'Look, you can't just run off. You owe me.'

They had to pause briefly between the third and second floors because Emma's feet had caught in the banisters. She uttered a groan but seemed unaware of the brothers' exertions.

'What gives you that idea?' Benny demanded.

'I saved your life.'

'Yet another reason for steering clear of you.'

'I know you hate me, but do you think I'd be here if I had any choice?'

They had at last reached the heavy, wrought-iron front door. Marc, who was bathed in sweat, had to support Emma on his own. Cold air streamed into the already chilly passage as Benny opened the door. Then he came back and they lugged Emma outside.

'Do me one last favour, Benny, please. Call a friend – you've got your contacts, after all. Check that number plate and get the owner's address for me, and you'll never see me again.'

'No.'

They sat Emma down on a graffiti-daubed ledge beside the entrance. Marc satisfied himself that she was safely propped against the wall. Then he went over to his brother, who was standing in the middle of the forecourt, feeling in his pockets for his car key.

'Why not, you bastard?' His breath emerged in dense clouds as he barred Benny's path.

Benny's block of flats was situated in a cobbled, traffic-becalmed street where the parking slots were arranged so as to slow the traffic. The numerous shops whose windows illuminated the district at night were in keeping with its character. Anyone who moved to Prenzlberg was hip, modern, eco-friendly, liberal-minded and fond of children. The residents tended not to be Berliners, so the local businesses were predominantly Spanish delicatessens, English-speaking kindergartens, Indian tea-houses and offbeat designer boutiques. The area around Kollwitzplatz was one of Europe's most child-abundant neighbourhoods, so it was no wonder the street felt as if it were in a city of the dead. Working parents still had two hours before their alarm clocks went off. As for the artists and students, they were either asleep or making a night of it two streets away, where there were bars and pubs still open.

'Hey, I'm talking to you. Why can't you do me one last favour before I get out of your life for good?'

'Because the number plate won't get you anywhere.' Benny screwed up his eyes and stared past Marc at the street behind him. Scenting a trap, Marc suppressed an urge to turn round.

'How do you know?'

'I already checked it.'

'How? You didn't call anyone.'

*Or had he? Had he texted someone unobserved, and had the message just been answered?* Marc wasn't sure. Far too many inexplicable things had happened in the last few hours.

'I didn't have to call anyone,' Benny said, pointing across the street. Marc turned to look and his heart stood still.

The ambulance was parked in the goods entrance beside a café on the opposite side of the street. As though in response to a word of command, the driver started the engine and inched out into the road.

The occupants behind the tinted windscreen were invisible this time, but not the illuminated licence plate: *B – Q 1371.*

'What on earth's going on here?' Marc demanded, swinging round. The ledge was deserted. Emma wasn't sitting on it any more; she was standing close behind them with the muzzle of Benny's automatic pointing straight at his head.

# 42

'So I was right!' Marc felt almost relieved at not being mistaken for once. Emma *was* a threat after all. She *wasn't* on his side of the abyss; or, if she was, only so as to push him over the edge.

*It had all been just a ploy. The papers in the hotel room, the photo of Sandra, the fainting fit that had enabled her to snatch Benny's gun while they were hefting her downstairs.*

'We have to get going,' Emma said hoarsely. She was still looking utterly drained. Her moon face was puffier than ever, her sweaty cheeks were threaded with dark-red capillaries, her eyelids quivering with fatigue, but she still had sufficient energy to transfer the automatic from brother to brother at one-second intervals. She also cast hurried glances at the ambulance, which was now driving past them at walking pace, presumably because the driver had spotted the gun in her hand and preferred to avoid another confrontation.

'What do you want me to do?' Marc asked quietly. His state of mind had automatically switched to the almost dispassionate mode he'd adopted during years of conflict resolution with his street kids.

'Over to my car, please!' Emma indicated her Beetle, which was parked in a bay some twenty metres away with one wheel on the kerb.

'Okay, I'll come with you,' Marc replied. 'But first you must give me that gun.'

'No!' she snapped. 'We're in danger, don't you understand? Quick!' She shouted the last words: 'We must get out of here!'

'Be quiet!'

They all turned their heads and stared at the entrance to the building next door, but the man who had shouted at them was nowhere to be seen. The door was wide open, but the passage beyond it was in total darkness.

'Who's there?' Emma called, glancing over her shoulder. The only response was a faint scratching sound followed by the metallic rattle of a chain being dragged across a hard stone surface.

'Hello?' she called again. Absurd enough already, the situation became more ludicrous still when a dog's furry head peered around the door post. The blackish retriever cross-breed looked straight at them, gave a cavernous yawn and ambled out into the rain. Its fur was so thick and matted the raindrops couldn't have penetrated more than a couple of millimetres.

'Come back, Freddy,' called the reedy voice that had just shouted at them. 'Come here and go back to sleep.'

*Just a tramp. We've woken a down-and-out.*

Emma's relief was palpable. The only witnesses to their altercation were a harmless vagrant and his mongrel sleeping rough in the entrance to a building. Refocusing her attention on Marc and Benny, she jerked the gun in the direction of her car.

'Where are we going?' asked Marc.

'Out of here for a start. Not him, though.' She indicated Benny, who just shrugged.

'Fine by me,' he said.

'Okay, Emma,' Marc said as gently as he could. 'We'll sort this out, but first you must give me the gun.'

She shook her head. 'No, I can't. Come on. . .' Close to hysteria again, she uttered the next words with desperate intensity. 'Otherwise he'll kill us too!'

Marc looked bewildered. He stared first at Benny, then at her.

'Kill us?'

'Yes, he's a bad man.'

There was something ominous about the remark, despite her childish choice of words.

'What do you mean, bad?'

'Didn't you smell it?' she shouted. The dog, which had returned to its master, started barking.

'Smell what?'

'You couldn't miss it. The stench in his flat.'

'What are you getting at?'

Marc's bewilderment and his headache intensified in equal measure. He needed to take a pill as soon as possible.

Emma opened the driver's door. 'He killed her. The girl in the bathroom. I traced the smell and found her.'

'The woman's paranoid,' said Benny, echoing Marc's thoughts.

'Please get in,' Emma pleaded in a slightly calmer voice. 'Just you, Marc, not your brother. You've got to trust me.'

'Trust you?' Marc fought for composure. All that prevented him from slapping her face was the gun in her hand.

'Yes, I can explain everything.'

'Then you'd better start with that licence number. Why did you lie to me?'

'It was all I could think of on the spur of the moment,' she said, trembling harder.

Benny started to say something, but Marc forestalled him. 'So you're in cahoots with them, are you? They've employed you to drive me insane.'

'No.'

'Why? Who'd be interested in destroying me?'

'That's the right question, Marc, but I can't answer it. Please,' she repeated, 'you've got to trust me.'

Benny laughed. 'Says the woman who claims she can smell dead bodies and threatens us with a stolen gun.'

Marc nodded, although something about Emma's tone of voice had puzzled him. Either she was a consummate actress or she genuinely believed she could justify her behaviour.

'Look, Marc, I know you don't believe I saw your wife. Even a photo of her wasn't enough for you.'

Using her left hand, Emma took her mobile from her jacket pocket, activated the display and handed it to him.

'You were so mistrustful of me, but I didn't want to be on my own again, so I quickly thought of a licence number – the first one that occurred to me. It's the number of the ambulance that's been tailing me ever since I broke out of the clinic.'

'That's another goddamned. . .' Marc was about to add 'lie' when Benny cut him short by snatching the mobile from his hand.

'One moment,' he said, turning the display through ninety degrees. 'Did you take this?'

Emma stared at him suspiciously. 'Yes. Why?'

'A yellow Volvo?'

'Yes.'

'With a dent in the side?'

Emma nodded more vigorously, although it was clear she didn't know where his questions were leading.

'Right side or left?'

'The dent? I don't know. Left, I think, towards the back.'

She started coughing again. The sweat was trickling down her cheeks now.

'What is it?' Marc broke in. 'Do you know that car?' He hugged his chest, although he didn't really know what was making him shiver, cold or fear; probably both.

Benny gave an affirmative click of his tongue. 'Yes. I drove it recently.'

'Really? So you know who it belongs to?'

Out of the corner of his eye, Marc saw a cyclist on the other side of the street get off his bike and look over at them with interest.

'Yes, I'm afraid so.'

'We must get going,' said Emma, who had also noticed the cyclist, but Marc wasn't listening.

'What do you mean, you're afraid so? Who is it, for Christ's sake?'

'Oh shit, you really don't want to know.' Benny handed back the mobile with a sigh, shoulders sagging.

'Why not?' Marc demanded. He was about to grab Benny's arm when his brother darted forwards.

The first shot that rent the air prompted the cyclist to pedal off as fast as he could. He didn't look back even when another shot rang out and the barking and cries of pain behind him steadily increased in volume.

# 43

Within the space of a heartbeat Benny had grabbed Emma's wrist and forced her arm upwards, complete with gun. The second shot went off right beside her head. The agonizing pain took only an instant to have the desired, paralysing effect.

She let go of the gun and sank to her knees beside the car with both hands clamped to her left ear. The blast had ruptured her eardrum.

'What have you done?' yelled Marc, slow to grasp what had just happened before his very eyes. All he saw was the blood oozing between Emma's fingers and staining the collar of her white jacket. For one horrific moment he assumed that Benny, the kid brother who'd never hurt a soul in his life, had actually shot her in the head. Then she tried to get up and although she was only emitting hoarse cries of pain, he guessed that her injuries could not be life-threatening after all.

'What now?' he demanded, more quietly. This time the question was directed at Emma as well as Benny, who had retrieved his gun.

'I'm going,' said Benny.

'You can't just push off!'

Marc knelt down beside Emma, at his wits' end. The bleeding was worse, if anything, and had plastered the hair to her temple. In a kind of displacement activity, he felt her forehead like a mother checking her child's temperature. It was burning hot.

'We must get her to a hospital. Please Benny, you'll have to drive us there...' Startled, he broke off and clutched Emma's hand, which had suddenly gone limp. She'd passed out again. 'At least help me get her into the car. Benny?'

He looked up, expecting some objection, but none came. His brother had disappeared.

'Shit, shit, shit. . .' Marc broke out in a sweat despite the cold. He was desperately tired and his headache had spread to his neck. He was afraid he didn't have the strength to manhandle Emma into the car.

*Damnation.*

He got out his mobile, intending to dial emergency, but the battery gave out after one keystroke.

*Shit!*

He patted Emma's jacket in search of her mobile. Then it occurred to him that Benny had had it last, so he'd probably pocketed it.

He rose to his feet, leant against the car and surveyed the buildings across the street. As far as he could see, there was no one at any of the windows, and the balconies were deserted.

*Why hasn't anyone called the police? Someone must have heard those shots.*

He was just about to bend over Emma again when he was startled by a voice he'd heard once before.

'Hello there, mate.'

Though very much quieter, the voice was definitely the one that had complained about the noise. Marc looked up. The old man was standing on the pavement with his dog on a length of chain.

'What do you want?'

The dosser seemed to take as much care of his clothes as the circumstances of his life on the streets permitted. It was easy to overlook the fact that he was destitute, because only close proximity revealed the crumbling layer of grime on his once expensive, crudely patched serge overcoat, beneath which lurked a sports coat far too big for him. Close proximity also enabled them to smell the cloying, rancid body odour that provided a further indication of his homelessness.

'No worries, mate,' the old man said with a toothless grin. 'I didn't see a thing.'

'It isn't the way it looks. I'm taking this woman to hospital.'

Marc caught hold of Emma under the arms and, with his last remaining strength, hauled her to her feet. Her breathing was fast and shallow.

The dosser just nodded indifferently and watched him struggling with his burden. He didn't start chuckling until Marc had managed to drag Emma to the other side of the car, open the passenger door and buckle her into her seat.

'Some night, eh?'

Marc turned to him, wiping the sweat from his brow. 'Look, if it's money you're after, I'm sorry. I'm skint myself.'

He made sure Emma's head couldn't sag forwards and shut the passenger door.

'I know.'

Marc, who was about to make his way round to the driver's side, stopped in his tracks.

'How?' he demanded.

'I'm sorry, I looked, but there wasn't anything in it. Here.'

The dosser extended a grubby hand. Only one of his four fingers boasted a nail and the thumb was missing altogether, but that wasn't what puzzled Marc so much. He stared at the wallet in disbelief, feeling in his pockets. It really was his own wallet the dosser was trying to return.

'Freddy found it. He's a great one for picking up things lying around on the ground. Aren't you, mate?'

The old man patted his dog on the head. It promptly rolled over on its back in the hope of further caresses.

'Thanks,' said Marc, still bemused.

'Don't mention it, I'm an honest man. Come on, mate.' He gave the chain a gentle tug and the mongrel got to its feet.

'But next time keep the noise down,' he said with another chuckle. He tapped his forehead and ambled off.

'Yes, sure,' Marc said pointlessly, turning the wallet over in his hands. He put it in his pocket. Emma had begun to whimper in the car behind him. She was evidently coming round.

He got into the Beetle, started the engine and put it in gear. Before driving off, he obeyed a spontaneous impulse and took out the wallet again. He opened it just to make sure his ID card – one of the few remaining proofs of his identity – was still there. Fortunately, it was in the pocket provided. He pulled it out, meaning to glance at the old passport photo in which he looked so much younger and fitter, but it resisted. When he withdrew it completely, a little piece of paper fell out on to his lap.

*What on earth. . .?*

He unfolded the slip of paper and stared at it incredulously.

*What's this?*

Marc felt sure he'd never seen the note before, let alone kept it in his wallet. He turned off the engine, undid his seatbelt in feverish haste, and got out.

'Hey!' he called in the direction of the dark doorway into which the dosser had just disappeared. 'Come back here!'

He broke into a run, although he hardly had the strength and already knew what awaited him at the end of his desperate sprint: *nothing.*

The dog and its owner, who had just brought him a hand-written message from his late wife, had both disappeared.

# 44

Many people make the mistake of wanting to repeat everything. Not content with a single memory, they long to experience their life's most blissful moments once again. They book another flight to the holiday resort they liked so much, watch the same film over and over, or sleep with an ex-partner although they're happily involved in a new relationship, only to discover that a second bite of the cherry will never, as a rule, taste as good as the first. Feelings of happiness can't be reproduced to order, can't be recalled at the touch of a button. Paradoxically, as Marc found out to his cost, this does not apply to pain, suffering and agony of mind. He had inadvertently visited their old home once before, and once before he had been almost overwhelmed with grief.

He got out of the car, leaving Emma behind. She had refused to be taken to A and E although the Martin Luther Hospital lay right on their route. Eardrums usually healed of their own accord, as he himself had found after a middle-ear infection. Besides, the car was hers and he needed it, both as transport and, possibly, as a means of escape. Even if Emma was paranoid and suspected his brother of murder for no good reason, she was the only person who could testify to the crazy situation in which he was embroiled. He couldn't tell friend from foe in any case, so it was better to keep an eye on his enemies – if indeed she was one of them.

He opened the garden gate. The small two-storeyed terrace house still seemed to be breathing. Unlike all its spick-and-span neighbours, whose well-tended gardens were enclosed by fences proof against wild boar, No. 7 looked rather neglected but, for that very reason, like an animate being – like an untidy nursery whose walls have been scribbled on in crayon but whose owners wouldn't exchange it at any price for a designer home in *The World of Interiors*.

Marc took another look at the note he'd found in his wallet.

*Meet you at the Villa Grunewald. Come quickly!*
*LOL – S.*

The simple message was unambiguous. It didn't prove she was still alive, of course. Sandra had often left similar notes on the kitchen table:

*Gone to the gym / Don't eat too much junk food, I'll cook us something / Last night was great – as usual / Don't forget to take the bottles back.*

At some stage, Marc had taken to signing his notes 'LOL' in the erroneous belief that it was short for 'Lots of love'. Sandra had rocked with laughter the first time she read it, because – as she patiently explained – teenagers used that acronym to acknowledge receipt of some amusing email or text message from a friend.

*Laughing out loud.*

Since then, appending an 'LOL' to nearly every message had become one of their private jokes.

That and the unmistakable handwriting were definite indications that Sandra had written the note. Another was the stated rendezvous. Their terrace house in Eichkamp was far from being a 'villa' – another of their private jokes.

Marc put the slip of paper away and got out his bunch of keys. The front door jammed, but it had done that months ago.

What greeted him inside was not the stale smell he'd been expecting. It was chilly – the central heating had been left on minimum to prevent the pipes from freezing – but the stuffy smell typical of an empty house was absent. Someone seemed to have aired the place not long ago. They had also taken the opportunity to polish the floor. The sofa's rubberized legs had left black scuff marks on the parquet, and these had disappeared.

'Hello?' he called. His husky voice sent metallic echoes reverberating around the bare walls of the deserted stairwell. He advanced slowly and cautiously, as if the route to the living room were a thin layer of ice. He wasn't sure which scared him more, being alone in the house or the possibility of coming face to face with his wife.

'Hello?' he called again. He would have liked to call Sandra's name aloud but he didn't dare.

Built on to the living room was a conservatory whose windows overlooked the neglected garden. He had turned on the exterior lighting, and the little halogen spotlights acted like a soft-focus lens. Everything looked fuzzy – veiled in a golden-yellow aura: the fruit trees, the rotting apples on the lawn, and the fish pond, which was overgrown with reeds and contained more mud than water.

A gust of wind tore some leaves from the silver birch immediately in front of the veranda. Marc was allergic to birches but had never had the heart to fell the proud tree. Now, looking up at it, he saw a crow soar into the sky from its topmost branch.

His tears seemed to be intensifying the soft-focus effect, because the tree had suddenly become much paler in colour. He rubbed his eyes, but the effect persisted.

*What the. . .?*

He put his head back and tried to analyse the strange glow, which bathed only a small part of the tree's foliage. When the wind stirred the higher branches, the truth dawned on him.

The tree was being illuminated not by the lights in the garden but by some other artificial light source. And this was located two or three metres above his head. On the first floor.

*Inside the house!*

Everything happened very quickly after that. He dashed back to the entrance hall and pelted up the stairs two at a time. Moments later he threw open the bedroom door. It was true. Although he had removed all the plugs and unscrewed every bulb, the room was ablaze with light.

His jaw dropped and more tears welled up in his eyes. He couldn't believe, couldn't grasp, what he was seeing as he blundered into the room.

*This is impossible! Why, Sandra? Why?*

He had got rid of all the furniture after the accident. The double bed, the louvred wardrobe units, the dressing table with the big mirror. A Pole and his son had come for them. They had dismantled them in his presence, carried them downstairs and driven them off in a trailer. And now, three weeks later, everything was the way it had been. The bed, the wardrobes, the dressing table – all were back in their old places. There was even a new addition, something that looked as wrong as the sight of a pregnant woman lighting a cigarette. Pale blue, with a snow-white canopy, and standing roughly in the middle of the room, was a brand-new, freshly made-up baby's cradle.

For one frightful moment Marc feared it might rock, propelled by some unseen hand in time to a discordant lullaby. But the cradle didn't budge a millimetre. It did something far more terrible: it started to speak.

# 45

'Help. Please help me.'

Marc shrank back. The voice grew louder. 'Don't go! Don't leave me here!'

Although he'd taken only a quick look and drawn the drapes aside for only a moment, he was sure the cradle contained nothing but a little pillow. He might have overlooked some pyjamas, a baby's toy or a blanket, but he certainly hadn't failed to see a living occupant, least of all one big enough to address him in such a deep male voice.

'Who's there?' he asked, convinced that he was talking to a recording.

He was all the more startled to receive an answer. 'Thank God you came, Marc.'

*It knows my name. How does it know my name?*

His heart beat faster. 'Who are you?' he demanded, reaching gingerly for the curtains. He was still a good metre from the cradle and had to force himself to approach it again.

'I'm the one you're looking for,' said the man. His hoarse, rather distorted voice sounded quite unfamiliar.

Marc drew back the curtain. The first thing he saw was the white pillow. Then he saw the numerals embroidered in red on the pillowcase:

*13 / 11*

Just as it dawned on him that this was today's date, he spotted the baby monitor. He picked it up, staring incredulously at the mouthpiece – and almost dropped it when the man spoke again. 'Please come and get me.'

He noticed the metallic echo only now, although the quality of the digital radio was several times better than that of a normal telephone.

He put the device to his lips and spoke straight into it: 'What is all this?'

'I. . . I'm an acquaintance. . .'

There was a hiss, followed by the sound of static on the line.

'. . . an acquaintance of your wife. Please help me.'

'Where are you?'

Another hiss, then the man said quietly: 'I'm down here. In the cellar.'

# 46

It took Marc three times longer to descend into the darkness than it had to dash upstairs.

He had always avoided spending more time in the cellar than absolutely necessary. Not from a childish fear that some faceless monster was lying in wait for him behind the boiler, but because he felt satisfied that people were no more born to live in windowless dungeons than they were to fly through the air at an altitude of ten thousand metres.

To him, cellars were like the dark bed of a lake. Much as you enjoyed being on the surface, you had no wish to know what was swimming around below you. Brave souls held their breath and duck-dived a couple of metres down, but no one swam right to the bottom, where mud harboured the lake's secrets, without a convincing reason – unless they'd lost something perhaps. A wedding ring, for instance, or a key.

*Or his wife.*

The plywood door leading to the steep flight of rough stone

steps had been bolted from the outside. Whoever was waiting for him below was locked in. Marc wondered whether he really wanted to know who it was.

He slid the bolt aside, opened the door and felt for the switch on the wall, an old-fashioned black knob like an outsize wing nut. He turned it twice clockwise, then in the opposite direction. The darkness persisted.

'Hello?' he called down the steps. No response. The intercom display, which had been flickering a moment ago, suddenly went out. He remembered that mobile reception on some networks got worse the lower you went. On the other hand, the phone in his hand was independent of any provider.

'Are you down here?'

He descended another step. His stomach gurgled and his persistent nausea sent bile surging up into his throat. Ignoring his body's cries for help, which urged him to go to bed at last, take his pills and sleep for two solid days, he groped his way slowly down the rope the previous owner had installed in lieu of a handrail. A psychologist by profession, he had turned the cellar into a makeshift consulting room by facing the walls with tongue-and-groove and laying some grey industrial carpet. Sandra and Marc had always wondered what sort of people had consented to entrust a stranger with their mental problems in the bowels of the earth, especially as the old house often emitted such mysterious noises that even hanging up laundry down there could be an unnerving experience.

'*The old girl's breathing,*' had been Marc's stock joke when the creaks and groans overhead became louder than usual. Built in the 1920s, the house should have stopped settling long ago.

There were no creaks to be heard now, and the central-heating pipes were silent.

Marc had reached the foot of the steps. Blindly, he opened

the fuse box secured to the wall in a niche beside them. He felt around, avoiding the toggle switches, until he found the lighter kept inside the box for emergencies.

The sulphurous yellow light of the little flame created an almost cosy atmosphere. Marc couldn't understand why the cellar lights weren't working. All the fuses were intact. Still, there were plenty of other more important things that were defeating him tonight.

'Where are you?' he called, raising his voice to drown the roaring in his ears. The quieter his surroundings, the louder his internal noises seemed to become.

With the lighter in one hand and the baby monitor in the other, he made his way into the passage connecting the former consulting room with the boiler room. They had removed the ugly, louvred sliding door, and Marc could see, despite the inadequate lighting, that the bare little room was deserted.

*That leaves only one possibility.*

He stepped over a redundant cable drum with the lighter held up in front of him like an Olympic torch-bearer. His shadow followed a few metres behind.

Just before reaching the grey concrete fire door he paused to give his thumb a rest. When the flame went out, darkness enveloped him like a cloak. Depositing the useless baby monitor on the floor, he thumbed the flint wheel again and shielded the lighter with his hand when the flame started to flicker. Then, although everything within him balked at doing so, he pushed the heavy fire door open and entered the boiler room.

He was so startled he uttered an involuntary cry.

# 47

'Christ! Who the hell are you?' he demanded when he had recovered himself sufficiently not to turn and run. The psychological shocks he'd sustained in the last few hours had sensitized him to such an extent that he was becoming more and more fearful – and taking longer and longer to calm down.

The man, who looked even more frightened than Marc felt, was lying in the middle of the room on a bare iron bedstead.

'Thank God,' he groaned faintly.

He raised his head. That was all he could move, because his wrists and ankles were shackled to the bed-frame. The flame of the lighter was reflected by the metal boiler on his left. As far as Marc could see by its feeble light, the man was wearing a suit and a tie, the knot of which had slipped sideways. It was hard to tell his age. Tall men tended to look older than they were.

'What on earth's going on here?' Marc demanded. He came a step closer.

'Water.'

The stranger tugged at his handcuffs. His fair hair was standing up all over his head. He looked like a comic-book character who has just received an electric shock.

'Please bring me some water.' His voice gave out on the last word.

'Not until I know what you're doing here.'

Marc caught a whiff of urine, presumably because the man had wet himself. Either from fear or because he'd been held captive for a considerable time.

*But by whom?*

For a moment Marc wondered whether it might be better to

go outside and tell Emma. But he still didn't know if he could trust her, and anyway, he doubted if she would be much help in her present state.

'Who are you?' he repeated.

'I. . .' The man paused to moisten a split lip with his tongue. 'I'm here to warn you.'

'About what?'

The man turned his head and looked towards the other end of the cellar, which was now in darkness. An old-fashioned mangle used to stand there, Marc recalled.

'About the script,' the man said softly.

'What script?'

The man looked back at Marc, who involuntarily retreated a step.

'My name is Robert von Anselm,' he said. His voice sounded suddenly monotone, as if he were reciting something he'd learned by heart. 'I'm your wife's attorney.'

*Nonsense.*

'You're lying!' The lighter flame flickered, Marc spat out the words so vehemently. 'I always dealt with her legal affairs myself.'

'No, no, no, you aren't listening. I wasn't your attorney or the family's, just your wife's.'

The bedstead creaked as the man's head sank back on the springs.

*Sandra's attorney? Why should she have employed a stranger to handle her affairs?*

'She came to see me shortly before the accident,' Marc heard the man whisper.

'What for?'

'To alter her will.'

*To alter it?* He hadn't even known there *was* a will. Sandra had always refused to make one.

'I assume she did so at her father's insistence,' the man added.

'I don't understand. What did she alter, and what does Constantin have to do with it?'

The man looked back at the dark corner on his right.

'You remember the film script your wife was commissioned to write?'

'Of course.'

*We'd been celebrating it on the day of the accident.*

'Do you know how much her agent sold it to the American production company for?'

'No.'

'One point two million dollars.'

Marc laughed incredulously. 'You're lying.'

The attorney coughed. 'What makes you so sure?'

'You don't get that kind of money for a film debut. Besides, Sandra would have told me. We didn't have any secrets from each other.'

'Really? Have you read the script?'

'How could I? She died before she could write a word of it.'

'Are you sure?'

*No, I'm not. After today, I'm not sure of anything any more.*

The man was still staring into the gloom on his right. Marc held up the lighter and peered in the same direction, then made his way around the bedstead. As he did so, the outlines of a desk came into view. It was standing right beside the gas boiler.

'But *I've* read it,' he heard the man behind him say hoarsely. 'That's why I'm here. I was going to drop it in to you. I wanted to warn you.'

Marc went over to the desk, which he'd never seen before. Looking quite as incongruous down here as the attorney shackled to the bedstead, it was far too small for an adult, with tiny little side drawers big enough to accommodate a textbook or exercise book at most. Stuck in the recess designed to hold the base of a reading lamp was the stub of an Advent candle.

Marc lit it. Lying on the desktop was a sheaf of paper held together on the left with a cheap plastic binding.

'Hey, what about my water?' the attorney croaked from behind him, in the dark once more.

The pages felt damp, as if they'd been lying in a box in the cellar for a while.

Marc brushed some dust off the top sheet and read the title:

## SPLINTER
## A screenplay by Sandra Senner

The stranger was whimpering now. 'Please untie me!'

But Marc was past replying. He had already turned over the page and begun to read. The very first lines were a shock.

# 48

## Synopsis of SPLINTER

Marc Lucas, a lawyer-turned-social worker who deals with problem children, loses his pregnant wife in a car crash for which he is personally responsible. A few weeks after her death he sees a newspaper advertisement for a psychiatric clinic. The programme 'Learn to forget' is looking for people who have undergone experiences of a highly traumatic nature — people who want to erase

> the memory of them permanently and are
> therefore willing to participate in a memory
> experiment: the deliberate actuation of
> total amnesia. Lucas sends an email to the
> director of the clinic, and...

'No!'

Marc groaned and bit the ball of his thumb. He felt so dizzy he had to lean on the desktop. His eyes roamed aimlessly across the page. Having already read the first paragraph twice, he began all over again in the hope that the letters would rearrange themselves into different words. But they didn't. The truth remained as terrible as it was inexplicable.

*This is my story. Sandra used my life as a...*

His hands were trembling, his fingertips so numb that he turned over three pages at once. He read on, but it only got worse:

> Marc's mobile phone stops working and his
> credit cards have been invalidated. His
> life appears to have been usurped by someone
> else.
> Returning to the clinic, he finds himself
> staring into a hole in the ground — a
> construction site. The building has disap-
> peared.

Once again, Marc couldn't bring himself to read the whole page; once again, he turned over impatiently, ever faster, ever more mystified by what he was reading. He knew it all at first hand – he himself had lived through it a few hours ago! Before long he was reading only snatches, only the lines that hit him in the eye.

```
...goes to the police...
...but this time the key fits...
...his wife never was in the flat...
...his father-in-law has also disappeared...
```

The more he read the less he understood. How could this be? How could Sandra have known all this? Worse still, how could she have foreseen the future?

He put the script down and stared at the title page, clasping the back of his neck.

## SPLINTER
## A screenplay by Sandra Senner

The numbness in his fingertips was slowly spreading up his arms, which now hung limply, wearily, at his sides. He felt an urge to turn and run, screaming, from the cellar. Nothing made sense any more. His life was a lie fabricated by a person he used to trust implicitly – someone who had risen from the grave and was trying to drive him insane.

*But do lunatics reflect on their condition? Isn't denial the very essence of a psychosis?*

His mouth opened and closed. Not that he was aware of it, he was talking to himself, uttering his thoughts aloud. Tears ran down his cheeks and landed on the cover of the script.

*Is this happening to me? Is it all real?*

A tear smudged the big, curved 'S' of 'SPLINTER' and left a black dot above it, transforming the character into the Spanish version of a question mark. He sniffed, fingering the plaster on his neck again. And then, in the midst of an avalanche of incoherent thoughts, he came to an entirely logical conclusion.

*This script must have an ending!*
He picked it up again.
*Why is all this happening? And how does it end?*
He turned to the last page.

# 49

Nothing. The last fifty pages were blank.

Marc riffled the script through his fingers from the back until, about a third of the way from the front, he came across two pages that looked as if they didn't belong. They were thicker than the rest and the edges were perforated and covered with rust marks. They were the concluding pages of the synopsis.

> . . . He eventually faces up to the ghosts of the past and obeys a mysterious summons passed to him by a homeless tramp: apparently, his late wife wants to meet him. He goes to their old home, where, down in the cellar, he finds a film script written by her. To his horror, he discovers that the synopsis on the first few pages are an exact reconstruction of his recent experiences. He turns to the end to find out what happens to him, only to find that the concluding pages are blank.
>
> So he turns back until he comes across two somewhat thicker sheets with perforated, blood-stained edges. At the foot of one is a handwritten telephone number. . .
> 020 7438 1209

Marc's gaze travelled downwards. Sure enough, the number looked as if Sandra had jotted it down on a menu card, though without the LOL.

His eyes stumbled back up the page until he found the line where he'd just broken off.

```
If Marc doesn't think his fear could become
still more intense, he's mistaken. Obeying
a sudden impulse, he opens the top right-
hand drawer of the desk...
```

He shut his eyes, then opened them and reread the last sentence. *Should I really...? What are you doing to me, Sandra?*

He hesitated for a moment, then stuck his finger in the hole in the drawer and pulled. It was unlocked.

```
... and finds a mobile phone.
```

There it was: an old model with big keys. The display flashed, indicating that the battery and signal strength were at full power. Like a man in a trance, Marc complied with the script's insane directions.

```
He takes it out and keys in the phone
number!
```

# 50

'At last! Thank God!'

A professional boxer's well-aimed punch couldn't have hit him harder. It was Sandra's voice that answered after the second ring, no doubt about it. A trifle sad, a trifle hesitant, but as unmistakable as a genetic fingerprint.

'You've called me at last.'

He had missed that slightly husky quality, which always sounded a little lethargic and was at its sexiest just after she'd woken up, as sorely as he had her touch, the lip-smacking noises she made when she was dreaming, and her laugh, which had never failed to infect him however low he was feeling.

'Sandra,' he said, torn between tears and laughter, 'where are you?'

For one moment, brief but long enough to bring more tears to his eyes, the whole crazy business was forgotten.

*The accident. Her reappearance. The tramp. The attorney still begging for water behind him.*

His joy at hearing her voice again was simply overwhelming. All that surpassed it was his disappointment when he realized it was a recording.

'I'm so sorry. I'll make it up to you, I promise.'

'What? What are you talking about?' Marc bellowed the words as if he could browbeat the answerphone into an explanation if he only yelled loud enough.

'I'll explain everything later. Soon, very soon. Just be patient for another few hours.'

*Another few hours? What happens then?*

He thought involuntarily of the hand-stitched pillow on the baby's cot. Of the date on the pillow case: November 13th.

*Today, ten days before the gynaecologist's earliest estimate of their child's date of birth.*

'Don't worry, darling, all will be made clear.'

*Don't worry? I'm losing my mind!*

'One more thing: if you're still down in the cellar, leave now. Get out of there at once.'

He felt a cold draught on the back of his neck. The candle almost went out, it was so strong, but the wick flared up again just in time.

'You forgot something, you see.'

'What?' he asked the machine.

'Robert von Anselm.'

A dark figure loomed up behind him.

'You didn't check his handcuffs.'

Marc swung round, dropping the phone and shielding his head with his hands, but it was too late. A fierce stab of pain, and he went plummeting down into a dark void. The candle went out before it even hit the floor.

# 51

*The first time they drove there he couldn't believe it was a proper road at all. The route that ran through the forest between Potsdam and Berlin, via Sakrow, was little wider than the average pavement. If you wanted to avoid oncoming traffic, you risked scratching your car's paintwork on the fir trees alongside.*

*At the moment, however, they had the road to Spandau to themselves and Marc could put his foot down.*

*'I wish you hadn't found out.' Sandra was gazing out of the window. 'Not so soon, at least.'*

*They often argued in the car. As usual, she avoided looking him in the eye.*

*'You shouldn't have taken me with you, then.'*

*She nodded. A moment later, still watching the trees flit past, she reached for his hand. 'Still, you do see we don't have any choice, don't you?'*

*His laugh was rather forced. Then, when she squeezed his*

hand so hard that it hurt, he said: 'You can't be serious, surely?'

He briefly contemplated pulling up, getting out and shaking some sense into her. His wife had clearly lost her mind.

'The end justifies the means,' she said. 'Isn't that what you always say?'

He speeded up. A yellow star lit up on the dashboard, indicating that the outside temperature had dropped below four degrees.

'Well, isn't that your motto in life?'

'You're crazy, Sandra. Killing is never justified.'

'But you can't prevent it.'

She let out a sob. As a rule, Marc always gave in when she started crying, but today it only made him angrier.

'Oh yes I will, believe me.'

The speedo needle crept past 70 kph and the fir trees beside the road dissolved into a grey-green blur.

He glanced sideways. The glow from the dashboard made the tears on her cheek look like blood trickling from a wound.

'You mustn't,' she protested. 'I won't let you.'

'Really? I already did it once. How do you propose to stop me this time?'

Now it was his turn to stare obdurately ahead. For a while they didn't speak, then they rounded a bend and the road became more undulating. Constantin's house had long since disappeared from the rear-view mirror.

She was sobbing louder now. He longed to put out a soothing hand and stroke the medicine ball of a pregnant tummy that bulged below her seatbelt. But then she did something unexpected. She unbuckled the seatbelt and turned round. He had the sudden feeling that someone was sitting in the back, a stranger who had been listening to their altercation the whole time. But

*Sandra turned back, with a photograph in her hand. Coarse-grained and greyish-black, like an ultrasound print.*

'*Look at it!*' *she shouted.*

*But before he could look back at the road there was an ear-splitting crash. The steering wheel bucked in his grasp, and although he strove with all his might to correct it he failed. His last sight was of Sandra's hands dropping the print and fumbling desperately for her seatbelt. Then lightning struck and everything went glaringly white. The next thing he saw was the worried face of an elderly man bending over him and patting his cheek.*

'*He's coming round,*' *said the face.*

And that was when Marc really did open his eyes.

# 52

For a moment he thought he was still dreaming, except that he wasn't in Sandra's car any more. He was in an antique shop, and the grey-haired owner had bedded him down on a sofa redolent of tobacco and wood smoke, its cushions so plump and yielding they threatened to smother him. He tried to raise his head, which was supported by a neck roll, but this quickly proved to be an impossible undertaking – unless he wanted to throw up over one of the numerous carpets covering the floor.

'Where am I?' he asked, remembering the attorney whose request for water he'd refused.

*And who knocked me out.*

He felt his head, which was still ringing, and noticed that his right sleeve had been rolled up. The plaster in the crook of his arm suggested that someone had taken a blood sample.

He blinked in surprise, and even that hurt. His eyelids were gummed together by a milky secretion.

'Don't worry, you're among friends,' he heard the antique dealer say. Now, having wiped the sleep from the corners of his eyes, he was able to get a better view of his new surroundings. The sofa's companion piece was a wing chair positioned so that anyone sitting in it could look out of the window and see the sofa and the fireplace at the same time. But that was the only set-up that made any sense. All the other furniture – bookcases, chests of drawers, upright chairs, a desk, even a tea trolley – was randomly arranged and mismatched in colour and style. The room reminded him of his own untidy flat, except that the removal firm's boxes were missing and every available surface was covered with medical textbooks, reports and articles.

'Friends?' Marc looked over at the fireplace.

Standing beside it, shoulder to shoulder with the elderly stranger, were Emma and his brother. Benny looked just as he had the last time they met – a weary, unshaven figure in cargo pants and bomber jacket – whereas Emma was looking somewhat better and had a white bandage over her left ear. Someone must have seen to it, and if Marc's inference from the medical diplomas on the mantelpiece was correct, he had a pretty good idea who it was.

'Who are you?' he asked the old man, whom he no longer took to be an antique dealer.

'I'm Professor Niclas Haberland.' The words were accompanied by a smile. 'But my friends call me Caspar.'

'How did I get here?'

'You can thank your brother for that. He brought you to me.'

Marc looked at Benny. He noticed only now that some of

his symptoms had disappeared. Although he still felt sick and his head was buzzing like a swarm of bees, he wasn't feeling as bad as he had over the last few hours. He wondered what the Professor had given him.

'I followed the two of you,' Benny volunteered.

'Why?'

'You know why.'

Marc nodded. The movement made his neck twinge. He hoped his fall in the cellar hadn't jolted the splinter nearer his spinal cord, and that it was only a trapped nerve.

*Yes, I know why. That's the reason I came to see you.*

'You asked for my help, you ass, and you know perfectly well how I react to that.'

'You did a runner.'

'Yes, I had some urgent business to attend to. But then, as I was sitting in my car, my conscience pricked me. You're still my brother, after all, no matter what's happened between us.'

Emma had gone over to the window. 'What a coincidence!' she said scathingly. 'First he tries to kill us, then he turns up like a fairy godmother.'

Marc ignored this. 'How did you find me?' he asked.

'You think I've lost my powers of intuition?'

Marc almost shook his head but remembered the trapped nerve just in time.

'You wanted to see Sandra again. The only likely place to start looking was your former home.'

Summoning up all his strength, Marc struggled into a sitting position. The room seemed to rotate for a moment, first one way, then the other. To his surprise he very soon felt much better than he had when he first sat up. His sense of balance gradually returned and his nausea, too, subsided.

'Anyway,' Benny went on, 'I drove out to Eichkamp and

spotted this nutcase outside the house, asleep in her Beetle.' He indicated Emma with a derisive jerk of his head. 'Then I waited a while. When you didn't come out after twenty minutes I went inside and found you down in the cellar.'

Marc looked first at Benny, then at Emma, and finally out of the window at the far end of the room, which evidently doubled as the professor's living room and study. The house they were in could not have been much bigger than the 'villa'. Judging by the clumsily split logs stacked beside the fireplace and the unbroken expanse of trees outside the window, it was quite possibly just a cabin in the forest.

'What about that attorney?' asked Marc, feeling the back of his head. There was a lump about five centimetres above the plaster over his splinter wound.

'What lawyer? You were alone down there.'

Marc's stomach muscles tensed. 'And the film script? It was lying on the desk.'

'Hey, I didn't waste any time looking around when I found you lying senseless on the floor. I simply humped you outside and drove you to the prof. That makes us quits.'

Benny folded his arms. Emma gave a contemptuous snort, almost as if she were about to spit on the floor.

'I don't believe a word you say,' she said.

'But I do,' said Haberland, who had been following this exchange from the wing chair. He glanced enquiringly at Benny.

'Go ahead, Professor, I release you from your oath of patient confidentiality,' Benny said with a smile, zipping up his bomber jacket. 'Deliver your lecture. I'm going outside for a smoke.'

# 53

Marc felt the room temperature take a sudden dive as his brother opened the door behind him and fresh air came streaming in. The icy blast suggested that they were well outside Berlin. It was just after eleven according to the digital clock on the desk, but the temperature could not have been above zero.

Haberland waited until Benny had gone out on the veranda and shut the door. Then he motioned Emma into a chair beside him. He did not begin to speak until she'd sat down, with an air of reluctance.

'Benjamin is a patient of mine,' he said, looking at Marc. 'That's probably why he brought you to me instead of taking you to a hospital. In the short time I was able to examine him at the clinic as an outside consultant, I became something of a friend of his. I don't set much store by publicity, which is why I live out here in the forest, away from the rest of the world.' He smiled, massaging his wrists.

'I remember reading your report,' said Marc. 'You were against discharging him, weren't you?'

Haberland raised one hand in a conciliatory gesture, causing the sleeve of his jacket to ride up. Marc wasn't sure, but before the professor tweaked it back over his wrist, he thought he spotted some raised scar tissue.

'It wasn't my job to decide whether or not your brother should be discharged. I merely diagnosed a disorder that had always been previously overlooked – one that renders it almost impossible for him to lead a normal life. It makes certain over-reactions, for instance suicidal tendencies, appear more under-standable.'

Haberland turned to Emma. 'Likewise, the question of why he followed you. Benjamin suffers from what is commonly termed the "helper syndrome". He's an HSP.'

Emma raised her eyebrows enquiringly.

'A highly sensitive person. If you went outside now and gave him your hand, he could sense your state of mind. Worse still, he would experience your mental state himself. Benny lives other people's lives. That's why he has to help them whether he wants to or not.'

'Nonsense.'

'No, it isn't,' Marc said firmly. Haberland's few words had struck home. The professor was describing him as well as Benny. Marc had known exactly what was going on inside his younger brother when the band split up. That was why, after the first flush of his affair with Sandra, he had tried to re-establish contact with him. By then, however, Benny was refusing to come home. He not only ignored all Marc's calls but dropped out of school rather than stay in touch with him.

Haberland continued to address his remarks to Emma, trying to explain the complex medical problems as simply as possible. 'It sounds a little hard to believe, I know, but I'm sure that you yourself have covered your eyes because you didn't want to watch some overly horrific scene in a film, for instance.'

He waited for Emma to nod.

'So you can at least empathize with the sufferings of others. Most of us become inured to being confronted by terrible sights day after day. We no longer notice the beggar shivering in the street, we avert our eyes from the woman burbling unintelligibly to herself on the Underground, and we no longer cover our eyes after the umpteenth horror film.' He paused. 'Most people become desensitized. But Benny is different.'

Emma looked out of the window. Benny was endeavouring

to light a cigarette. His hair fluttered in the wind as he shielded the flame of his lighter by turning to face the trees in front of the veranda.

Haberland, too, looked out of the window. 'Benny can't suppress his feelings,' he went on. 'For him, everything gets worse and worse. If he drives past a hospital he wonders how many people are dying inside. If he shuts his eyes he pictures all the terrible things that are happening at this moment – events of which we'll read in tomorrow's papers. He sees the baby shaken into a coma, the soldier whose torturers are crushing his genitals, the horse dying of thirst on its way to a Tunisian slaughterhouse. He can never forget anything he has seen, heard or sensed.' Haberland gazed at Marc intently. 'Just like you, am I right?'

The room was growing darker, the sky more overcast.

'No, it isn't quite as bad with me. Benny has always been the more sensitive one. Perhaps that's why I've managed to offset my helper syndrome by doing the work I do.'

Unlike his brother, Marc had succeeded in suppressing even his worst mental images as time went by. The best proof of that was that he'd given up chasing after Benny in the end. He had made many attempts to contact him and rescue him from Valka's clutches, but in vain. Benny's self-embargo was so complete that it had been months before Marc learned of his first suicide attempt. After that he'd even gone to court to see if Benny could be taken into care or made to undergo psychiatric treatment, only to be informed that, as long as his brother represented no threat to other people, he could do what he liked with his life. Marc had nonetheless felt guilty afterwards, suspecting that he might have given up too soon for reasons of personal convenience. In those days, life with Sandra was so infinitely less complicated than what would have awaited him with Benny at his side.

His train of thought was interrupted by a bird call. When he looked at the window his brother had disappeared.

'Okay,' Emma said belligerently, 'so how come such an allegedly peace-loving person tried to kill me?'

Marc shook his head. 'Benny hasn't a violent bone in his body.'

'What! He nearly blew my ear off and he forced me to drive out here at gunpoint.'

'That shot was accidental, I'm sure,' Marc protested. 'He never meant to hurt you. He'd be incapable of it.'

'I'm afraid that's not entirely true,' Haberland amended, raising his hand again. 'That's why he spent so long in a secure unit. Like any unstable personality, Benny suffers from extreme mood swings that threaten to tear him apart. It's the same with bipolar disorder. The switch can be tripped from one moment to the next, and all that your brother has suffered over the years – all that has been gnawing away at him – bursts forth. One little thing – that's all it takes to unleash his pent-up capacity for violence, either on himself or on others.'

'What did I tell you!' Emma said triumphantly. She took out her mobile, which Benny must have returned to her. She'd clearly had enough of this conversation and preferred to dictate the latest information to her voicemail.

Marc ignored his aching head and neck and struggled to his feet. To his surprise he succeeded at the first attempt.

'Okay, Professor,' he said, rolling his sleeve down. 'I've no idea what kind of injection you gave me – maybe I don't even want to know. It was very kind of you to minister to us, but now I must go. I'm afraid I don't have time to discuss our family's psychological problems.'

Haberland looked at him searchingly. There was a sudden hint of melancholy in his expression. 'Perhaps it would be wiser of you to *find* the time,' he said softly.

The lattice window trembled in a gust of wind. Although no one had opened a door this time, Marc felt the temperature drop again. 'What do you mean?'

'Well, your brother brought you to me because he wanted me to look at your head wound...'

'But?'

'But I'm not a general practitioner,' said Haberland. 'I'm a psychiatrist.' He looked years older all of a sudden. 'Perhaps I can help you to discover what's been happening to you.'

He went to the tea trolley beside his desk, picked up the quilted woollen jacket draped over it, and put it on.

'Come,' he said to Marc as if Emma wasn't there any more. 'Let's go for a stroll.'

# 54

The lake formed a horseshoe around the little cabin in the forest. A bird of prey was circling above its choppy surface just as they left the back door and emerged into the open air. Several ducks and a swan were flustered at first by the old dog, which lolloped down to the lakeshore and dabbled its forepaws in the water. They quacked and flapped their wings in a frenzy, then decided that the newcomers presented no threat and calmed down again.

'Easy, Tarzan!' Haberland called. Pale brown with a white muzzle, the animal had been lying so quietly in its basket that Marc hadn't noticed it until it jumped up, yawning, and accompanied him and its master on their walk.

'People always make the mistake of feeding wild animals,' said the professor, staring at the water. They had left Emma on her own in the living room, which Marc found slightly surprising.

Haberland didn't seem the sort of man to trust strangers in a hurry. At the same time, there was a look in his eye that conveyed long experience of worse horrors than any to be expected from an injured woman and a former patient.

'It disrupts the food chain,' Haberland went on. 'They become habituated to us, and that's wrong.'

'People do it because they're animal lovers,' said Marc, who had often tossed stale breadcrumbs to the swans on the Wannsee with Sandra.

'Yes, but it's a mistake all the same.' Haberland pulled up the zip of his quilted jacket, which ended well short of the hem of his sports coat. 'And it can never be right to do the wrong thing.'

They walked further along the shore. Marc wondered if they were really still talking about wildlife. Until recently his life had been governed by the principle that the end always justifies the means. Haberland must surely know about the false statement that had ultimately consigned Benny to a secure unit.

'You seem very unsure of yourself,' said Haberland, coming to the point at last.

The lakeside path, which now ran gently uphill, was separated from the water by a largish expanse of reeds.

'I am.' Marc inhaled the moist, aromatic scent of the forest flanking the path to their right. 'I no longer trust my memories.'

He gave the professor a brief account of what had happened to him up till then, ending with his most recent experiences in the cellar of his former home. 'Well, what do you think? Have I gone mad?'

Haberland paused to look back at his dog. Tarzan was making repeated attempts to forge a path through the reeds to the lake, only to give up when they pricked his muzzle.

'You're questioning your own existence. The mentally ill don't do that as a rule. They try to justify their confused state of mind by advancing flimsy theories. Like Emma, for example.'

Marc turned to face him. Their clouds of breath met and mingled.

'You think she's sick?'

'Only a charlatan would reach a diagnosis so quickly. Nevertheless, unlike you, she fails to ask herself the crucial question.'

'"Have I gone mad?", you mean?'

Haberland nodded. 'I had a long talk with her earlier on, while you were asleep. She made a feverish, nervous, edgy impression. The fact is, she's only interested in looking for evidence that will justify her conspiracy theory.'

'So you think she's paranoid?'

'Don't you?'

They passed a bench that had seen better days. The back was rotten and the seat seemed unlikely to be able to bear much weight. Haberland propped one foot on it and removed a wad of damp leaves adhering to the sole of his shoe.

'Let's assume you're entirely healthy, Marc – discounting your superficial injuries and your discoloured eyes, which worry me greatly, by the way. At least you aren't suffering from any psychosomatic disorder. The house, the lake, the forest – they're all real, and we're really having this conversation. How could you explain these occurrences?'

Tarzan trotted over to them. Not that Marc had noticed it before, the old dog avoided putting weight on one of its hind legs.

'Perhaps my memory was erased once before?' he theorized. 'Perhaps it didn't work properly the first time and I'm suddenly remembering facts from my former life?'

'Possibly.' The corners of Haberland's mouth turned up in a moue of scepticism. 'Or perhaps the exact opposite is happening.'

He picked up a stick and threw it in the direction they'd come from. Tarzan just stared after it with a weary eye.

'How do you mean?'

'I don't like talking about it, but for a short time I myself once suffered from almost total amnesia. Loss of memory occasioned by a trauma I wanted to suppress at all costs.' The professor rubbed his wrists again. 'Rediscovering my memory was a terrible process, but it did teach me one thing.'

'Well?'

'That the truth is often the opposite of what we believe.'

Haberland turned and followed his dog, which had set off for home. Marc hesitated for a moment, then hurried after him.

'You're afraid your memory has been tampered with. Erased. Possibly even for the second time,' Haberland said without looking at Marc. 'But what if it's being erased at this very moment?'

Marc shivered. 'How?'

'Well, I'm not sure how the Bleibtreu Clinic induces artificial amnesia in its patients. Up to now, losses of memory have always been an unintended by-product. However, it's conceivable that they subject their guinea pigs to shock therapy. And isn't that just what's happening to you now? One traumatic incident hard on the heels of another?'

'But why should anyone do that?'

They were almost back at the house now. Voices could be heard coming from beyond the veranda, probably those of Emma and Benny, who must have brought themselves to have a chat.

'To make you forget. The only question is, what?'

Marc shut his eyes, recalling a sequence from his recent dream.

'*I wish you hadn't found out. Not so soon, at least.*'

'I don't know,' he said truthfully.

'Then try to recall it.' The professor came to a halt and looked at him intently. 'Recall what you want to forget!'

'But how? How am I supposed to. . .'

Marc's wristwatch buzzed. He felt in his jacket pocket, then smacked his forehead with annoyance.

'What is it?' Haberland asked. His dog, too, seemed to stare at Marc enquiringly.

'I have to take my pills, but they're still in the glove compartment of my car.'

'What sort of pills?'

Marc touched the plaster on his neck.

'Oh yes.' Haberland went round behind him. 'I'm glad you raised the subject.'

'Why?'

'Earlier on, when I examined your head for superficial injuries, I took the liberty of changing the dressing. What's it for?'

'There's a splinter in my neck.'

The professor raised his eyebrows. 'Are you sure?'

'Of course. Hey, what are you doing?'

Marc couldn't react quickly enough to prevent the old man from ripping off the salmon-coloured plaster that held the gauze dressing in place.

'I know you can't see it, but go on, have a feel.'

*Why should I? Constantin told me the wound must remain sterile.*

'Well, go on.' Haberland guided his hand. Marc winced, but not in pain. He couldn't feel a thing. Nothing but bare, unbroken skin.

Haberland confirmed it. 'You don't have a wound there at all.'

*No splinter.*

'And it looks as if there never was one.'

# 55

The snow came without warning. Although it was still too fine and feathery to settle, Haberland advised them to leave as soon as possible. The rental car in which Benny had driven them there was fitted with summer tyres and would fail to negotiate the narrow forest tracks if the snow became heavier. And that, if the professor was to be believed, was a possibility to be reckoned with. By the time he said goodbye he was rubbing his wrists even more nervously than when they first started talking.

Marc couldn't understand why Benny was driving so cautiously. He dipped the headlights after only a few hundred metres and set the windscreen wipers at maximum. Ten minutes later it was as if the car had taken off, leaving the leaf-strewn ground behind, and was flying above a dense layer of cloud.

'What were you talking about with the professor all that time?' Benny asked, his fingers drumming nervously on the steering wheel. He sounded uneasy and faintly suspicious.

'Don't worry, he didn't tell me anything about you I didn't know already.'

Marc went on to describe the revelation that had occurred in the course of their walk.

'No splinter?' said Benny.

'No splinter.' Marc turned so that he could see his neck. 'He also said that no one would have prescribed an immunosuppressant for an injury like that. At most an antibiotic to combat inflammation.'

Benny shook his head in surprise.

They were bouncing along a track full of potholes. Marc still couldn't tell where they were, and visibility didn't improve until they turned out on to a deserted but metalled road. He now thought he knew what part of the suburbs they were in. He had been out here with Benny once before, years ago, when the future ill feeling between them wasn't even a cloud on the horizon. Not far from here must be the abandoned quarry in which they'd dumped their father's car.

'Twelve forty-five on the thirteeth of November. We're heading away from the Müggelsee and towards Köpenick old town,' Marc heard Emma dictate into her mobile behind him. 'All advice to the contrary, Marc Lucas is planning to go to the home of his father-in-law, Constantin Senner, in Sakrow.'

*Constantin.*

Marc managed to fade out her voice by shutting his eyes. He thought of the man he'd trusted more than himself. The man with whom he'd shared every possible emotion: joy, grief, anger, concern, euphoria, and dark, abysmal depression.

He had admired Constantin for being a man of integrity with clear aims, a man whose conservative political stance he had no use for, but whom he respected for his principles and the love he bestowed on anyone who meant something to his only daughter. Constantin had been his friend, confidant and mentor. And now he seemed to be the author of a plan designed to drive him insane.

'Why does Haberland live all on his own like that?' he heard Emma ask. He opened his eyes.

She had put her mobile away and was leaning forwards.

'Ever heard of the "Soul-Breaker"?' Benny countered. His

tone was less hostile, and the fact that Emma had addressed him of her own accord denoted a slight rapprochement between them. Clearly, Haberland's words had not been altogether wasted on them.

'You mean you haven't heard about the women who were abducted and later found buried alive in their own bodies, so to speak?' Benny glanced in the rear-view mirror. 'No? Just as well, probably.'

Marc turned to him, aware for the first time of being unhampered by any plaster on his neck – a pleasant but unnerving sensation.

'Where does Haberland come into it?'

'It's a complicated story – he told me it in outline during one of our therapy sessions. It took place on the other side of the city, more or less where you insist on going now.'

They passed a sign for the A113. On the other side of the street a knot of people had taken refuge from the snow in a bus shelter, but the wind was blowing it almost horizontally across the pavement, so only the ones on the inside were spared. Although Marc's seat was heated and a jet of warm air was blowing straight at his chest, he felt as unprotected as the pedestrians. The cold he was exposed to was of a different nature. It came from within.

*Constantin.*

Twice a week he'd gone to have his dressing changed. Twice a week he'd thought it exceptionally considerate of his father-in-law to attend to him personally instead of leaving the task to one of his nurses. He had lived with the threat of paraplegia and been advised to avoid violent exercise, forbidden to play any kind of sport, to touch the wound or even to get it wet, which had made showering awkward.

All lies, and all for one purpose only.

*No splinter, no wound. No wound, no reason to take pills regularly.*

That was why the chemist didn't have the medication in stock. Far from being immunosuppressants, the pills he'd been made to take every day had presumably served to throw his mind out of gear, to paralyse or even alter it. They were powerful psychiatric drugs, just as Inspector Stoya had told him at the station.

Marc took the plastic bag containing the unpaid-for medication from his jacket pocket and removed an aspirin. Although he was feeling better than he had a few hours ago, his basic symptoms – dizziness, nausea and leaden-limbed fatigue – had not subsided.

'What did Haberland give me?' he asked Benny, wondering how his stomach would react if he swallowed the aspirin without water.

'Nothing.'

Benny veered right on to the fast lane of the slip road leading to the urban expressway. The windscreen wipers were waging a furious battle with the snowflakes, which did not stick to the windscreen but hampered visibility nonetheless.

'The good professor had nothing handy in that shack of his,' Benny said, glancing at the plastic bag in Marc's hand. 'Your girlfriend back there got the last of the paracetamol.'

*But what about that plaster? That jab in the arm?* Marc was about to ask when he remembered giving a blood sample at the Bleibtreu Clinic. One of the preliminaries for an amnesia experiment in which he had never taken part yet seemed to be in the thick of.

*Am I feeling better because the effect of the pills is wearing off? Am I seeing things more clearly now I've stopped taking them? Did I just have temporary withdrawal symptoms, and am I now on the road to recovery?*

They drove north along the deserted expressway. Unlike rain, which regularly brought the traffic on Berlin's arterial roads to a thrombotic standstill, the first snow of the year always had a cleansing effect. The roads emptied, and if you were brave enough or drove a winter-proofed car you could make better progress than you ever could in rush hour. The lights of the vehicles ahead and behind them were so far away, even now, that they could hardly be seen.

External visibility was as blurred as Marc's inner vision. He still hadn't the faintest idea what part Sandra was playing in this crazy scenario, for which she even seemed to have supplied the script – one that anticipated all the traumas he was under-going. How was that possible? Why had there been a baby's cradle in their bedroom? And why had she wanted to alter her will, as the mysterious attorney had claimed? On the other hand, was there a will at all? Might it exist as little as the clinic that had vanished before his eyes?

*And even this invisible pointer is leading me back to Constantin,* Marc concluded in his mind. After all, he had spotted the Bleibtreu Clinic's advertisement in a magazine in his father-in-law's waiting room.

*Learn to forget.*

But what?

*What is going to happen today, 13th November?*

Professor Haberland's voice still resonated in his memory: '*Recall what you want to forget!*'

How was he supposed to do that?

Benny's mobile beeped, jolting him out of his reverie.

'What is it?' he asked when he saw his brother's face darken after he'd read the text message and replaced the phone in the tray between the seats.

'Nothing, just a change of plans.'

'Meaning what?'

'I can't keep you company any longer, Mark, I've wasted far too much time already.'

'Time on what?'

Benny smiled sadly. 'You don't need to know. I borrowed some money from the wrong people, and—'

Emma uttered a sudden cry. Simultaneously, Marc was thrown forwards against his seatbelt and flung up his arms.

'Bloody fool!' yelled Benny. He blew his horn furiously, but far too late to elicit more than a weary smile from the driver who had just cut in on them.

Marc froze.

The car that had changed lanes ahead of them and was now heading at breakneck speed for the Tempelhofer Damm slip road was a boxy, mass-produced saloon like thousands of others. The licence plate was illuminated but indecipherable, obscured by mud and slush. Despite this, Marc was in no doubt as to what had just overtaken them: the yellow Volvo photographed by Emma outside the police station. He was equally certain that the person who turned to look at them from the passenger seat was a fair-haired woman.

# 56

'After them!' Marc shouted, and before Benny could protest he had grabbed the wheel. The car swerved to the right. They were flung forwards with a force resembling that of a rear-end collision, but Benny had merely stamped on the brake so as to regain control of the car.

'What are you doing?' he yelled, almost in unison with Emma, who had luckily fastened her seatbelt in the back.

'Sandra,' was all Marc said, pointing ahead.

It was warmer in the city centre than beside the Müggelsee. The snow melted as soon as it landed on the asphalt and visibility was considerably better.

'Where?' Benny was now, willy-nilly, taking the exit road to Tempelhofer Damm.

'There, in that Volvo.'

'You're crazy.'

'Please!' Marc heard the desperation in his own voice. 'Do me this favour.'

Benny shook his head as if he couldn't believe what he was letting himself in for, but he put on speed.

They raced past the abandoned airport and along Tempelhofer Damm, heading in the direction of Airlift Square.

'You could be right!' Emma chimed in, hanging on to one of the grab handles in the back. The Volvo squeezed past a bus that was occupying two of the three lanes ahead of them. The road was further obstructed about a hundred metres ahead by a stranded lorry.

The Volvo was now out of sight and there was no possibility of overtaking it, but Benny sped towards the tailback without reducing speed.

'Stop!' Marc shouted, bracing himself for the worst. But instead of slowing down, his brother wrenched the wheel over and swerved on to the pavement. Emma started screaming, and all that prevented Marc from following suit was sheer bewilderment. A few seconds ago he'd had to urge Benny on, and now his brother was trying to kill them all. He didn't regain the power of speech until they were level with the slip road to the airport.

'Slow down, it isn't worth it.'

Benny's eyes flickered between the rear-view mirror and the road ahead. 'Just so you know. We aren't chasing anyone.'

'No?'

'We're being chased.'

Marc turned to look.

*Shit, what is it this time?*

The motorcyclist only two metres from their rear bumper was taking no more notice of traffic regulations than Benny. Instead of a helmet he wore a black balaclava and a blue-grey scarf wound around the lower part of his face. Mounted on a light motocross bike, he was steering with one hand and holding something to his ear with the other.

'Who on earth's that?'

Benny picked up his mobile, which seemed to be receiving another text message, and shot back on to the road via an unoccupied parking space. Their faceless pursuer did likewise.

'One of Valka's guys,' said Benny. He glanced at the mobile's display and put it down again.

'Valka? You mean you're still working for that psychopath?'

At that moment there was a flash outside the car. Benny had just driven across a red light at around 100 kph. The motorcyclist behind them had also ignored the speed camera.

'There, straight ahead!' Emma cried, pointing to the yellow Volvo, which had reappeared at last.

They were now speeding along Mehringdamm towards the city centre. All that slowed them down were the numerous delivery vans, more and more of which were double-parked.

Twenty seconds later, only a Smart car separated them from the yellow saloon and the motocross bike seemed to have disappeared. Marc didn't notice this until he realized he could no longer hear it blatting away behind them.

'Have we shaken him off?' he asked as they ignored another red light and turned right into Leipziger Strasse. It had now stopped snowing.

'No,' said Benny, and Emma uttered another scream. The motorbike had shot out of an entrance on their right and the man in the balaclava was alongside them.

'He's got a gun!' Emma yelled, ducking down. Benny braked hard before the man could pull the trigger, and this time it really was a collision that hurled them all forwards. The heavy 4x4 behind them had failed to react in time and was now propelling them across the carriageway with all its considerable weight.

'Bloody hell!' Marc shouted, but it was already too late. In the fraction of a second it took for the car to slew round, he recalled the last few moments before his crash with Sandra: the photograph of nothing identifiable, the sound of a tyre bursting, the steering wheel escaping from his grasp and the clump of trees coming ever closer.

Then came a crash, but not in his memory: in the present. They had hit the motorcycle. The rider toppled over sideways and disappeared under their bonnet. There was a frightful, protracted grating sound, worse than that made by ten finger-nails scratching a slate, and their car came to rest at last.

Benny was the first to open his door, after an instant's shocked silence, followed by Marc. Emma remained sitting in the back, trembling but unscathed. 'Where did he go?' she said.

Benny and Marc stared at each other in dismay.

The bike was lying wedged beneath the bonnet sideways on. There was no sign of the rider.

They were quickly surrounded by a gaggle of interested spectators. Traffic jams developed in both directions. Horns blared.

Marc went round the back to see if their pursuer had ended up beneath the wheels of the vehicle behind them.

'Are you crazy, you idiots?' yelled the driver of the 4x4, who had been inspecting his chromium-plated radiator grille, which was stove in. A man in his mid-fifties, he was wearing a tracksuit, sweatshirt and camouflage-green combat boots. 'You must have shit for brains!'

Marc took no notice of him, nor did he bend down to look for the vanished motorcyclist. He was staring uncomprehendingly into Benny's boot, which had sprung open on impact.

*What the. . .?*

In addition to a canvas bag, the boot contained a small arsenal: two knives, an automatic pistol, a pump-action shotgun and, unless his eyes deceived him, some secateurs, lying on top of a transparent plastic bag with some pink liquid sloshing around inside it.

Before he could reach for it Benny spun him around.

'Leave it!' he snapped.

'But what have you been up to?'

Marc indicated Benny's boot. His brother was now forcing the lid down with both hands.

'That's what I'd like to know!' bellowed the tracksuited figure behind them. 'Why slam on your anchors like that?'

Far away and faint as yet, police sirens could be heard approaching from Potsdamer Platz.

'You push off, I'll deal with this,' said Benny. He rammed the lid shut.

Marc stared blankly at the car's battered rear end.

'I'll explain later, I promise. There's no time now.'

Benny looked at the intersection where the Volvo had turned off before the shunt brought them to a standstill.

'There's always a traffic jam on Friedrichstrasse. You could still catch them.'

His brother had to repeat himself before Marc shook off his inertia and resumed the pursuit on foot.

# 57

He hadn't run far when he caught sight of her.

*Sandra.*

The driver of the Volvo had dropped her and disappeared into an underground car park in the next block, the illuminated sign above whose entrance proclaimed that there were still 317 spaces free. Sandra was waiting at some lights. She was wearing a cream-coloured winter coat with a synthetic fur collar and standing with her hands on her hips as if she had backache.

*Or as if she was pregnant.*

He was closing the gap between them and had covered half the block when the car park's digital sign changed to 316.

*What's she doing here? And who was driving her? Constantin?*

The pedestrian light changed to green and Sandra set off. She seemed in no hurry, in fact she was feeling for something in her outsize handbag as she went. Her golden-yellow hair bobbed up and down at every step. Marc felt so close to his wife he fancied he could smell the fragrance of her shampoo, although they were still at least fifty metres apart.

'Sandra!' he called, but the only response he got was some derisive remarks from a couple of youths slouching out of a mobile-phone shop. He clutched his side, breathing hard to relieve his stitch. Just as the urge to rest became unbearable, he spotted where she was planning to go.

*She's going shopping. Of course, it won't be long now.*

The window of the baby boutique was already decorated for the winter season. A snow cannon was showering the playpens and prams on display with fat flakes of artificial snow, and customers were being lured into the shop by an over-life-size snowbaby in pink rompers stationed outside the entrance.

Sandra slowed; she was now within arm's reach of him. He put out his hand, longing to stroke her hair and run his fingers over the little bump on the back of her head – the one he always had to knead when she got a migraine. He wanted to massage her neck, hold her against him and gaze into her eyes, imagining they would give him the answers to all his questions. In the end, all he ventured to do was tap her on the shoulder and say her name. Louder than he intended, in a hoarse voice he himself failed to recognize.

'Sandra!'

She swung round. For a moment she strove to retain her composure, wondering whether a smile or a word of greeting would be appropriate. Then fear gained the upper hand. The corners of her mouth began to quiver, and Marc could read her thoughts.

*What does he want?*

She retreated a step and opened her mouth, but it was Marc who spoke first: 'I'm sorry. I'm so sorry.'

He raised his hand.

Seen from the front, the woman bore not the slightest resemblance to Sandra. She merely shook her head in alarm.

'No, no, I'm not after your. . .' Marc stammered, pointing to the handbag which the far too old, far too heavily made-up blonde was clutching in white-knuckled trepidation. 'I'm sorry, I mistook you for somebody else.'

She backed away from him, not turning round until she had put a safe distance between them. Marc stared after her and repeated his apology when she looked back at him over her shoulder with the expression people normally reserve for tramps and beggars. Leaving the baby boutique behind, she merged with a party of Japanese tourists who were just alighting from a bus at the Friedrichstrasse intersection.

'So sorry,' Marc whispered in the direction the unknown woman had taken, disappearing like a name you can't remember.

*So sorry.*

Looking down, he noticed that he was standing in a puddle of melted snow and had lost control over his wet, trembling fingers. He was feeling hypoglycaemic but not hungry in the least, dead tired but as overwrought as someone who has drunk a whole pot of coffee on an empty stomach. All he wanted to do was cry. For his wife, his life, himself. But the floodgates refused to open.

*I'm losing my mind.* For the first time, he formulated it as a statement, not a question. Then he shut his eyes and buried his face in his hands, heedless of what the passers-by must be thinking as he got in their way.

Or did they exist at all? Perhaps he wasn't standing on a pavement with his eyes shut. Perhaps the big-city cacophony was just a figment of his imagination.

*Perhaps I'm lying in a hospital bed and the parking meter beside me is a drip. I'm wearing a catheter, not a pair of jeans, and the roar of passing traffic is the sound of my ventilator.*

He dreaded to open his eyes. He feared the worst – in other words, was afraid to confront the truth that would reveal his life to be a lie. When he finally brought himself to do so, he put his head back like a child trying to catch snowflakes on its tongue. The initial shock was not so great because the cloud-scape in the cement-grey sky distracted his attention from the scaffolding. Then the plastic sheeting fluttered, plastered against the office building by the wind.

*This is impossible.*

The realization exploded like a bomb, setting off an earthquake inside him. He reeled, although he didn't move.

Slowly, as if he really did have a splinter in his neck, Marc turned on the spot and scanned his surroundings like a 3D camera, storing items of information that vastly intensified his bewilderment. He saw the baby boutique, the car-hire firm, the medical bookstore, the entrance to the underground garage and, beside it, the inflatable mascot bobbing in the wind outside the mobile-phone shop. He remembered all these details, having seen them once before from a different perspective.

*While peeing. On the sixth floor.*

And then, when he had come full circle and returned to his original position, and when Emma cautiously put her hand on his shoulder from behind, he saw the final proof: the polished brass plate that discreetly identified the psychiatric institution situated inside the building:

## BLEIBTREU CLINIC

It was back.

And he was standing right outside its imposing entrance.

# 58

She spotted it at the same moment as Marc but reacted faster. He felt the hand on his shoulder relax its pressure and slide off. The next thing he saw was Emma's back. She was heading for the clinic's revolving door, carefully putting one foot in front of the other as if in response to a hypnotic command.

'Emma, no!' he wanted to cry, but it was too late. Two men had opened the glass side door and emerged into the cold with cigarettes and lighters at the ready. Emma squeezed past them and slipped inside before the door could shut.

Marc had no choice. He followed her.

The entrance hall looked at first sight like an airport's check-in area. A strip of red carpet led to a brushed-aluminium reception desk, and awaiting visitors behind it was a young woman in a kind of uniform. She was chatting to a white-haired gentleman who was standing in front of the counter with a cup of coffee in his hand. Classical muzak provided a soothing acoustic background.

'But that really isn't your job, Professor,' Marc heard the young woman say as he slowly came up behind Emma. She had paused about halfway to the reception desk and was looking up. Like the clinic itself, the lobby was a prime example of wasted space and energy. The atrium extended as high as the third floor, where the suites of offices began. The glass walls created the impression that one was standing in a gigantic aquarium from which the water had been drained. Every foot-step re-echoed, church-like, from the ceilings and walls.

'The silly thing is always going wrong,' trilled the receptionist, pointing to her computer screen. 'We couldn't even access the internet yesterday.' Neither she nor her companion had noticed them yet.

'We must get out of here,' Marc whispered, taking Emma's hand. It felt cold and moist.

'I told you so: the clinic exists. It hasn't disappeared.'

Emma was far too agitated to keep her voice down. 'They gave you the wrong address, Marc. They wanted to lure you to that building site – that's just what they were discussing when I overheard them.'

Her voice had risen steadily, attracting the attention of the blonde behind the desk.

'Can I help you?' she fluted. The white-haired man turned round. His expression conveyed a touch of annoyance at being disturbed while flirting with the blonde, who was forty years his junior, but his displeasure persisted only as long as it took for the coffee cup to slip through his fingers and smash on the marble floor.

'Thank God!' he exclaimed, half surprised, half relieved. He whipped out his mobile phone. 'Frau Ludwig is back. I repeat, Frau Ludwig is...'

Marc was now tugging harder at Emma's hand, but she seemed rooted to the spot. He couldn't get her to budge a millimetre.

*Back to the exit and out of here, fast!*

While he was wasting precious seconds the white-haired man bustled over to them, panting as if his short sprint from the reception desk had left him drained of energy. He raised both hands as a token of goodwill.

'Are you all right?' he asked.

Emma's eyes filled with tears. 'You remember me?' she asked timidly.

The man was now only two steps away. Marc had let go of her hand in readiness to beat a retreat on his own if necessary.

'But of course,' the man said. 'We've been looking everywhere for you.'

Everything happened very quickly after that. The lift on their right disgorged three male nurses, who came rushing out even before the aluminium doors had fully opened. It took them only a few seconds to force Emma to the floor and pin her hands behind her back. She was immobilized a moment later by a shot in the arm.

Marc, who didn't have a chance to help her, wondered why they had spared him so far – why they were tolerating his silent presence in the clinic's reception hall and when he would share her fate.

He shrank back as a figure loomed up on his right. It was the white-haired man, who did the last thing his brain, which was programmed for escape, expected. He put out his hand and expressed his thanks.

'You've been of great assistance and saved us a great deal of trouble. It's a real blessing you've brought her back.'

'Huh?'

Marc stared after the nurses, who had ensconced Emma in a wheelchair and were trundling her over to the lift.

'I hope she wasn't too much of a handful?'

'A handful?' Marc repeated.

A car sounded its horn outside, but to him it seemed like a signal from another universe.

'Frau Ludwig badly injured two of our nurses when they tried to apprehend her in the street yesterday. She tends to become violent when suffering from one of her bouts of paranoia. Where did you find our patient, Herr. . .?'

The white-haired man withdrew his hand, which Marc still hadn't shaken, with an air of disappointment.

'L-Lucas,' Marc said automatically. 'Marc Lucas.' He clutched the back of his neck. Another reflex action, even though the dressing was no longer there.

'Ah yes, I remember now. Weren't you a patient here?'

'You *know* me?'

'Yes, of course. When was that accident of yours? Six weeks ago?'

Mark's head started spinning. 'Who are you?' he asked. He'd never seen the man before in his life. Neither the jacket-crowned smile nor the high forehead nor the star-shaped birthmark on the throat, just below the chin, evoked the faintest recollection.

'Oh, forgive me,' said the man. 'I thought you knew where you were.' His smile vanished. 'I'm Professor Patrick Bleibtreu.'

# 59

Nobody stopped him. No burly figure barred his path, no one grabbed him by the sleeve or applied an armlock and pinned him face down on the floor. Yet he was so weak, so incapable of resistance, he would have been easy meat.

His head was in a whirl. If this really was the director of the clinic, who had he been with yesterday afternoon? Who had picked him up outside Neukölln public baths and subjected him to an hours-long inquisition?

The revolving door spat him back into the outside world, but he felt as if his inner self was still beside the white-haired man in the atrium of the Bleibtreu Clinic, waiting for him to return.

He turned and looked up. This was where he had been yesterday, but he wasn't in Französische Strasse; he was in a parallel street one block away.

*They want to destroy me. Someone wants me to lose my memory and is using dirty tricks to achieve his aim.*

The Maybach had driven down Französische Strasse and turned off into an underground car park connected to the office building on this side of the street.

Marc laughed hysterically. He'd never seen the Bleibtreu Clinic from the outside, and the draped scaffolding outside the windows had concealed the charade. Only the windows of the men's room were unobstructed, but their partial view of the intersection hadn't aroused his suspicions.

*And now? What am I to do now?*

He blundered aimlessly along the pavement. He was fighting an invisible opponent, unable to distinguish between good and evil, and he didn't even know the reason for all that was happening.

Perhaps Sandra was behind it all. Perhaps some PR consultant had advised her to engage in this conspiracy so as to boost her film's success when it emerged that the plot was based on fact.

*Except that the script had come first and the reality second!*

Of all the noises surging around him in Französische Strasse, it was – once again – a driver sounding his horn that broke in on his thoughts. He'd heard it in the lobby of the clinic, but this time it was much closer.

Glancing sideways, he saw his brother at the wheel of a dirty little Polo.

'Get in!' Benny called through the open window. 'Come on, we've no time to lose!'

# 60

The car appeared to belong to a young woman or a family with a young child. Numerous cloth elephants with sucker feet stuck to the rear windows and a Winnie the Pooh audiotape protruded from the slot in the cassette radio.

'I borrowed it,' Benny explained – not that Marc had asked him to. Neither of them had spoken for fifteen minutes, but his brother was growing steadily more talkative. 'I'll take this bus back to the multi-storey afterwards, honestly I will. I couldn't hang around when the law turned up, so I beat it and pinched this thing for us.'

Marc nodded mutely, unable to concentrate, because Benny's wasn't the only voice to be heard. Someone was singing in English. It took him a while to register that the music was coming from the radio. He turned it off and reached for the door handle.

'Pull up,' he said quietly.

Benny tapped his forehead. 'Like hell I will.'

'I want no part in a murder.'

'That's your nutty girlfriend speaking. Don't *you* start! I haven't killed anyone.' Benny drew a deep breath. The Polo stank of vomit and cheap scent. Presumably, someone had attempted to disguise the former with the latter.

'So why drive around with a plastic bag covered in blood and a small arsenal?'

'The guns aren't mine.'

'Whose, then?'

'Valka's.'

'What have you been up to?'

'Nothing. I borrowed some money, that's all.'

'What for?'

'A sure thing, but it doesn't matter now. I asked Valka to transfer the cash to my business partner's account, but the deal fell through. I was taken for a ride.'

'What about the cash in the sports bag?'

Benny glanced over his shoulder at the blood-stained canvas bag, which was lying on the rear seat.

'I hung on to some of it. Valka smuggled it to me in the hospital, but I'm missing the rest, so I can't pay him back in full.'

Benny was steering with one hand and massaging his right thigh with the other.

'And now you've got his hitmen on your tail?'

'More or less. Valka was going to scrub my debt if I did a job for him.'

They changed lanes and overtook a student looking for a parking place. The university and the next roundabout were still one traffic light away.

'What sort of job?'

'A journalist named Ken Sukowsky was researching Valka – researching him only too thoroughly. I was supposed to kill him and cut off his fingers, or maybe the other way round. Then I was to leave town pronto.' Benny looked in the rear-view mirror. 'I should have been in Amsterdam hours ago, damn it. Now I've had it.'

'Why?'

Benny sighed. 'Because I was only bluffing, of course. I went to see Sukowsky last night and warned him. Then I was going to do the rounds and say goodbye. You know, to all the people who've done me favours. Friends and acquaintances, or even strangers who helped me when I was in a bad way. Like the professor.'

He felt in the pocket of his bomber jacket and handed Marc a crumpled sheet of paper. Of the ten names on it, the first three had been crossed off, Haberland's included. Marc noted that his own name didn't appear.

'That was the real reason I drove you out there. While you

and Haberland were out walking I left some of Valka's cash on the kitchen table. The prof was one of the few people who really took care of me. He deserves it.'

'Like Leana?' said Marc.

They drew up at some lights. Benny looked at him in surprise.

'Did you also give your nurse some of Valka's cash?'

Benny nodded after a long pause. 'Yes, fifteen thousand. I thought I could leave town before Eddy wanted it back, but he gave me an ultimatum.'

'What was in that plastic bag?' Marc asked, still suspicious.

'A pig's head. My farewell present to him. He was meant to find it in the boot long after I was out of the country.'

The lights changed to green, and somehow they seemed to open the floodgates that had prevented Benny from talking until now. Everything came pouring out: how he'd been stopped at the checkpoint the previous night and narrowly missed being caught red-handed with the weapons he was supposed to use to kill the journalist. He even wound up by telling Marc about the murdered girl in his flat.

'Then you appeared on the scene with that madwoman. I couldn't get away in time, and now I've got Eddy's people breathing down my neck.'

Benny bore right and exited the Ernst-Reuter-Platz round-about at the last moment. They sped down Bismarckstrasse in the direction of the opera house.

'Why didn't you come to me with your money problems?'

Marc felt for the bag of pills in his jacket and discovered he must have lost them in the car crash. He only hoped his nausea didn't get any worse.

Benny glanced at him and laughed. 'Quite apart from the fact that we haven't exactly been close in recent years, you don't have €90,000.'

*Good God, as much as that?*

'What was it for, for heaven's sake?'

'It's better you don't know.'

Marc controlled himself with an effort. Quarrelling with his brother had never been productive. The more you probed him, the more he retreated into his shell.

'But why Valka?' he demanded. 'Goddamnit, Benny, I know people who won't top you the moment a debt becomes overdue.'

'Really? If that's a reference to your father-in-law, you must be joking.'

'Why?'

'He's broke.'

'*What?*'

Another set of lights changed, from amber to red. The vehicles beside them braked to a halt – unlike Benny, who construed it as a signal to accelerate away.

'What do you mean?' Marc asked in dismay.

'Broke, skint. Does the word have any other meaning?' Benny glanced in the rear-view mirror as if afraid they'd picked up another tail. Marc turned to look but could see nothing suspicious. 'It's that clinic of his. He overreached himself financially – don't you read the papers?'

*No. I've taken little interest in the outside world these last few weeks.*

'Added to that, one of his surgeons botched a cardiac operation – defective valve implant, or something. Not Senner's fault, but the damages will amount to millions. They say he no longer even owns the house we're on our way to right now.' Benny glanced sideways. 'That is where you want to go, isn't it?'

# 61

The human brain is capable of suppressing even incontrovertible truths which everyone must face sooner or later: age, illness, physical decline, death. All of these come to each of us, yet they seem unreal. Someone else shuffles the cards we play with, and much as we despair of the system, we're ultimately grateful for its mercies. After all, would we continue to make our way along life's road if we could see into the future?

That was the question Marc asked himself as he stood in the drive outside his father-in-law's house. Benny had remained in the car, even though he had his doubts about the plan that had brought them there.

'What are you looking for?' he'd asked as Marc was getting out.

'The truth,' Marc replied.

Was Constantin trying to drive him insane because of his debts? Did he want to get him declared legally incompetent so as to lay hands on the proceeds of the film script sale? Whatever the truth, Marc wanted his life back, even if it was that of a widower. He knew that Constantin stood between him and the truth and had to call him to account. That would clinch matters one way or the other.

He hammered on the door. Once upon a time Constantin had kept a spare key in the boathouse in case he locked himself out, but those incautious days were long past. A security expert had been employed after the burglary that had cost Sandra their first child three years ago. Since then a CCTV surveillance system had unobtrusively alerted those inside the house to the presence of visitors and, instead of a key, you needed a registered fingerprint. Today, however, Marc didn't have to apply his fore-finger to the cold key pad. The door was open already: it swung inwards at his touch.

'Hello?'

Marc made his way into the entrance hall. He sensed the change at once, even though everything seemed to be in its accustomed place: the little occasional table just inside the door, on which keys and mobile phones could be left; the big marble balls flanking both staircases; and the huge, silver-framed mirror in which visitors looked taller and slimmer than they really were. Normally, this gave visitors a good feeling as soon as they entered the house. In Marc's case, this didn't happen today, and not only because his father-in-law never left the front door unlocked.

But because he could hear people talking.

A man and a woman. They sounded like two good friends having an animated conversation, and they were somewhere overhead.

'Hello, it's me,' Marc called up the stairs. No response, just a muffled giggle followed by a long monologue on the man's part.

He set off up the stairs which he and Sandra had once climbed every other Sunday. His father-in-law used to hold a family tea party twice a month. They had all expected this tradition to lapse after his wife's untimely death, but Constantin had perpet-uated it, so they continued to drive over and exchange the latest news around the fireplace in the upstairs library. Every other Sunday. Until the accident.

Marc had reached the top step. The voices were more distinct now.

'Constantin?' he called hoarsely. It was hours since he'd had anything to drink, and his tongue felt like a foreign body in his mouth.

The passage stretched away in both directions. On the left were the guest bedrooms, on the right the library and Constantin's study, from which the voices were coming. Marc was near enough now to catch snippets of conversation.

'*Me, I wouldn't do that,*' the woman said brightly.

'*Really? I wouldn't be so sure,*' said the man. '*Think back to your most embarrassing experience.*'

'*Oh, that happened in the swimming pool recently, but I really can't tell you about it.*'

Marc found it odd that the couple didn't answer even though he'd advertised his presence more than once, so he decided to make as little noise as possible from now on. He turned right and tiptoed along the shadowy passage.

Mingled with the voices was a faint crackle of static. It grew louder the nearer he got to the study door, which was situated opposite a small guest lavatory about halfway along.

'*Coward!*' laughed the man inside the study.

'*No, honestly. Anyway, I don't really remember it.*'

'*Aha, here we go again!*'

Holding his breath, Marc depressed the heavy handle, opened the door, and froze.

The study in which the couple had been holding such an animated conversation was a scene of utter devastation. The standard lamp was lying sideways across the leather sofa, which had been slashed. The Persian carpet had been crumpled up like an outsize handkerchief and dumped in front of an empty set of shelves. All the books, pictures, photos and *objets d'art* they had once held were lying strewn across the floor.

Marc looked around for the couple and found them behind a dusty glass screen. The television set was lying on its side behind the shattered remains of an empty salt-water aquarium.

It was a miracle the old set was still working and hadn't given up the ghost like the numerous fish on the parquet floor.

'*Tell us what you think. We value your opinion,*' said the man on the screen, who looked like a caricature of a breakfast-show host. He was wearing a smile as bright as his vivid tie and jacket. The camera pulled back to reveal the studio set plus his platinum-blonde colleague.

'*No, I really don't want to think about it.*'

'*You see?*'

The picture flickered every two seconds and there was a smell of scorching. The television's lead had been fractured and was reacting with the spilt water.

Marc decided it was safer to leave the box turned on. He looked at the desk, the only oasis of calm in the midst of the devastation. Vast and immovable, as if made for some statesman who proposed to sign epoch-making treaties on its polished mahogany top, it stood facing the windows overlooking the lake.

Marc stepped over some smashed glasses and kicked aside an overturned globe that had once functioned as a minibar. He wondered what to do next.

The house was too big to search for hidden dangers – it contained six bedrooms alone. If the intruder was still on the premises, he would be taking a risk. On the other hand, he had no further reason to stay. The chaos here was such that he couldn't even find the remote control and turn off the drivel behind him, not to mention the answers he hoped would lighten the darkness of his psyche.

'*Yes, fine, but what if something goes wrong?*'

'*Okay, viewers, what do you think? Call us on the hot line below.*'

He was about to go when he caught sight of a drawer that

had been pulled out and left lying on the floor upside down. At first sight it looked like all the rest. It wasn't until he looked more closely that he spotted the dismaying difference.

*'Would you take part or not? Vote now!'*

Marc knelt down and ran his fingers over the numerals scrawled in a childish hand on the bottom of the drawer:

### 23. II.

His child's estimated date of birth.

*'Please press one for "Yes" or two for "No".'*

He turned the drawer over. Only one document, a sheet of grey-green paper, had lodged inside. Marc picked it up in his trembling fingers. It was a statement from Constantin's private bank.

*'We now come to a report made available to us by our esteemed colleague Ulrich Meyer. I'm sure it'll exert an influence on your opinion.'*

Bigger and bigger amounts had been withdrawn in recent days. The account was in the red and the last column bore the note 'Frozen'.

Marc looked at the television.

At this moment there was no difference between his inner devastation and that of the room in which he was kneeling. Someone had extracted all his mental drawers and tipped them out too. He found it impossible to order his thoughts. Everything was interconnected – Sandra, Constantin, the baby – but none of it made sense. Neither Constantin's debts nor the ravaging of his study. Nor Sandra's voice, which had just uttered his name loud and clear.

# 62

Marc stared dazedly at the screen, which was now showing Sandra in close-up. Her hair was sweaty and dishevelled and her eyes were bloodshot and puffy. She looked drained and desperate, but even though he had never seen her in such a state before, it was unmistakably his wife.

There followed a quick cut to a lanky young reporter. He looked rather too immature to be making an investigative contribution to a TV news magazine, but his deep voice made up for his lack of gravitas.

'Up to now, the Bleibtreu Clinic has been regarded as a reputable private hospital specializing in psychosomatic disorders. In the last few days, however, it has aroused controversy by conducting an unusual experiment. An experiment said to be taking place in the building just behind me, apparently without official authorization.'

The camera panned across the scaffolding in front of the clinic and homed in on the brass plate beside the entrance. The reporter continued in voice-over: 'MME, the memory experiment – that's the name of the programme whose participants are being brainwashed, ostensibly in order to eradicate their most distressing memories. It's a tempting idea, of course. Fatal accidents, unhappy love affairs, personal tragedies – what if we could permanently forget all the things that prey on our minds?'

The reporter reappeared. Inquisitive passers-by came into shot as they turned to watch him walking along the street in front of the clinic. 'But what if something goes wrong, as it did in the case of this patient whose records have been leaked to us?'

Marc gave a start. The television was showing a partially

blacked-out document. The names of the doctors in attendance had been obliterated, but his own name appeared on nearly every line, and his photograph in the top right-hand corner of the patient's record sheet had not been blacked out.

Unimaginable though it seemed, Sandra confirmed the evidence of his eyes. 'Yes, that's my husband's file,' she said, sounding even more desperate than before. 'Please quote his name and publish his picture. It may help him to recover his memory.'

The camera pulled back to reveal all of her. She was lying in a hospital bed, her body more bloated than ever.

Marc began to shed silent tears.

'My husband underwent treatment there, I've no idea why, and now he can't remember a thing.'

Another cut to a hand-held camera shot of the Bleibtreu Clinic's reception desk, in front of which Emma had so recently been overpowered. Suddenly a hand shot up and obscured the lens. A tussle ensued, and the camera's view of the lobby went haywire.

'Unfortunately, the clinic's medical director declined to comment on these accusations. Our camera crew was forcibly ejected.'

The report wound up with a final shot of Sandra in hospital. 'He can't remember a thing,' she repeated. 'Not even me or the baby.' Tears were streaming down her cheeks. 'Good God, he doesn't even know there are complications.'

*Complications?*

His wife was now addressing the camera direct. 'Marc, if you're watching this, I need you here with me. Please!' she sobbed. 'There's something wrong with our baby. They're going to have to deliver it prematurely.'

There the report ended. Back in the studio the two presenters resumed their appalling patter, grinning as if they'd just concluded a live broadcast of the Oktoberfest.

'*There, you can carry on voting now,*' the man said with a laugh. '*Would you have yourself brainwashed into not remembering any nasty experiences?*'

'*Or,*' the woman added, '*will you say no, that's not for me – I don't want to wind up like Marc Lucas. His wife is giving birth this very afternoon, by the way. Her baby is due to be delivered any minute – by Caesarian section at the Senner Hospital – and it's really tragic that the father won't. . .*'

Unable to bear it any longer, Marc stood up and put his fingers in his ears, yelling in an attempt to drown the presenters' voices.

At that moment, down in the drive, a shot rang out.

# 63

Just as Marc got down there, his brother's head slammed into a garden lamp post. He must somehow have managed to escape from the car and wrench the assailant's gun from his grasp. It was lying half a metre away beside an ornamental shrub, and its owner was preparing to kick Benny in the kidneys as hard as he could.

Marc had no idea if it was the motorcyclist or another of Valka's henchmen. He wasn't wearing a balaclava and, from the back, he looked too bulky for a motocross enthusiast.

Benny had failed to get back on his feet and was trying to crawl out of the danger zone on all fours. To no avail. His assailant kicked him in the crotch from behind and he jackknifed. Then the man bent over him.

Meanwhile, Marc had tiptoed around the car, which was now minus its windscreen. He was only two metres from the pump-action shotgun with which the thug must have shattered the perspex. He was about to make a dive for it when the beefy figure swung round.

'Think I'm stupid?' the man said with a laugh.

Marc raised his hands. Now that he had a full-face view of his brother's would-be killer, he recognized him at once.

'Hello, Valka.'

He was even fatter than he remembered.

'Well, if it isn't our worthy social worker! This is just like old times.'

With a supercilious grin, Valka checked the magazine of the pistol he was holding. Unlike the pump-action lying beside the bush, which needed reloading after the last shot, Benny's automatic had plenty of rounds in it.

'A shame you ran out on the band because of that slag of yours.'

'Since when do you do your own dirty work?' said Marc. Although his breath was steaming, he didn't feel the cold wind blowing across from the lake. Fear was warming him from within.

'Ever since your brother tried to fuck a fucker,' Valka retorted, aiming a kick at Benny's unprotected face every time he said the F-word. Strangely enough, Benny was shielding his stomach with his arms, but not his head. Blood was oozing from his mouth and nose.

'Ah, so you're an Eddie Murphy fan,' Marc said quickly, before another kick could land.

Valka stopped short. 'What?'

'That was a quote from a film: "Never try to fuck a fucker" – something like that. It comes from *Trading Places*, but never mind. You should be in the movies yourself, Eddy.'

Valka grinned. Then he looked down and addressed himself to the human bundle at his feet. 'To think this smart aleck put you in the nuthouse!'

'Get stuffed!' croaked Benny, spitting out a front tooth.

From far away came the sound of a barge hooting as it made its way downstream to Glienicke Bridge. Marc looked round. The gardens in this area were so big the houses couldn't be seen from the road. No one would come to their aid and the pump-gun in front of him was just a useless lump of wood and metal. Valka was three car-lengths away; he would empty an entire magazine into Marc's chest before he'd covered half that distance.

Marc knew this as well as Valka, who didn't even trouble to aim the pistol at him. He knelt down with the metal toe of one cowboy boot only millimetres from Benny's right eye. Then he grabbed him by the hair and lifted his head off the gravel until his own mouth was close to Benny's blood-stained lips.

Valka jammed the muzzle of the automatic under Benny's chin. 'Okay, Benjamin, ready to die?' he asked quietly, sounding like the psychopath he was.

To Marc's horror, his brother just nodded – wearily, like someone resigned to his fate. Then he said something to Valka in a whisper so soft that it was carried away by the wind whistling in the trees. Saliva flecked with blood trickled down Benny's chin. For some strange reason, his eyes conveyed something akin to profound gratitude before he shut them.

'All right, you maniac,' said Valka, 'go to hell!'

And then, just after Marc had decided to court certain death rather than stand there idly, Valka did something altogether illogical.

He gave Benny's cheek an affectionate pat. Then he straightened up, flung the pistol away as far as he could and, without a backward glance, strode off down the drive to the gate.

# 64

'Why did he do that?' Marc had to shout to make himself heard above the headwind, which seemed to be scything into his face with the velocity of a tornado. Valka had blown out the windscreen but only perforated the driver's seat when Benny hurled himself aside at the last moment.

'Why did he just walk off like that?' Marc looked back at Benny, who had made it back into the car and was lying sideways across the rear seat with his knees drawn up, mopping his mouth with the bottom of his T-shirt.

'No idea. Must be my lucky day.'

Benny heaved, then turned on his side and threw up over the floor mats. It was a while before he could go on. 'I reckon he didn't want to get his own hands dirty. His people will find me soon enough.' He groaned. 'It's all over anyway.'

Marc shook his head uncomprehendingly. 'We're almost there,' he shouted above the wind.

Just to make matters worse, it was sleeting again. The wet snow was blinding him. Cars, pedestrians, road markings, the buildings on either side – all were dissolving into a blur before his eyes.

Benny tried to raise his head. 'Where are we going?'

'To the Senner Clinic.'

A people carrier behind them flashed its lights, but Marc couldn't drive any faster, much as he wanted to. He removed one cold, wet hand from the steering wheel and blew on it, then felt in his pocket for the pistol, which he'd retrieved from a puddle of melted snow. Even the magazine was still in place.

'Where are we, for God's sake?' Benny tried to prop himself

on his elbows, but his strength failed and he subsided again. They were driving through a suburb so neat and tidy that it could have passed for a picturesque Bavarian village. The pubs were called The Coachman's Rest or The Village Inn and there were almost as many churches as livery stables. It was no wonder the locals attending the weekly street market turned to stare at their shot-up car as if it had materialized from outer space.

Marc let go of the wheel and wiped his streaming face. The sleet was turning to snow, causing him to slow down even more.

'There's something I must tell you,' he heard Benny groan. He looked in the rear-view mirror.

'When you dropped out of the band and I swallowed those pills. . .'

'It was bad, Benny, I know. I should have taken more care of you.'

'No, I don't mean that.' Benny coughed. 'I didn't do it because of you.'

'So why did you?'

'Because of Sandra.'

The words smote Marc in the face, cold as the sleet. *Sandra?*

'You weren't the only one who was in love with her.'

Marc turned round.

'Don't worry,' Benny said defensively. 'I never had an affair with her, though she wavered at first.'

Marc stiffened. His fingers tightened their grip on the steering wheel as he tried to sort out his whirling thoughts.

*So that explains it. . .*

That was why Sandra had kept him dangling for so long at the start of their relationship. She'd been unable to decide between him and his brother.

'Why are you telling me this?'

'So you don't worry about me any more,' Benny said haltingly.

'The truth is, Sandra fell in love with you very soon. I was just an aberration – the pathetic younger brother who confused her for a short time. We met three times, then she realized you were the right one for her. I accepted that, but afterwards I simply couldn't bear being anywhere near you both.'

*Does that mean...*

The jigsaw puzzle was forming a picture piece by piece.

*... his first suicide attempt stemmed from a broken heart?*

'You never left me in the lurch, Luke. I was the one who severed contact. And then...' His voice tailed off.

'Then what?' Marc insisted.

'One day, quite by chance, I bumped into her again. It was when she was pregnant the first time.'

Marc could scarcely breathe.

*Three years ago? Was Benny the reason for her odd behaviour? Was it him she'd been with at that café in Neukölln?*

'Believe it or not, I was in an even worse state then than I am now,' Benny said. He spat out some more blood. 'She saw at once that I was in a bad way and automatically blamed herself – as if her decision to fall in love with you was the reason for my hitting the skids.' He gave a hollow laugh. 'That was crap. The responsibility was mine alone.'

His voice was growing steadily fainter. It sounded almost dreamy, and Marc began to grasp the truth.

*Damn it, he's still in love with her. After all this time...*

'Her relationship with me was very much like yours, Marc. She wanted to help me – to make up for what she thought of as her mistake. I'm afraid she even had second thoughts about her relationship with you and wondered if she'd made the right decision. But hell, Marc, she was a pregnant bundle of hormones at the time. I'm sure you experienced her mood swings for yourself.'

'I still don't understand what you're trying to tell me.'

'It's quite simple. Sandra and I met on several occasions, and each time she ended up feeling worse. She couldn't talk to you about it. Your marriage was at stake, after all, and she knew how rocky our own relationship was. In the end she turned to her father for help. She meant to ask him to help me. With his money and his connections, I mean.'

Marc glanced over his shoulder. He had seldom seen his brother look as sad as he did now.

'Now do you understand?' Benny demanded hoarsely. 'If it hadn't been for me, she wouldn't have lost her first child. She'd have been with you on the day of the break-in, not out at Constantin's place.'

Marc sensed that he'd been holding his breath for far too long. Greedily, he sucked in lungfuls of icy air. Then he coughed, and the cough relieved some of the tension that had built up in the last few minutes.

'Forget it,' he said. He brushed some bits of shattered windscreen off the passenger seat and deposited Benny's pistol on it in case of another attack. 'You weren't to blame.'

'Yes, I was.'

'No. It was chance – a quirk of fate. If anyone failed, we both did.'

After a couple of minutes, during which Marc silently digested his brother's confession, they pulled up at a red light. The wind had veered, and he took advantage of the delay to mop his eyebrows, mouth and nose with a handkerchief.

'We both got it wrong, didn't we?' he said.

Benny grunted.

'And now?' Marc glanced at the rear-view mirror. 'Will we manage to straighten things out?'

'I don't know. We could always consult the radio oracle,' Benny quipped through gritted teeth.

*Radio oracle. . .*

The very words triggered a host of old memories as numerous as the snowflakes that were once more whirling into the car. If he remembered rightly, the last time they'd played it was the night they dumped their father's car in the flooded gravel pit.

'Shall I?' he asked.

'Yes,' Benny called back. He coughed. It might also have been a laugh; Marc couldn't tell. They were just turning into Heerstrasse.

'Okay, the question is: "Dear radio oracle, how will everything turn out today?"'

Marc slowed to 50 kph and turned on the radio at random.

*A commercial.*

'We don't have time. Skip it!'

Marc pressed the search button. They landed on some instrumental jazz, then on a classical programme. After that came talking or news broadcasts. They didn't succeed until the seventh attempt.

'I know, I know what's on your mind,' sang a strikingly high-pitched male voice. 'And I know it gets tough sometimes.'

'You can say that again,' said Benny.

Marc glanced over his shoulder. 'Know who it is?'

Benny didn't open his eyes. He shrugged apologetically, the cuts and bruises on his swollen face conveying some idea of the pain he was in.

'Do you?' he asked almost inaudibly.

They came to a bridge over the Havel. The tyres skidded on the icy surface, and Marc slowed down, although everything inside him was urging him to head as fast as possible for the hospital, where Benny could be attended to.

*And where Sandra was just giving birth to their child?*

He almost welcomed this opportunity to occupy his mind with this puerile game. It meant he didn't have to reflect on the fact that he was on his way to see his late wife giving birth to their child.

'I'll think of it in a minute,' he said as the refrain began.

''Cause it's all right, I think we're going to make it.'

He dried his face on his sleeve. His skin, his lips, even his tongue seemed to have gone on strike. Not long to go now, though. He could vaguely discern the high-rise building in the distance.

The Senner Clinic marked the boundary between Spandau and Charlottenburg. Most of the buildings in the complex were at most two or three storeys high and almost hidden from Heerstrasse by a dense belt of trees. But the new fourteen-storey hospital block, which also housed a hotel for convalescents and patients' families, jutted into the sky like a phallus and served as a guide to drivers on their way to open-air concerts in the woods. Here, at the latest, was where they had to turn on their indicators.

'I think it might just work out this time.'

'Hear that? Everything's fine. We're going to make it.'

*All right.*

Marc knew it was a silly, irrational, childish superstition but he couldn't help feeling heartened by the radio oracle's prediction.

They left Heerstrasse and turned down a private approach road. Notice boards warned drivers to proceed at a walking pace. The outside lights were on already.

'Okay, but what's the singer's name?' Benny was coughing again, and this time it didn't sound like laughter.

*Had Valka shot him after all?*

Fear for his brother dispelled his irrational euphoria.

'I don't know,' Marc said quietly. The road narrowed and came out in a visitors' car park.

'Shit, you know what that means.'

Marc nodded mutely. Of course he knew the rules; he'd invented them himself over twenty years ago. The radio oracle didn't count unless you knew the singer's name. If you didn't it brought bad luck.

'Yes, it's a bad omen, but I'll think of it in a minute.'

*Criss, Christoph, Chris Jones, Christopher. . .*

It was on the tip of his tongue when a mobile phone beeped in the footwell. He looked down in surprise. 'Hey, somebody wants you.'

The Nokia's display was flashing. He bent down and picked it up. A sealed envelope was indicating the receipt of a text message.

'It fell out of my pocket earlier on,' said Benny.

Marc gave a start. Then every muscle in his body tensed.

'What is it?' Benny asked, but Marc was staring at the phone, transfixed.

*It can't be true. Not this on top of everything else. . .*

Benny had activated the preview function, so Marc had two seconds to read the sender's name and message:

**Where are you, Benny?**
**Hurry, it's almost time.**
**We can't start without Marc!**
**Constantin**

Marc stared aghast at the rear-view mirror, which dealt him his next shock. All he saw at first was Benny's hand reaching for the grab handle. Then his face came into view.

Benny made a sudden lunge for the passenger seat, but Marc was too quick for him. He braked hard and the pistol fell to the floor. The car spun round ninety degrees, slithered another half-metre, and came to rest just short of a stop sign.

Reaching down, Marc retrieved the automatic and put the muzzle to his brother's blood-stained forehead.

# 65

'Keep away from me!' Marc yelled. He almost lost his footing on the icy ground as he got out of the car in his rubber-soled trainers. 'Stay where you are, you two-timing bastard!'

There was a stench of petrol and the little car's radiator fan was humming like that of a clogged vacuum cleaner. Marc gave up holding his brother at bay and stumbled up the driveway as fast as he could. It ended in front of a plain, flat-roofed building with two ambulances parked outside. Unlike Bleibtreu's establishment, the Senner Clinic did not spend its private patients' money on fancy architecture or interior decoration. Constantin invested it in ultra-modern equipment and well-trained staff, so the entrance differed little at first sight from that of a public hospital: an aluminium reception desk, a kiosk with the obligatory newspaper racks and bookstall, a big noticeboard beside the lifts and, in the background, the entrance to the visitors' cafeteria.

*Where to now? Where should I go?*

Turning round, Marc bumped into an empty wheelchair left there by a young male nurse, who was chatting with the commissionaire. He only saved himself from falling over by grabbing the reception desk.

'Where is he?' he shouted, brandishing the automatic. The

nurse turned pale and shrank back, hugging his clipboard. A commotion broke out behind Marc. He heard shouts, hurried footsteps, raised voices. Doors banged and cold air streamed in from outside, but none of this was happening in his world.

'Constantin Senner – where's he hiding?'

The commissionaire, a thickset man with bloodshot eyes and a triple chin, threw up his arms and trundled his swivel chair swiftly backwards as if he could lessen the impact of a bullet if only he put enough distance between himself and this demented gunman. He opened his mouth, trembling, but couldn't get a word out. He was as silent as the hospital's endless-loop publicity film, which was running ad infinitum on a plasma screen just above their heads.

'Where?!'

'In theatre,' the commissionaire croaked eventually. He mopped his moist forehead with the sleeve of his cheap blue uniform. 'Number 3, third floor.'

'Okay, now call the police, understand? Until then, I won't. . . Hey, what's *that*?'

Marc broke off and looked up – at his father-in-law. The promotional video depicted Constantin showing a prospective patient's family around the hospital. He was convincing the happy group – and, by proxy, the viewer – of the advantages of private treatment.

Marc blinked nervously.

The young wife and laughing child were complete strangers to him. Not so the actors playing the husband and grandfather. The latter, who was just admiring an operating theatre, had introduced himself to Marc as Professor Bleibtreu, and the former liked to be shackled to iron bedsteads in cellars. The video suddenly showed a sturdy male orderly pushing a grey-haired patient into the cafeteria in a wheelchair. It wasn't the first time Marc had seen either man. The one in the wheelchair had passed him a message from his late wife in the guise of a tramp. As for the lanky orderly, his face had seemed familiar to Marc last night, when he refused to let him into the 'Beach'. He probably knew the actor from other television commercials.

'It isn't what you think.'

Marc spun round and looked into his brother's face. Benny was cautiously approaching him, favouring his left leg.

'Beat it!' The automatic swung in his direction.

'Put that gun down and let me explain.'

'No, get lost!'

They were now on their own in the lobby. Anxious faces were pressed against the glass doors flanking the reception area and several people were jabbering excitedly into their mobile phones.

'Please. I'll take you to Sandra.' Benny hobbled towards him with his arms outstretched. 'Please,' he implored again, in a voice drained of emotion.

Marc gulped and ran a hand over his face. His legs started to tremble and he felt sick. He was so exhausted he could hardly hold the pistol straight.

'You're lying,' he said, in tears now.

'No,' said Benny. 'Come on, there's still time.'

# 66

Glaucoma surgery, coloproctology, minimally invasive surgery, gastroenterology, oncology – Constantin had considerably expanded the spectrum of treatments available at his hospital in recent years. Originally designed as a facility for specialized surgical operations, it now housed a rheumatology department, a plastic surgery department, and the obstetric wards to which Marc's brother was now conducting him.

It took them a long time to climb the three flights of stairs. Benny seemed to be suffering from concussion as well as dragging his right leg, but Marc kept the pistol jammed into his back. His brother had deceived him long enough. First rejection, then his offer of assistance and reconciliation, and now, perhaps, he might be faking his injuries.

They reached the top floor of the flat-roofed building and opened the glass door leading to the wards.

A blue noticeboard said 'Perinatal Centre' in white lettering. The arrow pointed to the right.

'Where are we?' Marc asked as they set off along the corridor. The walls of the children's ward he'd once inspected with Sandra had been hung with colourful pictures including photos of happy babies in the arms of even happier parents expressing their thanks to doctors and nurses. Wherever possible, an attempt had been made to mitigate the typical characteristics of a hospital, for instance with orange walls, hospital gowns adorned with appliquéd Disney motifs and soothing classical muzak in the passages.

*Childbirth isn't a disease,* Constantin had always said, but his motto didn't appear to extend to this part of the hospital.

'This isn't the delivery room,' said Benny.

'No?'

Marc looked at another sign: 'OP III/Neonatal Intensive Care Ward.'

'This is where the problem cases come.'

*'Good God, he doesn't even know there are complications...'*

'What sort of problem cases?'

Marc's question went unanswered, because at that moment a door straight ahead of them swung open and a hospital bed was wheeled through. And, on it, his wife.

# 67

*Sandra.*

She was deathly pale. Her eyelids were half closed, her hands folded as if in prayer on her mountainous belly. Tubes led from her arms to some medical apparatus attached to the bed-frame. The nurse wheeled her on down the corridor.

'Wait!' Marc called. He hurried after the bed to make sure, but she was no more of a hallucination than she had been when she opened the door to him yesterday.

*Sandra.*

He recognized the lips he had so often kissed and the curve of the eyebrows he had so often traced with his finger that the time he'd spent doing so could have been measured in hours.

'Who are you?' the nurse demanded, alarmed by the sight of the gun in his hand. She reached for her bleeper.

'It's me, Marc,' was all he said, gazing fixedly at Sandra.

*Is it really me? Am I standing here, looking into the eyes of my late wife, or don't I exist at all? Am I living in a horrific world of illusion?*

He started to sob. Putting out his hand, he parted her lips with his forefinger as if trying to help her to speak, because she seemed to find it a superhuman effort to open her mouth. At last, after what seemed like an eternity, he heard the words he longed to hear.

'I love you, Luke.'

Boundless relief surged through him.

'I love you so much.' Her speech was slurred and her gaze glassy. She smiled like someone on drugs.

Tears sprang to his eyes. He raised his arms in a helpless gesture and turned to Benny, who had been watching them both in silence. Then he dropped the gun unheeding and gripped the metal frame of the bed, which the nurse was now wheeling further along the corridor. He was incapable of articulating even one of the countless questions that were striving to cascade from his lips all at once. *Why are you still alive? What have you all been doing to me? What's wrong with our baby?*

'Why?' was all he managed to say.

'Please leave her alone. She's already been given her pre-meds. I must get her to the theatre.'

Marc scarcely heard what the nurse was saying, but he made no further attempt to delay her. He walked alongside and bent over Sandra, whose lips were moving silently.

'What?' he asked. 'What did you say?'

'I'm sorry.'

'For what?'

They were now only a few metres from the glass doors beyond which the sterile area began.

'We went too far.'

'Too far in what way? What did you do?'

The drugs inside her body were numbing her from within, bearing her away from him and into oblivion. Her tremulous voice sank to a whisper. 'But we had no choice, understand? We couldn't let you remember.'

She made a last effort to sit up, but the nurse gently forced her back on the bed. Marc felt a hand on his shoulder pulling him backwards – backwards and away from his wife, whose bed was being wheeled through the airlock and into the theatre.

'We couldn't let you remember,' Sandra repeated despairingly before she disappeared from view.

*For ever.*

As the double doors closed behind her, Marc felt that he had lost his wife for good.

'Come,' said the voice belonging to the hand that was holding his arm in a vicelike grip. 'It's time. I'll explain everything.'

Turning round, Marc gazed into his father-in-law's drawn, weary face. Constantin Senner had never looked so old.

# 68

'She's alive!'

'Yes.'

'So there never was an accident?'

Constantin had ushered Marc and Benny into a spacious consulting room. Standing as far apart as possible, they formed the extremities of an invisible right-angled triangle.

'Yes, but it wasn't fatal. Sandra escaped with superficial injuries. Your airbag, on the other hand. . .' Constantin was breathing heavily. He pursed his lips before going on. '. . . your airbag failed to inflate. You hit your head and passed out instantly.'

Benny pulled up a swivel chair and sat down with his back to a full-length glass door. Beyond it lay a spacious terrace running the full width of the new hospital block.

'We brought you here to the clinic,' said Constantin, who had remained standing in front of the desk with Marc facing him across it. 'When you recovered consciousness you couldn't remember the last few hours before the accident. That was our chance.'

'What on earth are you talking about? What chance?' Marc was overcome with ice-cold rage.

'We had to make every effort to maintain your partial amnesia until today, but we realized that the trauma you sustained in the accident wasn't severe enough to suppress your memory long-term. So we decided to give your brain something else to occupy it.'

'You faked Sandra's death?'

'It wasn't easy for us, believe me. We wanted to discontinue the process more than once. My daughter most of all.'

Marc recalled the photo of the yellow Volvo that Emma had taken outside the police station and shown to him.

*They were arguing, the two of them, that's the only reason I took the picture.*

'What about the Bleibtreu Clinic? Does it even exist?'

'Oh yes. Patrick is a good friend of mine – he often treats my in-patients. He examined you after you regained consciousness here. Your amnesia would probably not be of long duration, he told us, but he didn't want to include you in his programme, not officially. I can well understand that. After all, he really does carry out serious research, whereas what we were doing was highly unethical. Still, he did at least place one floor of his clinic at our disposal.'

*Then Emma really is just a patient!*

Marc didn't know whether to laugh or cry. His closest confidante, the person who had helped him most, was a paranoid refugee from a hospital. Perhaps she really had overheard a conversation between Constantin and the genuine Professor Bleibtreu and jumped to certain conclusions. She'd escaped from the clinic to warn him and worked herself up into a paranoid psychosis at the same time.

'I still don't understand,' Marc said with a catch in his voice.

He pressed both hands to his burning cheeks. 'Why go to such incredible lengths?'

'Because it's a matter of life and death, Marc. We never wanted to hurt you, believe me. Your grief was simply meant to delay the process of recollection, and it worked really well for the first few weeks. However, then you began to dream of the moments immediately preceding the accident, and we knew it would be only a matter of time before you caught on and put two and two together. So we placed the magazine containing that bogus advertisement in my waiting room.'

*Learn to forget.*

'In the end we needed only one more day. Just another twenty-four hours in which you couldn't be allowed to remember. We couldn't set up the operation before, and it would have been too risky to deliver the baby earlier.'

Marc hesitated one last moment. Then he couldn't restrain himself any longer: he vaulted over the desk that separated him from his father-in-law.

'What was I meant to forget?!' he yelled, and punched him in the face. Constantin staggered backwards with Marc's hands around his throat.

'Tell me!' he cried, squeezing hard.

'Marc,' Benny called in the background. 'Let go of him.'

Constantin's eyes bulged, and his cheeks turned puce, but he made no attempt to defend himself.

'You'll never find out that way.' Benny sounded calm, almost detached, and it might have been his oddly dispassionate tone of voice that brought Marc to his senses. He gave one final squeeze, then let go.

Constantin fought for breath, clasping his blotchy throat, and started to retch.

'Hurry up and give me some answers or I swear I'll kill you!'

His father-in-law stood there with his head bowed, coughing. Then he straightened up, took a folder from the desk and went over to a metal-framed light box on the wall. He turned on the halogen light behind the frosted-glass screen, removed a photograph from the folder and clipped it to the screen.

'This is a greatly enlarged ultrasound picture.'

All Marc could see were black and white splotches. He didn't know whether they were benign or malignant, yet he recognized the photograph.

The last time he'd seen it was a few seconds before the crash – in Sandra's hand.

*That was why she undid her seatbelt, to get this ultrasound picture from the back of the car! But why?*

'We're looking at your unborn son's abdominal region. And this. . .' Coughing, Constantin cautiously tapped a shadowy area on the photograph '. . . is his liver. The problem is quite apparent.'

He gazed at Marc with a sorrowful expression. 'The baby's bile ducts are missing.'

'What does that mean?'

'He suffers from the illness that killed your father, Marc, only far more severely. The bile cannot drain away. The baby will be born without a functioning liver.'

'What. . . what can be done?'

'Nothing. A human being without a liver isn't viable.'

Marc felt he was rotating on the spot, not that he'd budged a millimetre. 'You're saying my son is bound to die?'

Constantin nodded.

*But why all this? Why deliver him by Caesarian section ten days earlier than planned?*

An actor had gone through the motions of examining him at the Bleibtreu Clinic. The hours of tests, the blood samples, the pointless psychological questionnaires he'd had to complete –

these were just a way of gaining time while they set up the ensuing charade, which involved wiping his mobile phone and changing the lock and name card on the door of his flat. But why? So that other amateur actors could pass themselves off as the manager of his office, a handcuffed attorney, and even himself? The bogus film script, the answerphone recording of Sandra's voice, the forged bank statement, the video at Constantin's house that looked like a news magazine's report but was really a fabrication – all these things had been intended to nudge his memory in the wrong direction and, at the same time, get him to this hospital at this particular juncture. *Why?*

'I know what you're thinking,' Constantin said in an attempt to get through to Marc, who was staring at the illuminated photograph like a man in a stupor. 'How could we have done this to you? How could I have lied to you? How could I have treated you for an imaginary splinter so you had to take pills that reinforced the suppressive process? It was a matter of life and death, my boy, don't you see? You think I enjoyed swapping your SIM card or turning on that confounded dolphin lamp just to bemuse you, then hiding behind your lavatory door and shutting myself up in the bathroom while you combed the rest of the flat for me? I didn't concoct all this myself, believe me. I employed a company that specializes in role play – it usually arranges murder-mystery weekends. They didn't know what was actually at stake, so they probably went too far. The film script you found at Eichkamp, the attorney in your cellar, my wrecked study and, last but not least, the furniture in your house – that was wrong beyond a doubt, but in the last analysis we had no choice. You do understand, don't you? Good God, he's your son! My grandson!'

Marc had only taken in snatches of Constantin's outburst. His thoughts had drowned out one word in three.

*No, it still doesn't make sense. Why should they have wanted me to forget about my son's terminal condition if he's doomed in any case?*

*Unless.* . . The truth hit him like a blow in the face. 'You need a donor!'

Constantin stared at him blankly. 'Yes, of course. I thought. . .' He turned to Benny. 'Didn't you explain it to him?'

Benny shook his head. There was a look of infinite sadness in his eyes. 'I leave the talking to you. I just do the dirty work.'

'You intend to carry out a transplant?' Marc broke in.

'Yes, though an infant's chances of surviving a liver transplant aren't a hundred per cent, as you know.'

'So you need someone with the same DNA as my son?'

Constantin nodded warily. 'A donor with a compatible blood group is sufficient.'

'Someone whose liver can be surgically tailored to fit into the body of a newborn baby?'

'Yes.'

Click! The first truth was like the bead of an abacus sliding into place. 'How soon after the birth do you need the organ?'

'Immediately.'

'And how long after the death of the donor can you transplant it?'

Constantin glanced nervously at his watch. 'Only a few hours.'

Click! Click! Two more beads, two more truths. Only one question remained.

'Would I survive the operation?'

'No, I'm sorry. That's why we had no choice – that's why we couldn't let you remember.'

Constantin's bleeper went off. He nodded with finality, as though confirming that a bargain had been struck.

'Right, that's it.'

He went over to Benny's chair and laid a hand on his shoulder. 'I can depend on you, can't I? A straightforward shot in the head. Brain-dead, but the heart must go on beating. Do it the way I showed you.'

Benny nodded, took the automatic from his pocket and flipped the safety catch as Constantin left the room, closing the door behind him.

# 69

*'The end justifies the means – aren't you always saying so yourself? Isn't that your motto in life?'*

*'You're crazy, Sandra. The end never justifies taking a human life.'*

Marc's memory of their argument before the crash drowned the roar of the blood being pumped ever faster through his body by his pounding heart.

So that was their plan.

They hadn't been able to kill him any sooner because they didn't need his liver until the child was born.

Haberland had been right about everything.

*'Well, I'm not sure how the Bleibtreu Clinic induces artificial amnesia in its patients. Up to now, losses of memory have always been an unintended by-product. However, it's conceivable that they subject their guinea pigs to shock therapy. And isn't that just what's happening to you now? One traumatic incident hard on the heels of another?'*

'Turn round,' Benny told him. He checked his magazine once more, then drew the curtains. The only source of daylight now was the door to the terrace.

'You're crazy.' Marc had lost all sense of time. It was still snowing outside. Seen from up here, the city might have been wrapped in dirty cotton wool. Everything looked at once real and unreal.

'Please turn round. They're delivering the baby right now. We don't have much time. It must be operated on immediately.'

'But why? Was all this really necessary?'

Marc tried to catch his brother's eye, but Benny avoided his gaze. His hand was trembling too, even though the gun gave him control of the situation.

'You could have looked for a compromise.'

'Sandra didn't want to take that risk.'

*'I wish you hadn't found out.'*

'There really isn't any other solution.'

Marc clasped his head in despair. 'Damn it, Benny, you know me. Don't you think I'd have sacrificed myself willingly?'

'Would you?'

Marc's knees were threatening to buckle.

*Would I have had the courage? Or would I have copped out?*

'You know me. We're brothers!'

'I know, but I've no choice.' Benny sniffed. He was standing in the gloom beside the desk, and Marc couldn't see the tears streaming down his brother's cheeks. He, too, began to weep as he slowly, very slowly, turned to face the wall. He gazed at the light box displaying the ultrasound picture of his son. The first and last picture of his child he would ever see. Then he shut his eyes.

'Why couldn't they simply transplant part of my liver?' he asked. 'Why does anyone have to die at all?'

'You see? You'd have looked for a compromise. You were too much of a threat to our plan.'

Marc's chest rose and fell like that of a patient hyperventi-lating. Sweating all over, he tried to think of the son he would never hold in his arms. He would never stand silently beside his bed and watch him breathing in his sleep, never take him to school, never see him swimming in the sea, never slip him the cash for a night out with his first girlfriend. And the thought that his child would survive thanks to him did not detract from his fear of dying. He was no hero; he was simply a debilitated, exhausted man with a terrible fear of death.

'*But you can't prevent it.*'

'*Oh yes I will, believe me.*'

'Shit, I really wish I didn't have to do this,' Benny muttered. 'I wish you'd never come to see me, and I wish I still hated you. I'm so sorry.'

Then the black specks stopped dancing before Marc's eyes and a last, lovely memory of Sandra came back to him.

'*If one of us dies – no, please hear me out – the first of us to go must give the other one a sign.*'

'*By turning the light on?*'

'*So we know we aren't alone. So we know we're thinking of each other even if we can't see each other.*'

'Benny,' Marc said, opening his eyes again.

'Yes?'

'You don't have to do it.'

'I do.'

'No, I'll do it myself.'

'That's not on.'

Benny's voice sounded muffled, as if he had a handkerchief over his mouth.

Marc spun round, but he was too late.

His brother was holding the automatic two-handed with the muzzle in his mouth. He pulled the trigger.

# 70

'Nooooo!'

Marc's senses had been so overstrung by his fear of death, he thought the detonation would burst his eardrums.

But there was no report, no blood and no slew of brain matter soiling the curtains over the window facing the terrace. Just a metallic click like that of a cheap ballpoint pen, but even that was almost unbearable. Perhaps the ammunition had been of inferior quality and the damp primer hadn't been ignited when the firing pin struck it. Perhaps there had been no round at all in the chamber because grit or dirt had obstructed the recoil spring. Perhaps it wasn't even down to the puddle of melted snow into which Valka had hurled the automatic and there was quite another reason why the bullet hadn't ploughed through Benny's brain and shattered his skull.

Not the first time, at least.

Feverishly, Benny worked the slide mechanism and replaced the muzzle in his mouth.

'Nooooo!'

Marc felt he was having one of those nightmares in which you try to escape from some threat, only to find yourself running on the spot. Sluggishly, as if restrained by invisible rubber bands, he made for his brother. Time seemed to be flowing backwards, or at least to be standing still. He had never crossed a room so slowly.

In reality, it all took less than half a second. Marc reached the desk, snatched up the heavy brass lamp, and smashed the base against his brother's shins.

Benny doubled up in front of the window, clasping his legs and howling with pain.

'You idiot!' he yelled. 'You fucking idiot!'

Marc picked up the gun, which had slithered across the floor and ended up by his feet. 'Why?' he yelled almost as loudly. 'Why do that?'

'You mean you still don't understand?' Benny was rocking back and forth like someone with autism. He screwed up his streaming eyes and shouted the words into his clenched fist. The words that made sense of everything at last.

'You've got it too!'

'What?'

Benny said it again, spitting out the words one by one. Saliva trickled down his unshaven chin. A thread of spittle landed on his chest.

*Of course.*

*I've got it too.*

# 71

Marc studied his reflection in the glass door to the terrace with the snowflakes dancing behind it.

It was obvious once you knew: the yellow-tinged eyes, the fatigue, the ever intensifying pains in his head and limbs, the itching. All symptoms of cirrhosis.

In front of him, Benny was trying to haul himself back on to his chair. 'Your liver's fucked,' he gasped. 'Not as badly as your son's – he doesn't have any bile ducts at all. You've got a bit more time, Marc, but not much more. Understand?'

No, he didn't. His brain registered all the facts but his mind refused to recognize the connections between them.

'You mean to sacrifice yourself?' he asked, dumbfounded.

'We don't have any choice.'

Benny had struggled to his feet and was clinging exhaustedly to the back of the chair. 'Your baby's liver damage was discovered long before the accident – by ultrasound, during a routine examination here,' he explained hurriedly. 'Constantin was shocked, but he didn't tell either you or Sandra. You weren't supposed to find out until he'd located a suitable donor.'

'You!'

Benny nodded.

'He began by checking the official donor databanks and put the baby on the waiting list, but how likely was it that an infant belonging to a compatible blood group would die in time?'

*Zilch.*

'So he examined all the potential donors in the family.'

Although everything within him rebelled, Marc began to draw the right conclusions. So that was why his father-in-law had persuaded him to undergo that health check three weeks before the accident. Fatigue, nausea and aching limbs – Constantin had identified the cause of those symptoms but concealed it from him.

'You inherited your liver damage from our father and passed it on to the baby, Marc. I'm the only close relation who was spared.' Benny laughed. 'Ironical, isn't it, that I should be the broken link in the chain?'

While his brother was talking to him persuasively, almost imploringly, Marc recalled the cryptic words of Benny's nurse, Leana Schmidt, which now made sense to him:

*'Benny's behaviour changed the day after he had an MRI scan... We normally scan the brain for anomalies, but they only scanned the lower part of his body... I got hold of the pictures... He's perfectly fit.'*

'You propose to die for my sake?' Marc asked. The very question sounded inconceivable.

Benny rose with an effort. 'Yours and the baby's. That's the plan. Constantin told you when you met him at his house on the day of the accident.'

*Which I wasn't supposed to remember.*

'Is there really no other potential donor?' Marc asked help-lessly.

'No.' Benny looked at him sadly. 'Neither legally nor on the black market. I've tried everything.'

*So that's why you needed the money...* The words flashed through Marc's mind. Ninety thousand euros. Benny had borrowed the money from Valka to purchase an organ illegally, to save his life and that of his child, but the deal had fallen through.

'Marc, look at me.' Benny thumped his chest with his fist. 'I've got a healthy liver and a compatible blood group, unlike Sandra. You won't find that combination in a hurry. Don't you see what it means?'

Marc nodded. His brother was the ideal donor. That was why he had suddenly changed his lifestyle, working out and eating a healthy diet. All in readiness for the forthcoming operation. And that was why Valka had let him go. Benny must have let him into the secret at the last moment, probably after he'd been dragged out of the car and beaten up in the drive of Constantin's villa. Valka had refrained from shooting Benny only because he knew he would soon be dead in any case. Why soil his hands when his victim was going to kill himself?

'Sandra loves you,' Benny said quietly. 'So does Constantin. They arranged all this so as not to lose everything at a stroke – you *and* the child. So please,' he entreated, 'give me back the gun. Let me get this over.'

Marc retreated a step. Even though his memory of their last meeting at Constantin's villa was still incomplete, he now knew exactly what they had been arguing about in the car on the way home.

'*Still, you do see we don't have any choice, don't you?*'

At the end of her tether, Sandra had agreed to this murderous plan to save her child *and* her husband. He had vehemently opposed it, and had it not been for their accident on the return trip, he would undoubtedly have thwarted his brother's suicide attempt a second time.

'But why did you go to such lengths?' he asked desperately.

'Sandra told you: things got out of control. On the one hand, Constantin wanted to maintain your amnesia so you didn't prevent my death. On the other, he had to prepare you for the operation. That was another reason why you had to go and have your dressing changed so often.'

'Why didn't he simply drug me or abduct me?'

'What, Constantin?' Benny shook his head. 'Your father-in-law may be unscrupulous but he isn't a criminal. On the contrary, he wanted to save your life. At first he thought a single lie would do the trick, so he shut you up in a mental prison far harder to break out of than any form of physical restraint – do you understand? He couldn't just let you disappear either. First you had to retract your statement to the board of examiners, otherwise I would never have been discharged from that psychiatric hospital.' Benny coughed. 'It all went pear-shaped, of course, and when Emma suddenly appeared on the scene the chaos was complete. The script didn't contain a part for an escaped lunatic. We hadn't allowed for her, any more than we expected you to ask me, of all people, for help. Damn it, Marc, I'd meant to spend the last few hours before my death saying goodbye to everyone, but all at once I had you, Valka and that paranoid creature breathing down my neck.' Benny's voice shook. 'Sandra wanted to back out at one stage. She begged Constantin to ditch the whole scheme and come clean with you, but by then he wasn't behaving rationally any more. All that drove them both in the end was panic and fear.' He swallowed hard. 'Fear for you, fear for the baby. Have you got it at last?'

*Yes, alas.*

They had traumatized but not meant to kill him. The whole business had merely served to protect him. He was to forget in order to survive.

'And now?' said Marc. His physical and mental strength had finally run out. 'Where do we go from here?'

# 72

Benny smiled sadly and glanced at his watch.

'The liver is the only divisible organ in the human body,' he said after a short pause. 'Your son will get the left lobe and you the larger one. That's how Constantin explained it to me. It'll work as long as it's done quickly, so please. . .'

He put out his hand for the gun. 'Come on, I was going to do it anyway. At least my death will have some meaning.'

'I can't let you do it.'

'Everything's ready. Your son is waiting in the theatre. He hasn't a chance of surviving unless I die. Nor do you.'

'Maybe,' said Marc. Then he quoted an elderly man he'd met only a few hours earlier – the one person who had always been honest with him. 'But it can never be right to do the wrong thing.'

His brother stared at him in surprise. 'One person dies, two survive. What can be wrong with that?'

'Death isn't a mathematical equation!' Marc shouted.

Benny rolled his eyes. 'You can't understand, is that it? You want a reason. All right, listen and I'll give you one.' He brushed a lock of hair out of his eyes. It was matted with blood and sweat. 'You remember that day in May?'

*The burglary, Sandra's miscarriage.*

The question pierced Marc to the quick. 'What are you getting at?'

'It was me.'

'What?'

'I shot my mouth off to Valka – told him that Sandra's father was asking to be burgled.'

'No.'

'Yes. I swear I didn't mean them to break in. All I did was bitch about the stupidity of a fat cat who left his house so insecure. During one of our meetings Sandra had mentioned the spare key in the boathouse, just in case I needed a bolt-hole and no one was at home.'

Benny's eyes were misted with tears.

'She tried to help me, damn it – that's why she lost her baby. Your baby. I struggled with my conscience, really I did, but it became too much for me in the end. That's why I slit my wrists.'

For a moment Marc felt the ground give way beneath his feet. He had just, for the second time, prevented the suicide of a man who was responsible for the death of his first child. A tidal wave of rage and sorrow broke over him.

*Is Haberland mistaken? Can it be right to do the wrong thing?*

Thinking of his work with young people – of Julia, whose life he had saved by means of a psychological trick and simultaneously sent back to hell – Marc realized that the principle he had always lived by was now being put to the most terrible test of all.

*Does the end justify the means after all?*

'I confessed to Sandra immediately,' Benny said, 'but she

wouldn't give me away.' He gulped. 'For your sake. You were never meant to learn the true reason for her doubts. Besides, she knew there could be no greater punishment than my own self-hatred.'

Marc recalled what Constantin had said: '*A tragedy can form a tremendous bond between people who love each other.*'

That was why Sandra had found her way back to him after the miscarriage, and that was why she and Constantin had so readily accepted Benny's self-sacrificial offer.

'Please,' Benny entreated. 'Let me make up for what I did. To you, to the child. And to Sandra.'

Marc's lower lip trembled as he thought of the consequences of the choice he now had to make. If he prevented Benny from committing suicide he would be risking his own life and, at the same time, sealing the fate of their child.

He raised the gun, checked the safety catch and worked the slide mechanism to insert another round into the chamber. He was prepared for what happened next. Gritting his teeth and ignoring the agonizing pain in his injured leg, Benny sprang at him and tried to wrench the gun from his grasp. Marc dodged aside and made for the door to the terrace. He almost failed to grab hold of the handle because Benny caught him by the sleeve.

Wrenching the door open, he hurled the automatic far out over the balustrade with Benny yanking at him from behind.

The two of them stumbled and fell, and for a moment they lay panting side by side, hurt and exhausted.

Marc wanted to look away, but he couldn't. He was experiencing an unprecedented emotion, torn between a father's desire for revenge and brotherly love. In the end he gazed into Benny's tearful, dark-brown eyes, not knowing what to say. But he didn't have a chance to ponder the matter, because this time he was unprepared for what came next. It all happened far too quickly.

Benny drove his elbow into Marc's face, jumped up and hobbled out of the open glass door, dragging his injured leg and groaning with pain. The flagstones on the terrace were slippery, and Marc was too far away to have a chance of catching his brother as he prepared to leap over the balustrade.

# 73

It was quite deliberate. Benny vaulted the balustrade like an exhausted hurdler, right leg leading and arms waving as if bidding farewell to the leafless weeping willow in the hospital grounds, which topped the three-storey block by several metres. He flung out his chest and arched his back, looking for a moment like a skydiver just before his parachute opens. Then his left foot caught in the rail.

The ice-sheathed metal uprights trembled. Benny appeared to have tried to turn in mid-air and reach back with his right arm. Marc's suspicion was confirmed: it was no accident. Benny had checked his progress in an attempt to prevent himself from falling and clutched the handrail at the last moment.

*But why?*

Stars danced before Marc's eyes as he tottered out into the sleet-filled darkness.

Benny's hand had slipped off the handrail, but he had at least caught hold of an upright. He was now hanging by one arm, legs kicking. He tried to get another handhold, but the metal uprights were so icy his hands kept losing their grip.

*He wants to haul himself up again. He's had second thoughts.*

Marc hurried to his aid, slithering rather than walking in his rubber-soled trainers. Meanwhile, Benny's fingers had completely lost their grip on the upright. He was now clinging to a narrow ledge with both hands.

By the time Marc reached him, he was hanging by his fingertips.

Marc leant over the balustrade. Looking down, he realized why Benny had checked his fall.

*It's too high.*

He had picked the wrong place to jump.

*'Brain-dead, but the heart must go on beating. Do it the way I showed you.'*

It was doubtful if his organs would have survived intact, even after a fall from three floors up, but here the drop was far greater. In front of this east wing Constantin had had a pit excavated for an annexe, an underground garage or a swimming pool for convalescent patients. Its exact purpose was unclear from up here, but not the effect of a fall from this height.

*Benny will smash himself to pieces.*

Especially as the bottom of the pit was sheathed in steel mats. No shrubs, no grass, no soil. There was nothing down there to break his fall.

'Shit,' Benny hissed between his teeth. He made no attempt to move for fear of slipping off. His fingers were numb and bloodless. He wouldn't be able to hang on for much longer.

'I'll help you,' said Marc. He couldn't do anything from his side of the balustrade, so he climbed over the handrail and balanced on the narrow ledge Benny was clinging to. His rubber soles could get little purchase on the wet stone.

'Okay,' he said, grabbing hold of his brother's sleeve with one hand and hanging on to an upright with the other. 'I've got you,' he lied. He was weak and exhausted and aching all over.

He could scarcely hang on himself, let alone haul his brother back over the balustrade.

'Shit,' said Benny. 'I'm too stupid even to die.' Marc gave him an agonized smile. 'I'll manage,' he lied again.

'Forget it.'

'Fuck that.'

'Let go of me or we'll both be done for.'

Marc's fingers slipped on the smooth material of the wet bomber jacket, but he quickly recovered his grip. For the moment.

He looked down in search of help, but the hospital grounds were deserted in this weather. An ambulance with a red cross on its white roof was uselessly parked fifty metres away.

'I'm sorry,' he heard his brother say as he continued to stare at the roof of the ambulance. A sudden thought occurred to him. It was so absurd and so utterly inappropriate he couldn't help laughing.

'Cross!'

'What?' said Benny.

'The radio oracle. The singer's name was Christopher Cross.'

Benny looked up with a feeble smile. All at once he ceased to look like someone clinging to a ledge for dear life. Although every muscle in his body was taut as a bowstring, he seemed to be at peace – resigned to the inevitable.

'Let go of me,' he asked for the last time.

*All right.*

Marc nodded.

Then, summoning up all his strength, he gripped his brother by both arms. Although he himself was now unsupported, he managed to raise him at least a few centimetres. Not as much as he would have liked, but he simply couldn't do any better – he didn't have the strength left.

It wasn't ideal, nor did it eliminate every element of risk, but in the end, at the very last moment, just as he thrust himself and his brother away from the ledge and plunged to the ground, an inner voice told him that his plan would work.

# 74

## TODAY

The fire on the hearth had not lost its magnetic attraction. Marc could scarcely tear his eyes away from it while Haberland was talking, and the flames seemed if anything even brighter now.

He had kept Haberland covered at first, but when the old man took absolutely no notice and continued his account with ever greater insistence, he put the automatic on the coffee table and ended up forgetting all about it. Now that Haberland had finished and was looking at him expectantly, Marc felt simultaneously relieved and apprehensive.

*That's how it happened. That's just how it was.*

Haberland's descriptions were so vivid that the memories had unfolded in his mind's eye like a film.

'May I have a glass of water, please?' he asked hoarsely. It must have been hours since he'd had anything to drink, and his throat felt raw and dusty. Strangely enough, many other negative sensations had receded far into the background. The dislocated shoulder, cracked ribs and loose teeth were transmitting only muted signals to his brain.

Haberland showed no sign of having heard Marc's request. 'So you accept that you really experienced all those things?'

Marc nodded with an effort. Haberland leant forward with an air of interest.

'In that case, what leads you to believe you may have lost your mind?'

*'Please, you've got to tell me. I don't know what's happening to me.'*

Marc stared past him at the bright, leaping flames in the fire-place, then at the window. It seemed to be still as dark outside as it had been when he arrived.

'How do you know all this?' he asked in a low, almost detached voice. He couldn't help thinking of the first thing Haberland had said to him that night.

*'I really wish you'd come sooner. Time's running out.'*

'Were you just another of Constantin's play-actors?'

'No,' Haberland said with an amiable smile. 'On the contrary, Emma and I were the only ones not in the know. Benny only brought you out here so that I could look at your injuries. He also wanted to gain time and say goodbye to me.'

He took a big wad of notes from his inside pocket and showed them to Marc for a moment before putting them back.

'I think Benny didn't like it at all when I found there was no wound beneath your dressing.' Haberland's smile broadened. 'Didn't you notice how nervous he was when you drove off with him after our walk beside the lake? Your brother was very much afraid I'd given your memory a helping hand. But I knew nothing of the conspiracy.'

Marc digested this, then shook his head sceptically. 'I don't believe that. If you weren't implicated in it, how do you have such a detailed knowledge of what I've been through in the last few hours?'

'Hours?' Haberland queried. He glanced at the little digital clock on his desk.

11.04. Precisely the time at which they'd visited him yester-day.

Marc blinked in bewilderment. 'Has it stopped?' he asked. Haberland shook his head.

*But. . . That's impossible, it can't be. . .*

He tried to get up but failed to extricate himself from the soft, yielding sofa cushions. His arms had gone to sleep – the blood didn't appear to be circulating properly. He turned towards the door.

'How did I get here? And how. . .' He looked down at his useless arms, which he couldn't move of his own volition. 'How could I have survived the fall?'

*A ten-metre drop? On to steel mats? Without medical attention?*

Haberland gave another amiable smile. 'You're starting to ask the right questions at last. I told you you'd find all the answers by yourself.'

'Have you ever heard a story and wished afterwards that you'd never found out the ending?'

Marc was overcome by a sudden urge to tear away the invisible cobwebs on his skin: dusty threads that cocooned his mind as well as his body and concealed the truth he so badly wanted to fathom. The truth embodied in a single question: 'Do I exist?'

Haberland smiled again and folded his hands. A log collapsed on the hearth, sending up a shower of fiery red sparks. At last he said: 'Yes, beyond a doubt. Where Benny's experiences were concerned, I had to improvise a little. I reconstructed them from the conversations you and your brother had in the last few hours, so some of them may have been misrepresented, but everything I told you about yourself really happened to you. You're real enough.'

He paused. Then he said quietly: 'Unlike me.'

The room was invaded by an icy draught just as it had been

yesterday, when Benny went out on the veranda to smoke a cigarette.

The memory of his brother brought tears to Marc's eyes.

'You know what they say about the last few seconds before death?' Haberland asked, rubbing his scarred wrists.

Marc nodded. 'The whole of your life is supposed to pass in review before your mind's eye – or parts of it, at least. Experiences that have left a lasting impression on your psyche. Passing an exam, getting married, the birth of a child. Negative experiences too, though. . .'

He broke off.

*Like a car crash?*

'Of course,' Haberland went on, 'no one has ever crossed the threshold and returned, but many people who have been resuscitated claim that their near-death experience consisted in talking with people who meant a great deal to them.'

*Like Sandra, Constantin, Benny and. . .*

The professor nodded, as if he could read Marc's thoughts. 'Scientists have ascertained that all they are, these final moments and the dazzling light towards which one appears to be moving, is a biochemical disturbance in the dying brain.'

The fire flared up even more brightly than before. Marc's eyes were smarting. Everything around him seemed to become clearer, practically transparent.

'Who are you?' he asked.

'I'm just a memory.'

The professor rose from his wing chair. All of a sudden, Marc no longer felt the leaden inertia that had kept him on the sofa until now. He got to his feet effortlessly.

'Come, Tarzan.' Taking an old knitted cardigan from the tea trolley, Haberland bent over his dog. The weary animal raised its head and stretched, then crawled out of its wicker basket beside the window.

Marc looked first at the fire and then at the professor, who was patting his dog's head.

'So it was all for nothing?' he asked. 'All the suffering?'

Haberland looked up.

*Should I have let Benny fall after all?*

'I don't know. I can't see into the future, no one can. I can only tell you what's already present in your memory.'

Marc nodded. The film was at an end. The last reel had fallen off its spindle.

'But then, you know what I think.'

*It can never be right to do the wrong thing.*

The floorboards creaked faintly as Haberland shuffled over to the veranda door with his dog in tow. From behind, they looked tired but contented.

It was growing lighter outside. To Marc, the scent of wood smoke from the fireplace seemed suddenly more intense, but that might just have been his imagination – just another biochemical disturbance in his brain, like the image of the professor, who turned with his hand on the door handle.

'Come on,' he said. 'Let's go for a stroll.'

LOCAL NEWS

# THE END AND THE MEANS

Today, at the Senner Clinic in Berlin-Charlottenburg, doctors turned off the life-support system of a man whose fate has aroused widespread public sympathy.

Mystery still surrounds the circumstances in which Marc Lucas and his brother Benjamin fell from the roof of the hospital where Marc died after lying in a coma for ten days. His death, which occurred at 11.04 a.m. today, resulted from the severe internal injuries he sustained.

By an ironical quirk of fate, or so it seems, his death saved two human lives. Had he not hit the ground first, he would not have broken his brother's fall. Benjamin Lucas suffered numerous fractures but survived without any internal injuries. This enabled him to donate the left lobe of his liver to a newborn child – none other than the dead man's son, who was suffering from a fatal liver condition and had been delivered only minutes before his father's ultimately fatal fall.

Because of the mysterious circumstances surrounding the case, it is now under review by the district attorney's office. There are many indications that it may have involved suicide for the purpose of an illegal organ donation, particularly as the hospital's medical director is Constantin Senner, the father of Sandra Lucas, the dead man's wife. An operating theatre had been prepared and a team of surgeons was standing by in readiness to carry out the transplant, a difficult operation on a newborn child. Moreover, the baby had been on a waiting list for donor organs for weeks beforehand.

It is also rumoured that another surgical team had been standing by to operate on Marc Lucas, who is said to have needed a liver transplant himself. This would seem to corroborate the district attorney's suicide theory, because Benjamin Lucas could never have donated *both* halves of his liver and survived. On the other hand, if he had wanted to save the lives of his brother *and* the unborn child, why did he jump in company with Marc Lucas?

An unnamed source in the district attorney's office doubts that charges will be brought. 'Establishing the facts in a family drama of this kind is always difficult. Constantin Senner could undoubtedly be struck off the medical register for unethical conduct, but he intended in any case to cease practising and sell his hospital because of financial problems.'

It is doubtful, therefore, whether the underlying circumstances will ever be entirely clarified. Marc Lucas will probably take most of the truth to the grave with him. As for his brother, who is now out of intensive care, he has invoked his right of refusal to testify. He does at least appear to have made a good recovery from his living-donor operation, which is permissible between relatives and when only part of an organ is involved. If any blame attaches to Sandra Lucas, on the other hand, she may have been sufficiently punished. Not only has she lost her husband, but it is still uncertain whether her brother-in-law's lobus sinister, or left lobe of the liver, will be accepted or rejected by her child's body. The baby is doing well, all things considered, but it is still far too early for a definite prognosis.

Ken Sukowsky

# 'BOSS OF THE BOUNCERS' ON TRIAL

**Berlin** – The trial opens today of Eduard Valka, head of the criminal organization that controls the city's nightclub and disco doormen. He stands accused, in addition to other charges, of procuring the murder of Magda H., an underage prostitute from Bulgaria, and of conspiracy to murder a journalist employed by this newspaper, who was conducting research into Valka's criminal activities. In view of the evidence against him, which the district attorney's office describes as overwhelming, an early verdict is expected.

Sunlight slanted down through the barred windows, projecting an elongated trelliswork of shadows on to the floor. Although the patient's room was regularly cleaned and aired, the minuscule motes of dust dancing in the sun's rays lent them the appearance of a spotlight.

'She's not responding,' said the doctor in charge. A peppermint – a vain attempt to disguise the stale cigarette smoke on his breath – glinted between his teeth as he spoke.

'How long has she been like this?' asked Marc Lucas. He propped the unwieldy cardboard tube, which he'd had to bring all this way, against the foot of the bed.

'For ages.'

The doctor stepped aside and cast a judicial glance at the drip that was giving the old lady an electrolytic infusion. The plastic container was still full.

'I wasn't even working here when she was admitted, but according to her record her psychosis was already very pronounced.'

'Hm,' Marc grunted. He took her hand, which was lying on the starched bedspread. It felt rough and heavy.

'Who sent her here?' he asked.

'Her mother was still alive then. If you ask me, the court should have appointed a legal guardian far sooner. The situation was too much for the poor woman. Her first mistake was to begin by putting her daughter in the Bleibtreu Clinic. You know the old story?'

Marc pretended he was hearing it for the first time.

'No? It made quite a splash in the press. Anyway, her paranoid episodes, some of which were schizoid, got worse in there. At the start of her treatment she thought she was an interpreter, although she didn't speak a single foreign language. Then she believed herself to be taking part in a secret amnesia experiment – the Bleibtreu Clinic was actually conducting one, but only with the aid of volunteers. Having overheard a conversation between two doctors and jumped to the wrong conclusion, she felt threatened and ran away. She was recaptured, fortunately, and her mother at last managed to ensure that she was confined in a secure and respectable hospital.'

The doctor crunched up his peppermint with a satisfied air. The idea that his hospital had been preferred to a private institution evidently pleased him.

'We couldn't cure her. Still, at least she now knows she isn't an interpreter, and that nobody means her any harm. Don't you, Frau Ludwig?' The doctor gave her knee a clumsy pat through the bedclothes.

The elderly patient seemed unaware of what was going on around her. She was asleep with her eyes open and breathing exclusively through her mouth.

*She looks thin,* Marc thought. *Almost emaciated.* Quite unlike his mental picture of her.

'Look. . .' The doctor cleared his throat. 'No offence, Doctor, but I can't imagine how you hope to get through to her. She's very suspicious of strangers.'

'I'm not a stranger, actually,' said Marc, removing the lid of the cardboard tube. 'Can you hear me?' he asked, turning to look at the woman as he turned it upside down and carefully shook out its contents.

No response.

'What on earth is *that*?' the doctor asked a minute later, when

Marc had completed his preparations. He went over to the wall with his hands extended in the direction of the canvas which his young visitor had temporarily secured to it.

'An heirloom,' Marc replied. From now on, he concentrated on the patient alone.

'Look.'

He stepped aside to enable her blank gaze to dwell on the picture facing her bed. 'I've brought you something.'

'Haberland's House?' queried the doctor, reading the little inscription in the bottom-right corner of the painting. He turned round. 'All I can see is a white expanse.'

Marc took no notice of him. He was now standing right beside the old woman, at the head of the bed. In spite of her severe mental illness, her face hadn't entirely lost its gentle expression.

'My uncle Benny told me you liked it a lot,' Marc whispered, too softly for the doctor to hear. 'You were the only one who grasped what it was meant to represent when you spotted it in his flat. Benny took it to the house in the forest later on. Do you remember?'

No change. Still no response.

'You see, my young friend!' The doctor sounded almost triumphant. 'She won't let anyone get through to her.'

Marc Lucas nodded absently.

'I'll leave it here for you,' he whispered in the old woman's ear. 'And I'll come again. Next weekend. Perhaps you'll feel like talking to me about my father then.'

*About the man to whom I owe my life in every respect.*

'I think you were a great help to him.'

Marc continued to whisper, although Emma's face betrayed not the least sign of comprehension.

'Anyway, you knew him better than I do.'

He brushed the hair off her forehead and stepped back. Emma Ludwig's mind really didn't seem to be in the same room as he was. Her face remained blank and expressionless as she gazed inertly at the coarse-grained white canvas.

She didn't react when he gave her hand a farewell squeeze, nor did she stare after him when the doctor escorted him out.

She didn't even blink when, a long time afterwards, her eye shed a single, impotent tear.

# LEARN TO FORGET

We are a self-help group looking for former participants in a psychiatric amnesia experiment. You yourself may have been a patient and cannot now remember the experiments to which you were subjected. If you have the **slightest doubt** about your memories, please visit our self-help page on the internet under:

**www.mpu–berlin.org**

There you can check whether you have ever participated in an amnesia experiment.
Many thanks.

# About the idea underlying SPLINTER

Before I started work on SPLINTER there were many things in my life I would sooner have forgotten. For example how I once, when utterly exhausted and befuddled by jet lag, went astray in my own hotel room. I'd meant to go to the bathroom but found myself outside in the passage. The door had swung shut, needless to say, and my key was on the bedside table. The only other thing you need to know is that I'm not a pyjama fetishist. All I wear as a rule is a short T-shirt, with the emphasis on short.

My ride down in a fully occupied lift, the horrified expression of the woman behind the reception desk and the giggles of the bellhop who escorted this half-naked German back to his room — I would have swallowed an amnesia pill on the spot if it had blotted out my memory of this toe-curling episode.

I would have done so then. But that was before I started to write SPLINTER and made a closer study of the subject.

Hand on heart: Would you take a lovesickness pill if one existed?

Or an amnesia injection after a particularly embarrassing or — worse still — tragic experience?

You may think that this question — and with it the entire theme of SPLINTER — belongs in the realm of science fiction. But don't be misled. Scientists (criminals too, alas) have long had access to substances that can eradicate recollections from our short-term memory — and I'm not just talking about mental blackouts occasioned by excessive alcohol intake: Flunitrazepam, for example, which has sadly gained notoriety as a so-called date-rape drug. In combination with other narcotics, it ensures that rape victims cannot remember the horrible crime perpetrated on them.

But research into drugs that erase long-term memory is ongoing. Biologists from New York and Rehovot, Israel, have discovered an active substance that blocks an important protein in nerve tissue if injected into the cerebral cortex. This, however, induces complete amnesia.

Mark Bear of the Massuchusetts Institute of Technology is conducting some rather more specific research in this field. He wants to get rid of bad memories without affecting good ones. 'Wouldn't that be nice?' he asked in the 14/2008 edition of DER SPIEGEL for 31 March 2008, under the title 'Der Sprache des Gehirns' ('The Language of the Brain', an extremely readable article by Jörg Blech on the present state of research, which I link with my website, **www.sebastianfitzek.de.**)

Bear, who assumes that traumatic experiences etch themselves more deeply into our nerve tissue than positive ones, is looking for a pharmacological substance that will focus solely on these deeper 'engravings'.

I myself am in the fortunate position of not having so far undergone any experiences as traumatic as those inflicted on Marc Lucas in the novel you're holding in your hands at this moment, so I won't presume to pass judgement on people so desperate that they yearn for deliberately induced amnesia. While writing SPLINTER I came to realize more and more that I don't want to relinquish a single one of my memories. Neither of the day I received the news that my first book was to be published, nor of the night my mother died. I believe that people are the sum of their memories, and if there is any reason for our presence here on earth, it may be to accumulate as many of them as possible during our journey through life.

## Before I forget...

It has become almost a tradition for me to begin my acknowledgements by thanking the reader. So thank you.

To be quite frank, you aren't in the forefront of my mind while I'm writing. I've so far received thousands of emails addressed to **fitzek@sebastianfitzek.de** (which I really do answer personally, by the way, even if it sometimes takes me a while), and many of them contradict each other. What one person likes another thinks is stupid, and vice versa, so I stick to what I did in my first thriller, THERAPY: I simply write a story I would like to read. That's why I'm so grateful I'm not alone, and that there are other people, like you, who spend time with my books. That's precisely why I thank you and hope you had an entertaining hour or two. If not, I know the address of a clinic in Berlin that can help you to forget this novel in short order...

This book is dedicated to my brother Clemens Fitzek. We are seven years and eight hours apart, the eight hours being what it seems to take to drive along the urban expressway between Charlottenburg and Köpenick. Although we see each other so seldom, I feel profoundly attached to you. Thanks so much, and not for your medical advice alone.

Sabine — the same goes for you, of course. I'd have been lost without all the invaluable professional tips you gave me.

I owe a very special debt of gratitude to Dr Marcus Schuchmann, who gave me some valuable medical advice in the cheap Berlin restaurant where we'd taken refuge from a shower of rain. Unfortunately, I can't reveal your field of expertise without giving away the end of the thriller. Next time, you'll get more than a measly hamburger, I promise!

Sandra, I thank the screenwriter who wrote you the leading role in the film of my life, even though I now have to get to grips with its side effects: for instance, the little remarks that upset the endings of my stories — and improve them as a result!

BB, how glad I am we didn't dump your father's car in the lake that time. We really came within an ace of doing so. I thank you today for the experience I was able to incorporate in *Splinter* and hope your unwitting father never reads this.

Gerlinde, you're crazy but wonderful. A lot of things have changed, but your unstinting friendship and support endure. I can't thank you enough for them (and for introducing me to the radio oracle).

Zsolt Bács, you got rather short measure in my last acknowledgements, even though you gave me one of the most helpful tips for my thriller THE SOUL-BREAKER when I was suffering from writer's block. You'll get something nice for it, but remember Santa Claus: one big present is enough.

I sometimes come across people who look more innocuous than me but are even crazier. For instance, Thomas Zorbach and his team from vm-people. Anyone who manages to induce his colleagues to stage my book readings by lying down in mortuary refrigeration drawers (thanks, Oliver Ludwigs) has more than earned his place in these acknowledgements.

People who work with me have to be prepared for the worst every day. My editor, Carolin Graehl, got a shock when she returned from holiday and overheard Andrea Ludorf (who looks after my reading trips) terminate a phone call with the words: '... Fine, so I'll get hold of a wheelchair for Sebastian Fitzek.'
Carolin's fears were groundless. I hadn't had an accident; I simply needed the thing for my reading (better not ask why).
Christian Meyer, a very good friend who had really only wanted to accompany me to the reading, had to push me on to the stage in the said wheelchair. I had previously bullied him into wearing a surgical gown and mask.
Thank you all for joining in this tomfoolery. Take seriously what you do but never yourself. That's my favourite motto, and it applies to Manuela best of all. You not only do a splendidly professional and meticulous job (you're my quick-out brain!) but laugh at all my silly antics

as well. What I thank you for most, though, is your friendship.

If I look like a fighting machine at my next reading it'll be down to Karl Raschke, former personal trainer to Graziano 'Rocky' Rocchigiani, who thinks, for some obscure reason, that he has to develop me into an iron man. I'm so exhausted by the end of a workout, I don't have the energy to cancel our next appointment. Thanks, Kalle. But for you I'd still be a fat, lazy couch potato. In other words, I'd still be happy.

Sabrina Rabow, only a fantastic press agent like you could have kept my criminal record out of the papers all these years. (I'm joooooking!) Thanks so much for that and for always being there for me.

I hit on the basic idea for SPLINTER during a conversation with the neurosurgeon Professor Samii at his clinic in Hannover. He startled me with the following remark: 'Most people are looking for new techniques and ways of storing knowledge in their brains more easily and quickly. Very few concern themselves with how one learns to forget.' **Learn to forget. . .** Thank you, Professor Samii, for that wonderful quotation.

The following have earned a place in my acknowledgements' eternal Hall of Fame:

Dr Hans-Peter Übleis and Beate Kuckertz.
Thank you for letting a child like me run riot in your publishing house. What publisher could

suit my thrillers better than Droemer? After all, it's an anagram of 'Moerder'!

Carolin Graehl and Regine Weisbrod. Damn it, I always think after the first draft: 'That's it, there's nothing more to be done.'
And then you come along and improve the book so much with your editing I can scarcely believe it myself. You're wonderful. It isn't your fault if people don't like my thrillers, and that's a fact.

It seems a lot of people clear off if they've had to work with me for any length of time. It started with my first editor, Dr Andrea Müller, who discovered me, and to whom I'm eternally grateful. She was followed by marketing boss Klaus Kluge, who has also defected to the competition. Well, you'll soon discover what a tough sell obscure authors like Dan Brown and Ken Follett are. :-)
Seriously, though, I'm delighted for you and grateful to you for all you did for me.

I now know so many Droemer staff whose daily work ensures that my books get read I could type out the entire in-house telephone directory. On behalf of them all, I express my thanks to Andrea Ludorf, Andrea Fischer, Dominik Huber, Susanne Klein, Monika Neudeck, Sibylle Dietzel, Iris Haas, Andrea Bauer, Georg Regis, Andreas Thiele, Katrin Englberger and Heide Bogner, but the list is far from complete.

My thanks go also to Claudia von Hornstein, Christine Ziehl, Uwe Neumahr and everyone else in the team from AVA International, my literary agency and, first and foremost, of course, to Roman Hocke. He's the agent who first made an author of me, but I wouldn't recommend him to anyone else. He'd have less time for me if I did!

The same applies to Tanja Howarth. If you've got a book and want it published in Britain and the USA, take an amnesia pill and forget her phone number. Tanja is mine.

And now for the cheap seats, which I'll polish off in a single sentence. (<u>No, it's not just that I don't have much room left. You're important to me, honestly, but these acknowledgements are already so long and paper is getting more and more expensive. . .</u>)
  So thanks to Ivo Beck, David Groenewold, Oliver Kalkofe, Arno Müller, Jochen Trus, Thomas Koschwitz, Dirk Stiller, Iván Sáinz-Pardo, Peter Prange, Christian Becker, Stefan Bäumer, Dagmar Miska, Christoph Menardi (thanks for your surname), Kossi, Fruti, the Alzners, Simon Jäger, Michael Treutler, and, of course, my father Freimut Fitzek, who was second to none in encouraging my love of literature. My next book is for you — not that it'll be much use to you.

So. . . Have I forgotten anyone? Ten to one I have, and I can't, alas, blame that on any pill. If, after reading this book, you aren't so sure you can remember everything in your life — if you feel you may have taken part in an amnesia experiment at some stage — there's a website on the internet where you can find out:

**www.mpu-berlin.org**

Drop in there sometime. It'll be worth it!

I shall end by addressing the question I'm always being asked: Are my stories based on fact? To be quite honest, I can't really remember.

> **Sebastian Fitzek**
> **Berlin, March 2009**